MIDDLE SCHOOL MAGIC

LUMINESCENCE

MIDDLE SCHOOL MAGIC

LUMINESCENCE

BRADEN BELL

SWEETWATER
BOOKS

AN IMPRINT OF CEDAR FORT, INC.
SPRINGVILLE, UTAH

ISBN 13: 978-1-4621-1405-4

LIBRARY OF CONGRESS CATALOGING-IN-PUBLICATION DATA

Bell, Braden, author.
Luminescence / Braden Bell.
    pages cm. -- (Middle school magic)
    Summary: When Dr. Timberi's sigil sails into Lexa Dell, it creates a connection that tells Lexa, her twin Conner, and friends Melanie and Pilaf that he is alive--and suffering terribly at the hands of his Darkhand enemy, Lady Nightwing.
    ISBN 978-1-4621-1405-4 (perfect)
    [1. Magic--Fiction. 2. Middle schools--Fiction. 3. Schools--Fiction.] I. Title.
    PZ7.B3889145Lu 2014
    [Fic]--dc23
                            2013041572

Published by Sweetwater Books, an imprint of Cedar Fort, Inc.
2373 W. 700 S., Springville, UT 84663
Distributed by Cedar Fort, Inc., www.cedarfort.com

"Angel Lullaby" from *My Turn on Earth* used by permission from Deseret Book

Cover design by Kristen Reeves
Cover design © 2014 by Lyle Mortimer
Typeset and edited by Melissa J. Caldwell

Printed in the United States of America

10 9 8 7 6 5 4 3 2 1

To my family and students.

With special gratitude to Vickle, the best daughter I can imagine. You have been a gift from the beginning.

And to Leah, Avery, and Emma, each of whom has a special place in my heart.

ALSO BY BRADEN BELL

MIDDLE SCHOOL MAGIC:
THE KINDLING
PENUMBRAS

THE ROAD SHOW

Contents

✳ Contents ✳

✳ Contents ✳

CHAPTER 1

SHADOWS AND DARKNESS

CONNER DELL DIDN'T MEAN TO BLOW UP the substitute teacher.

Not that he minded, since the guy was a jerk to the gazillionth power. And, to be fair, that incident wasn't completely his fault. Lexa and Melanie helped with that too.

Conner also didn't mean to zap every power line and transformer in Nashville like popcorn in a microwave. Things like this just seemed to happen when young Magi were around, the natural combination of adolescence, strange powers, and a secret battle raging between the followers of Light and Dark.

At the moment, though, Conner wasn't worried about the cosmic battle between the Magi and their Darkhand enemies. For now, his main battle involved his algebra homework.

Alone in his room, he glared at the textbook, stifling a burning hatred for whatever idiot had first shoved letters and numbers together.

X *makes a sound!* he thought. *It's not a number.*

As his frustration rose, he pounded a clenched fist onto his desk.

Bad idea.

The desk cracked and crumpled to the floor.

The Light gave all Magi a special gift or ability when their powers first Kindled. Conner had superstrength and speed, which came in handy when fighting bad guys. But superstrength also led to a lot of damage in the off-hours.

He reached down and grabbed the algebra book from the top of the wreckage, resisting the urge to hurl it through the wall. Instead, he grabbed a football and pounded it back and forth from hand to hand. The sharp slap matched his frustration, and so he threw it harder, ignoring the burning numbness.

He considered asking Melanie for help. Melanie Stephens—his sister's best friend, and Conner's . . . well, Conner didn't know what to call her officially, but excitement flutter-kicked inside his chest as he thought about her peach-scented red hair and sparkling Dr. Pepper–brown eyes. And with the Light enhancing her already supersmart brain, Melanie could do algebra as easily as Conner could break stuff. Asking her would be easy. Since the Trio—he, Melanie, and his twin sister, Lexa—had Kindled, they could head-talk, or communicate telepathically.

Conner started to open his thoughts to call Melanie, but a whispered hiss filled his ears.

Conner Dell.

Across the room, the shadows on the wall came to life, pulsing with energy, like black jellyfish in the air.

When the shadows whispered his name again, Conner

dropped the football and opened his mind to them. He couldn't understand them as clearly as he had when he'd come out of the Shadowbox. Since the Lucents had healed him, the guilt and darkness of the soul-torture had faded. But he also couldn't connect to the shadows as easily or understand them as well.

Sometimes he got close, mostly when his emotions grew hot and strong. At those times, the raw strength of his feelings seemed to connect to the shadows the way a tourist in a foreign country might yell loud enough to be understood occasionally.

And now, with his frustration creating a connection, Conner felt a mental click as a pathway opened between his mind and the shadows.

He stretched his arm out, and the shadows flew at him from every corner of the room, pouring through the air like black syrup at high speed. Soft and cold, they landed in his hand, wrapping his stinging fingers with the sensation of icy silk.

The sensation triggered an avalanche of feelings as Conner remembered the first time he'd felt shadows. That memory stabbed deep inside of him with a sharp, burning blade.

Responding to the power of his emotion and reflecting Conner's memory, the shadows slid and bubbled, shaping themselves into the image of a smiling, middle-aged man. Dr. Timberi, Conner's teacher and Magi mentor.

Conner choked on bitter emotion as he recognized Dr. Timberi's smiling, triumphant face. He remembered that night. Remembered the excitement on Dr. Timberi's face when they first realized Conner could control shadows . . . *Our side just split the atom!* Dr. Timberi had said, beaming with excitement. *Now we must figure out how to build the bomb.*

Magi could control Light. Darkhands controlled the Darkness. But Conner could do both—the only person with that power. It was an unexpected side effect of surviving the Shadowbox, and Dr. Timberi gleefully assured them it would provide a major advantage to the good guys. They only had to figure out how to use and apply Conner's new powers.

But before they could do anything: a fight, some smoke—and Dr. Timberi was gone.

Conner gulped against the growing bitterness in his throat.

Right then his phone pinged, breaking his focus. Excavating the phone from the debris of his desk, he read a text from his friend Pilaf. "Hey guys, I'll pass out invitations later, but you're invited to my birthday party this Saturday, so don't plan anything."

Pilaf's message tugged Conner's scowl up into a brief smile. Good old Pilaf. No other eighth grader still passed out birthday invitations. And to Conner's joy, the text had gone to Melanie. Which meant that they'd be together. Conner, Melanie, Pilaf—and Lexa.

Conner's happy thoughts vanished, and he scowled as he thought about his twin sister, Lexa.

Following the strength of his anger, the shadows boiled and blended together into the form of a thirteen-year-old girl. Lexa, sticking her chin up in a defiant pose. *I hate him!* Her voice still rang in Conner's memory. Some of her final words to Dr. Timberi. A parting gift to the man who sacrificed his life for her freedom. *He's a mean, stupid jerk, and I hate him! I hate him!*

It was Lexa's fault Dr. Timberi was gone. Her drama-queen tantrum had led to his being captured. All because she didn't get the stupid lead in a stupid play. Now, the man who had saved their lives multiple times, the man who had helped heal Conner's broken mind and spirit, the man who had been their teacher, director, guide, and loyal friend was in the clutches of his worst enemy. And it was Lexa's fault.

Looking at Lexa's image brought Conner's frustration screeching back, bigger than before. He clenched his fists tighter and tighter until a loud crack reminded him of the phone still in his hand.

Dropping the phone, he punched the shadows instead. As his fist scattered them, something crackled, and he thought he saw a few black sparks.

Alive or dead? That was the question. One week had trudged by since Lexa shocked the mourners at Dr. Timberi's funeral by insisting that he was alive. One week since the funeral, and three weeks since his capture. Three weeks with no news.

Conner wondered if Lexa had just made it all up to deflect blame from herself. Maybe she even really believed it—but did that make it true?

Something like a cold kiss grabbed his attention. The shadows had slithered up his arm and now brushed against his face. As he brushed them away, Conner struggled again to understand the difference between shadows and Darkness.

Shadows were simply the absence of light. Darkness, on the other hand, was alive—a real power, an evil intelligence of some kind. Shadows were smooth and subtle, but not evil or bad. Not like the sharp, sizzling Darkness the Darkhands hurled. They had to be related, but Conner didn't understand how, and until he did, his new powers couldn't help Dr. Timberi or anyone else.

Somehow the Darkhands twisted shadows into something that could kill.

Or torture.

Conner clenched his eyes shut, trying to squash the images of Dark flames lancing from Lady Nightwing's fingers into Dr. Timberi's body.

Assuming Dr. Timberi was still alive, what was Lady Nightwing doing to him now? Conner had been her prisoner. He understood exactly the ways she could inflict pain on body, mind, and spirit. And Dr. Timberi had been at her mercy for three weeks. So while everyone else worried that Dr. Timberi might be dead, a quiet part of Conner worried that Dr. Timberi might still be alive—but wishing for a quick, merciful death.

Conner whispered yet another silent prayer for Dr. Timberi's safety as a warm tear snuck out of his eye.

The shadows in Conner's hand shifted again, gliding into a perfect representation of Lady Nightwing. Tall and regal, she carried the hypnotic beauty of a deadly snake.

His stomach clenched with bitter, stewing hatred. How many lives had this evil woman destroyed? How many spirits had she maimed and crippled?

Driven by growing fury, Conner flung the shadows away. They scattered but came flowing back, oozing into a different shape now: a pale man with long hair hanging down over eyes that burned with hate.

The Stalker. That was what they'd called him at first. But his real name was Timothy. Timothy Timberi. They'd just discovered that he was Dr. Timberi's son.

Conner's anger screamed inside of him. How could any son be like that? Conner had seen Timothy fight Dr. Timberi multiple times, trying to kill his father. Those attempts had all failed, but Timothy had tried. Again and again. But after all that, when Lady Nightwing turned on Timothy, Dr. Timberi had bargained with his own life, giving himself in exchange for his worthless son—and the safety of his students.

The shadows divided now, taking three shapes: Lady Nightwing, cackling with triumph on her smug face. Timothy looking sneaky and evil. And Lexa, striking her tragic-martyr-drama-queen pose.

Conner's anger exploded into a raging fury. The combustion propelled his fist forward, and he threw a punch at the shadowy images.

The chilly tingle of shadows cooled his hand as his fist connected with Lady Nightwing, but then sparks appeared in the air—hot, black sparks that sizzled around his clenched fingers. As his fist continued through Lady Nightwing and into Timothy, the sparks grew and spread, merging with strands of shadow. By the time his fist crashed through Lexa's image, shadows and sparks had blended into a ball of black fire in his hand, burning like flames wrapped inside of dry ice.

The momentum of Conner's punch hurled the ball of black flames across the room, drawing in more shadows and consuming them like gasoline. By the time the fireball crashed into his window, it had doubled in size. It vaporized the glass, flew outside, and collided with the power lines.

The black flames exploded, crackling as they danced

down the wires. The electricity in the lines merged with the black fire, creating eerie flames flashing back and forth from light to dark.

The scent of ozone filled the air as the strange fire converged on the transformer hanging from the telephone pole. For a few seconds, the flames disappeared inside the large metal bucket. Then a series of pops crescendoed, followed by a fountain of sparks that erupted out and rushed down the lines on either side, creating more of the flashing fire. The flames grew and multiplied as they rushed down the power lines.

As every light in Conner's neighborhood disappeared, the total darkness allowed him to watch wave after wave of explosions in the distance. Every light within his range of vision vanished, immersing him in darkness.

As a faint red glow lit Conner's room, it took him a few seconds to realize the glow came from him. Red was his signature color when he performed Lightcraft, and without conscious effort, his Light illuminated the area just around him, keeping the overwhelming darkness at bay.

In that silent moment, he felt safe. Peaceful. Even with darkness all around, it couldn't come inside him. Not unless he let it. His light might not be large enough to light the world, but it could still defy the darkness.

Sirens sounded in the distance, and dogs barked, interrupting the peace of the night. The air around him crackled, then hot, jagged streaks of white Light flashed through the room, blinding him. This wasn't his Light—and the color didn't belong to anyone he knew. Fearful now, Conner tried to run away, but as the Light began to swirl around him, he found himself frozen, unable to move.

THE CHERUB

IN THE QUIET OF HER ROOM, MELANIE STEphens sighed and pushed her homework aside. For once, she drew no comfort, or even distraction, from diagramming sentences, memorizing dates, or even solving algebra.

The clock, placed with precision in the center of her nightstand, changed from 11:59 to 12:00.

Melanie scrunched her nose and took deep breaths, pushing against the fiery jabs of panic that came with the new time. Staying up late to do homework was not new. Staying up late and having no homework done to show for it was very new. And disturbing.

Focus, Melanie. Focus. If x *equals—*

"Who cares?" she yelled. "Who cares about stupid *x*?"

She slammed the book shut and slid it away.

For the first time in her life, homework seemed trivial. In fact, school seemed meaningless. Normally, she celebrated the beginning of each school year, relishing the routine, the challenge, and the constant feeling of success she experienced. She always knew the answer to every problem. She was always the one who could help other people.

Until now. When it really mattered. Hot tears began to burn her tired eyes. She looked at her wall. Pages and pages of notes had been tacked up—pages and pages of ideas and thoughts about where Dr. Timberi might be imprisoned. She had grilled every Magus she knew for information, had asked them to talk to everyone they knew, and had kept careful track of it all.

So far, though, the whiteboard in her head sat still and silent. The whiteboard that had never let her down and had solved every problem she'd ever confronted. Until now.

And that hurt, bringing pain at an elemental level. When the answer really mattered, she didn't know it. When the problem was serious, she couldn't solve it. And when someone she loved truly needed her help, she had none to give.

Looking back at her desk, Melanie's bleary eyes locked on her script for *The Sound of Music.* Stupid, hateful, evil play. She wished it had never been written. If it hadn't, then Dr. Timberi would still be there. If Lexa had not been obsessed with being cast as Maria, if she had been gracious and not insisted on going to argue with Dr. Timberi at the school that night, nothing would have happened.

If, if, if . . .

Melanie knew she shouldn't blame Lexa. Initially she had, and then at Dr. Timberi's funeral, they'd all bonded in a wonderful, healing moment.

But as time passed, the sweetness faded, and Melanie struggled to not to blame Lexa.

A quiet, simple thought appeared and interrupted Melanie's brooding. Standing in sharp contrast to the more tumultuous thoughts filling her mind, it caught her attention like a single, quiet student raising her hand in a rowdy classroom.

The thought told her to organize a sigil.

It seemed random, so she ignored the thought and went back to work. But the thought persisted.

It couldn't cause any harm. A sigil was a small piece of the soul blended with the Light and given visible form. Magi used them often to communicate with each other or to fight with Darkhands.

Feeling a little silly, Melanie raised her hand and flicked her fingers. A unicorn, made entirely of pink Light, galloped into the air.

A second later, a small light appeared near her face. Followed by another. And another. After blinking several times, Melanie realized the lights were not illusions generated by tired eyes. Dot after dot of light appeared, filling her room like large, colored fireflies.

Lucents!

Mysterious beings of Light, the Lucents were basically baby cherubim. No one knew much about them, except that they had great power and seemed to take a special interest in Conner. The Lucents had healed him after the ordeal in the Shadowbox had damaged his soul. They revived him after becoming a junction for Dark and Light had nearly killed him. And when the Darkness had dragged Conner underwater in the ocean, they had saved him from drowning.

Now the Lucents filled her room.

They didn't speak in words, or even thoughts. Instead, an image flashed through Melanie's head. She recognized the old-fashioned key hanging around her neck. Dr. Timberi had given it to her the night he was captured so that she and the others could escape. Melanie, Conner, Lexa, and Dr. Timberi's son, Timothy, had scampered off to safety while Dr. Timberi surrendered to Lady Nightwing.

Melanie pushed those memories away. They led somewhere far too painful for her to go.

As she pulled the key out, the Lucents gave Melanie an image of herself turning the key. She hesitated for a moment. Turning the key would open the Otherwhere—a strange dimension guarded by the cherubim. Frequent trips through the Otherwhere had taught Melanie to be cautious around the cherubim. Fierce and fiery beings, they saw inside human souls, and Melanie always felt unsettled and frightened around them.

She hesitated, but that was the image the Lucents gave: her opening the Otherwhere and talking with the cherubim.

Melanie grabbed the key, fighting against the emotions that boiled up when she remembered the last time she'd used it. She pushed it into the air, and it disappeared inside the Shroud, an invisible barrier between the two worlds. As she turned the key, the air in front of her parted like a pair of curtains.

Normally, humans stepped through the Shroud and into a corridor, but this time, a person-sized white light of blinding intensity met her at the opening. Managing to be both soft and blazing, the light combined the cold brilliance of a star with the warmth of a bonfire on a cold night. As always, the light around the cherubim burned so brightly that no human eye could see what they looked like.

Waves of power washed over Melanie, radiating from the form in front of her.

You opened the Shroud between our worlds, Melanie Stephens. Cherubim spoke telepathically, so the words came as thoughts surrounded by intense feeling.

I'm sorry, Melanie said in her thoughts. *I didn't mean to disturb you. The Lucents—*

Do not apologize, Melanie Stephens. This cherub sounded both soft and strong, a downy layer of kindness wrapped around a core of steel. Or perhaps it was the reverse.

I sent the Lucents to find you. They gave you the idea to form a sigil. You were right to follow your impression.

Why?

Because it is very difficult for us to move in your world. Lucents move there more freely than cherubim, but even they cannot simply appear anywhere. They need some Light as a foundation before they can come. Your sigil gave them something to which they could connect, an anchor for them in a hostile world.

The cherub paused. *Melanie Stephens, the key you used to open the Shroud. To whom does it belong?*

Morgan Timberi. But he's gone.

And did Morgan Timberi give you a password to prove that he gave you that key?

Yes, ma'am—Melanie thought the cherub was a female—*His password was* Nicole.

Nicole. The name of Dr. Timberi's dead wife.

Murdered by the Darkhands, Nicole was the long-lost love of his life and the mother of his wayward son.

You are correct; that is his password. You are troubled, Melanie Stephens.

Troubled? Melanie almost shouted. *Yes! Dr. Timberi is missing, and I can't help him!*

I know about Morgan Timberi, the cherub said. *But there are other things that trouble you.*

Since Cherubim could read people's souls, Melanie saw no point in hiding anything.

My relationship with Conner is super complicated and awkward right now. We liked each other this summer, but then I fell for Lady Nightwing's trick and believed that Conner had become evil. But he hadn't. So I owe him an apology, but I feel way too dumb to bring it up. So that awkwardness hangs over everything else. Plus, Conner's mad at Lexa because he blames her for Dr. Timberi being captured. And, to be honest, I'm mad at Lexa too. I know I shouldn't be, but I am. Everything's so messed up.

You are honest, Melanie Stephens. That is a start. The cherub scanned her mind and heart. *You blame Lexa Dell to some degree for Morgan Timberi's capture. But your anger comes mostly because she is always the center of attention, good or bad. You are diligent and disciplined; she is careless and sloppy, and yet she can perform Lightcraft and you cannot. You feel that Lexa causes problems but gets affection and attention. For example, Morgan Timberi's Last Sigil chose Lexa to deliver his message and provide shelter.*

You are angry with Lexa Dell. But in reality, much of the anger comes because you are angry at yourself, angry that you are not all you wish to be. You feel that you live in her shadow.

Yes. Melanie felt very small and petty. The cherub's words rang true. She was tired of Lexa always being the center of everything. Melanie felt like she was just Lexa's assistant or sidekick, her perpetual backup singer.

Melanie Stephens, if you must live in a shadow, it is more important than ever to find the light. Sometimes you must be the bridge that brings the light into the darkness. Sometimes you must be the light that glows in the darkness. Do not be angry with Lexa Dell. Even more, do not be angry with yourself.

Melanie didn't want to talk about this anymore. It didn't really matter anyway. Not compared to more important things. *Can you tell me where Dr. Timberi is? How can I find him? How can I help him?*

Do not trifle with my words or push them aside! The cherub's thoughts grew stern and strong. *Melanie Stephens, you and your friends are like sparrows, clinging to great rocks and wondering why you cannot fly. If you would fly, you must release your grip on the rocks that weigh you down. Only then can you possibly help Morgan Timberi. How can the Light work through you when you hold onto Darkness? You form one side of a powerful triangle, and you can do nothing for Morgan Timberi until that triangle is once more complete and strong. I must go now. Ponder my words.*

The cherubim faded and Melanie found herself alone in the dark. Complete darkness. Looking out her window, she saw no lights anywhere in Nashville. Apparently power had gone out in the whole city. But, hidden in the dark, she sensed something that worried her. She felt Darkness all around, as if it had exploded, leaving traces everywhere.

Unnerved by the Darkness, Melanie called up the

Light. Soft pink Light—her signature color—bloomed around her fingers, pushing the darkness back.

Lexa? Conner? She reached out in her thoughts. If Darkness was exploding through the skies of Nashville, they needed to know.

Hi! Conner's soft voice sauntered through her thoughts, giving her pleasant chills. As usual. For as long as she'd known him, Conner Dell had given her chills.

Did I wake you up? she asked quickly, hoping he hadn't heard her thinking about getting chills.

No. I was already up. His thoughts turned sheepish. *I, uh, just sort of blew up the power lines. From what I can see—or not see—out of my window, I think I did a pretty thorough job.*

Are you okay? Could he sense the anxiety in her thoughts?

Yeah, fine, he replied. *Just feel pretty stupid. I was trying to figure out how to use Darkness and it sort of got out of hand.*

Should she talk to him now? Just get everything out in the open, apologize, and—

Because Melanie was connected to Conner's mind, she heard the heart-shredding screams coming from the room next to his. Terrible, terrified cries.

Conner, what's that? What's wrong? she asked.

Something's wrong with Lexa! he said.

But she didn't hear anything else. The air around Melanie crackled, and then hot, white Light flashed, dancing through the room in jagged streaks. White fire shot up from the floor, and Melanie couldn't move.

CHAPTER 3.

A Mother's Touch

Some part of Lexa Dell woke up, only to find herself still trapped in a dark, viscous dream, suspended in a nightmare like a grape in Jell-O salad. She thrashed around, disturbed by something she couldn't understand even as she swam in a pit of darkness and terror so thick it seemed tangible.

Something else troubled her as well, a dizzy feeling that muted her mind and made thinking clearly almost impossible. And pain. Terrible pain. Should nightmares hurt?

Struggling against the dream, Lexa realized that she was screaming, and those screams pulled her out of whatever trance had been smothering her.

Disoriented, she stared around her room as hot sweat gushed through every pore. Her room seemed unusually hot. And dark. No street lights or anything. The power must be out—

Lexa jumped, screaming again, as her bedroom door exploded open and a shadowy figure ran in.

"Lexa!" Red Light appeared in the figure's hand, revealing Conner's worried face. "Lexa, are you okay? What happened?"

"Lexa!" Lexa's mom burst into the room now, waving a flashlight, and followed by her dad, armed with a baseball bat. "Lexa, are you okay?"

Lexa! Melanie's voice echoed in her head, surrounded by a cloud of worry. Somehow that worry made Lexa feel warm inside. *Are you okay? I felt your screams in my head.*

Lexa looked at all the worried faces. "I'm okay."

Her dad knelt by the side of her bed. "Are you sure everything's okay, Lex?"

Lexa's mom sat on the edge of the bed and stroked Lexa's hair.

Now that her pulse had slowed down to the speed of a hummingbird's wings, Lexa tried to pull a few thoughts together.

Something had happened while she was sleeping. Something upsetting and frightening and painful. But what?

With every second, it faded, becoming more distant and less real.

"I'm fine," she said. "I think I just had a dream—not a regular bad dream. More like a vision. But I don't remember anything about it. Actually, it wasn't even like a vision. It was something else—but I don't know what. Instead of dreaming something, it's like I was experiencing something in my sleep. Something really bad." The Light sometimes gave Lexa dreams or visions that provided insight and information. She also had frequent flashes of insight or intuition she called *theelings* since they seemed to combine both thoughts and feelings.

Lexa grabbed her hair, pulling it into a ponytail and giving it a nervous tug. She looked at Conner—a little nervous to talk to him. He always got so mad at her lately. And now that she wasn't in danger, he looked annoyed. *Why is it so dark anyways? What time is it?*

It's 1:15, Conner said. *And I sort of blew up all the power lines in Nashville. With Darkness.*

What? Lexa forced herself not to squeal.

I was experimenting with shadows and things got out of hand.

Oh my gosh! Are you serious?

Conner practically snarled at her. *I didn't* mean *to. Sheesh, Lexa!*

"You're doing that thing where you talk in each other's heads, aren't you?" their mom interrupted.

Still scowling, Conner looked down at the ground. "Yes, ma'am."

"And," she continued, "I'll bet you're talking about Magi things and why Lexa is screaming in the night."

Their mom sighed, and her parents looked at each other for a minute. "We need to talk, you two," her dad said, nodding at her mom. That meant they'd been planning a lecture. "I'll be right back." Their dad took the flashlight and left the room, lit now by a red glow from Conner and a yellow one from Lexa. He returned a few seconds later holding a framed picture. As he shined the light on the photograph, the glass gleamed and the silver frame sparkled in the darkness.

Lexa didn't need the light, though. She had the picture memorized.

The picture showed her mom and dad, each rocking

a new baby. An infant Conner filled their mother's arms, and Lexa snuggled against their dad's chest. The picture had been enlarged and hung in the master bedroom above the now-empty rocking chairs.

Looking at the picture, Lexa could hear the lullaby her parents used to sing.

"Now listen, you two," her dad said. "I understand that teenagers don't want to talk to their parents. And it complicates things even more since we're not Magi and don't understand a lot of this stuff. But we've tried to be supportive, even though there's a lot we don't understand."

"Your father is right about being supportive," her mom jumped in. "Look at how Melanie's dad reacted. We didn't do any of the stuff Frank Stephens did."

Mr. Stephens had never liked Dr. Timberi. Then, when the Trio had Kindled and Dr. Timberi trained them to become Magi, Melanie's dad freaked out.

"We're your parents," her mom said, pointing at the picture. "To us, you will always be those babies and we need to take care of you. We need to know what's going on. And even without powers, we still might be able to help you."

Now it was their dad's turn. "Conner, if you had told us about the Shadowbox when it happened, we could have helped you work through that a lot sooner. And, Lexa, if you had talked to us before shooting over to the school to argue with Dr. Timberi after you didn't get the part you wanted in the play, we would have talked you down." His voice got soft and tender. "You wouldn't have gone, and you wouldn't be struggling with all the guilt you're dealing with now."

Awkward silence stumbled through the room, and tears scalded Lexa's eyes. She couldn't count how many times she'd relived that night in the last three weeks or how many times she'd wished she could have changed it.

But she hadn't considered this. Her dad was right. If she'd just talked to her parents, things could have been much different.

Lexa felt as if she had shrunk, compressed by the weight of her own stupidity. She hated to admit it, but her parents were right. Both she and Conner had suffered— and made other people suffer—unnecessarily.

"Just keep us posted on what's going on, okay? We love you guys." Her mom ended the lecture.

"I'm not hiding anything," Lexa said. "I just a had a bad dream. Or something. But I don't remember any more."

"Okay, well, keep us posted. Let's get back to sleep," Lexa's dad said. "You still have school tomorrow."

"Uh, Mom and Dad," Conner said. "I blew up the power lines. That's why there's a blackout."

"Conner, this is no time for joking around," their mom said.

"I'm serious," he said. "Come see my window. I sort of blew it up."

"Con, this better not be a joke," their dad said, following him out.

"Good night, sweetheart," her mom said, smoothing Lexa's hair. "You're crying! You never cry. What's wrong?"

Lexa shrugged. "I cry most nights now."

Through the wall, she heard her dad yell. He must have seen the window.

Her mom squeezed her hand. "I had no idea, but this is exactly what we're talking about. We need to know these things." Her voice got soft. "Is this about Dr. Timberi?"

Lexa nodded, and her mom hugged her. Neither of them spoke.

"Everyone hates me," Lexa said. "And I deserve it."

"No one hates you, sweetheart."

"Conner does."

"No, he doesn't. He's angry, but that's different. It will go away." Her mom paused. "You're not the only one who is struggling and suffering right now." Her mom cut off the protest Lexa started to make. "No, hear me out. Conner loves Dr. Timberi fiercely. He believes Dr. Timberi is the reason he didn't go completely crazy last summer. Except for our family, and maybe Melanie, Dr. Timberi means more to Conner than anyone in the world. Conner misses him, but there's more. You have to understand something, Lexa. Good men protect those they love, and in Conner's eyes, he failed."

"What?"

"Conner blames himself for Dr. Timberi being captured. He thinks he should have stopped it and torments himself by wondering what he could have done differently. The thought that he escaped and left Dr. Timberi behind eats at him the way your decision to go confront Dr. Timberi eats at you. All of that guilt and sadness is boiling around in Conner like a pressure cooker."

"But he shouldn't feel guilty," Lexa said. "Dr. Timberi told us to escape—he made us promise. Conner shouldn't be upset at himself. That's ridiculous."

"Is it any more ridiculous than the way you're beating

yourself up?" Her mom paused, and Lexa saw the trap she'd walked into. How had she not seen that one coming? Her mom snapped the trap shut. "Yes, it was your fault Dr. Timberi was at the school that night. But that doesn't mean that everything else that happened is your fault. Other people made choices that evening as well, including Dr. Timberi. You are not responsible for those choices. Or the final outcome."

"But I said I hated him!" Lexa allowed a sob to escape. "He heard me say that."

That, more than anything, seared Lexa's heart. A red-hot coal no amount of tears had extinguished.

Her mother's voice got firm. "Lexa, you told me about the message Dr. Timberi's Last Sigil gave at his funeral." At Magi funerals, the mourners opened a container that housed the deceased's Last Sigil. This sigil communicated the person's final words to loved ones. Then, with no body to anchor the soul to this world, the Last Sigil faded away.

"You told me his sigil spoke beautiful words of love and forgiveness. What happened next?"

"Mom—"

"I want you to say it out loud." Her mom loved to make her think through her problems.

Lexa grabbed her ponytail and tugged. "His Last Sigil didn't fade. Which means he's really alive."

"And what happened next?"

"His sigil went inside of me." Lexa remembered the warmth and overwhelming feeling of love and peace she'd felt in that moment. "And I knew he'd forgiven me."

"Lexa, out of hundreds of Magi at that funeral, Dr. Timberi's sigil went inside of you. Think about that. He had dear friends there, and all kinds of high-ranking, important Magi. But his sigil—that piece of his soul—chose you. Why is that?"

"Because I've had sigils go inside of me before?" Lexa said. "This lady named Notzange sent a sigil and it found me a few months ago. Maybe sigils can get in easier since I'm a Seer."

Her mom frowned. "Maybe. But I think it was Dr. Timberi's way of letting you know he forgave you, that he still loved you."

"You don't know that, Mom."

"No, but I knew Morgan. And that's the kind of person he was."

"Is," Lexa said in a firm voice, tilting her chin up.

Her mom smiled. "That's the spirit. Lexa, you told me that when the sigil came inside of you, Dr. Timberi gave you a message."

"He asked me to help him, asked me to come find him."

"Exactly. Now, in the week since the funeral, what have you done to help him?"

Again, Lexa was grateful for the darkness covering her face. She didn't like the answer to her mother's question: Nothing. Nothing at all. Great. Now she had something else to feel guilty about.

"Sweetheart, it's time to stop feeling guilty and time to get to work. You can wallow or you can work."

"But what can I do?" Lexa yelled in frustration.

"I don't know. I'm not a Magi. But the Lexa Dell I know wouldn't sit around moping. She'd come up with a dozen wild plans and schemes that were completely impossible—and then she'd make them work anyway. The

Lexa Dell I know would plow ahead with single-minded determination, ignoring anyone who said it couldn't be done." With gentle but firm hands, her mom pushed Lexa down onto her pillow. "Lexa, I understand having regrets. But it's time to move past them. You certainly don't do Morgan any good by beating yourself up." She bent down and kissed Lexa's cheek. "Good night."

"Good night, Mom."

As her mom left the room, Lexa's mind whirled around at light speed. Her mom's advice had changed her perspective and—

The air around Lexa crackled, then hot, white Light flashed, lancing through the room in jagged streaks. White fire shot up from the floor, and Lexa couldn't move.

CHAPTER 4

THE SUMMONS

LEXA WATCHED, PARALYZED, AS THE WHITE flames bent and turned, forming a spinning pinwheel, which threw off sparks as it rotated faster and faster.

Bright silver Light exploded out of the pinwheel, taking the form of the Magi emblem: an eight-pointed star surrounded by a crescent moon. A woman's voice said, "Please prepare for a message from the Magisterium." Lexa went from feeling uneasy to panicking. The Magisterium was the White House or Vatican of the Magi world—the ultimate authority over all the Magi everywhere. Were they coming to get her because she'd been responsible for Dr. Timberi being captured?

The air grew hot, and the temperature must have increased by at least five degrees as the light formed a strange creature. Half-eagle, half-lion, the beast looked at her and growled with just the hint of an eagle's shriek.

"You are Lexa Dell?"

"Yes, sir." Lexa didn't know what to say. "Or ma'am."

The griffin stared at Lexa. "Hold still for identity confirmation."

Two thin rays of Light shot out of the griffin's eyes. One ray stopped in front of Lexa's left eye, turning into a miniature whirlpool, swirling in the air in front of her. The other line shot into her forehead, then slid down her face. Warm but not painful, the Light scanned her face, and then both rays disappeared.

The griffin nodded. "Your identity is confirmed. Alexandra Louise Dell, you are hereby summoned by the Magisterium of the Sodality of the Midnight Stars to testify at a Tribunal of Inquiry. Examiners from the Chambers of the Supreme Magistrate will arrive within the next seventy-two hours to collect all relevant memories."

"But—"

"The tribunal will be held one week hence. Your presence is required."

"But—"

The griffin faded, leaving only the still-swirling pinwheel of white fire surrounding the Sodality emblem. The star flashed and the woman's voice came back.

"This communication from the Magisterium is now complete," she said. "We thank you for your attention."

Guys? Lexa called Melanie and Conner. *Did you just get a message from the Magisterium?*

Yeah, Conner said. *Right after I blew up the power lines. I thought it was because of that.*

Me too, Melanie replied. *Right after a cherub came to visit me. I thought maybe I was in trouble for that.*

Why are they busy having tribunals anyway? Lexa asked.

They should be out looking for Dr. Timberi! Wait, Mel, what did you say about a cherub coming to visit you?

Brown Light flashed in the air by Lexa's head, forming the shape of a rattlesnake. "Dell, you still awake?" A familiar voice, deep with a heavy Texas accent, filled the room—Colonel Lee Murrell, one of Dr. Timberi's oldest friends and the commander of the Twilight Phalanx, an elite Magi fighting force.

"Yes, sir," Lexa said.

"Good," the rattlesnake sigil replied. "We've got a big problem, and I need you to get over to the school five minutes ago. I'm here in Mona's classroom." Mona was Madame Cumberland, the French teacher at Lexa's school, and one of the Magi.

"Okay, I'll be over in a minute. Should I bring Conner and Melanie too?"

"Sure, but hurry!"

"Yes, sir," Lexa said. "We'll be right there."

Did you guys hear that? Lexa asked.

Of course we did. We're in your head, Lexa, Conner snapped. She almost snapped back but stopped, remembering what her mom said about how Conner had been feeling lately.

I'm going to stream over, Lexa said. Streaming was a form of Lightcraft where Magi turned into comets so they could travel at incredible speeds. *Do you want to come?*

I can't stream. Melanie's thoughts grew chilly. For some reason, Melanie hadn't learned to stream yet. It was a sensitive topic, and Lexa couldn't believe she'd just mentioned it like that. As Lexa stammered for something to say, Conner said, *I'll give you a ride, Melanie.*

CHAPTER 5

SNEAKING OUT

MELANIE TURNED HER THOUGHTS OFF SO that no one would hear her mental squeals or the high-speed tap dance her heart started. Conner was going to give her a ride!

After calming herself, Melanie opened the link again. *Sorry, I got cut off,* she said. *A ride would be great. Thanks so much.*

Wait. What do you mean a ride? Lexa asked. *Didn't you already try that?*

Melanie cringed at the memory. A few months earlier, Conner had sort of kissed her. In the excitement of the moment, he'd turned into a comet and had tried to carry her with him. But Melanie couldn't stream. And, when a Magus streamed, any non-streaming person or object they carried became many times heavier than normal. So Conner had dropped her on the ground. While Lexa watched. Awkward, to say the least.

Melanie figured something out a few days ago, Lexa, Conner said. *If she phases, then she's full of Light, so she's basically weightless and I can carry her.*

Cool! Lexa said.

Thanks. Melanie felt justified in her pride at the discovery. Although she would have preferred the ability to stream instead of being a smart-but-defective Magus who couldn't stream but figured out ways around it.

I'll be right over, Melanie. Conner's words drew a big, silly smile on Melanie's face.

Melanie placed pillows under her blankets, simulating her sleeping body just in case a parent looked in. As she worked, her smile faded into a frown. If she'd discovered this streaming work-around sooner, or if she'd learned to stream in the first place, everyone would have escaped from the school well before Dr. Timberi was taken. Conner, Lexa, and Dr. Timberi all could have streamed away that night. They remained because they didn't want to desert her.

Everyone knew it was Lexa's fault that they had been at the school in the first place. But so far, no one seemed to notice it was Melanie's fault they stayed.

Which explained why Melanie shouldn't blame Lexa for what happened. Any fingers she pointed at Lexa might eventually point back at her.

But that didn't mean Lexa didn't do plenty of annoying things.

Lexa had caused this whole problem in the first place but was invited to secret midnight meetings with senior Magi. Lexa, who never studied or practiced Lightcraft but could do anything she wanted. Lexa, who lurched around like a bull in the china shop of life—making messes that everyone else had to clean up.

Meanwhile, Melanie was allowed to tag along to Lexa's important meetings, like a dutiful secretary—

A flash of red Light outside of her window signaled Conner's arrival. Melanie pushed her frustrations aside, opened her gateway, and connected with the Light. She tried not to giggle as the familiar ticklish sensation ran all over her skin. In streaming, Magi merged with Light, becoming a comet. Phasing involved using the Light to alter the way a human body absorbed and reflected Light. It meant being covered and cloaked by the Light, so that a Magus became invisible. And, it turned out, basically weightless.

Sneaking down the stairs, Melanie thought she heard a noise, and froze. She listened but didn't hear anything. It must have been her sister, Madi, rolling over or something.

Melanie took a deep breath, trying to calm her raging pulse. She'd never sneaked out of the house before. And even though she was invisible, her absence would be obvious if anyone woke up and looked too hard. And if her parents discovered that she'd sneaked out of the house, they would kill her.

Once downstairs, Melanie took another deep breath and walked through the wall next to the front door. She stopped phasing, returned to her normal state—and her pulse rushed into a raging torrent again.

Conner stood there smiling, his dimple flashing in the September moonlight—

She began phasing again to hide her blush. Even other Magi couldn't see you when you phased.

Melanie? he asked. *Where did you go?*

When she felt a little more in control, she un-phased again. *Sorry,* she said. *I thought I heard something. Where's Lexa?*

Conner jerked his head upward. *Up there in a holding pattern.*

Melanie looked up and saw a bright yellow comet sketching wide circles in the sky.

Ready? Conner asked, turning around. Melanie took a slight running start, then jumped up, perching piggyback on Conner.

Being so close to him triggered a series of tingly chills, from head to toe. The spicy scent of his cologne enhanced the chills. She wrapped her arms tighter around him, enjoying the increased closeness.

He must have felt the same way because he began to shake and tremble. Melanie sighed. The recent awkwardness between them seemed gone. Knowing he was overcome felt so romantic—

Conner gasped. *Choking me,* he wheezed.

Oh.

Relieved that he couldn't see the hot blush smoldering on her face, she let go of his neck. *Nice job, Melanie. Nice. Job.*

Thanks, he said. *That's better.*

Oh well. Dr. Timberi had warned her to not let the romance with Conner grow too far beyond friendship. "Be friends," he had said. "Good friends. Affectionate friends. But leave it at that. If love is real, it will grow along with you until you are both mature enough for a durable relationship that will shelter and feed it."

As Conner blurred into a comet, Melanie phased. Both of their bodies changed, transformed by the Light into more refined matter. Conner had compared streaming to a runner's high on steroids, and Melanie thought that captured the exuberance. She'd never felt so free and unrestrained.

Shooting through the sky at comet-speed made time slow down. In that form, at that speed, no one could talk or even head-talk. Words were too slow and clumsy, and you shot past them before they could even be formed. Instead, streaming created a shared consciousness, a merging of feelings and thoughts the second they occurred.

Since Melanie could sense what Conner felt, she wondered how much he experienced her feelings. Could he perceive the way she got fluttery and excited when he was around?

His thoughts flowed back into her, and she realized he did—and he loved it.

Shooting through the sky with a boy she liked after sneaking out of her house made Melanie feel a little wild.

Giddy now, Melanie decided to tell him all the things she wanted to say. How she felt about him, and how sorry she was for misjudging him over the summer. She started to open her feelings, ready to let them flow into his mind— but a heavy, lead-like sadness interrupted her.

Lexa had streamed up next to them, and her consciousness seeped into the mix, overwhelming Melanie with the heavy anvils of guilt and regret Lexa carried. The weight of self-reproach pulled down on Lexa to the point that Melanie didn't understand how she could manage to walk, let alone fly. She'd had no idea of the burden Lexa carried.

But Melanie also felt something else inside of Lexa—a strong desire to save Dr. Timberi. It burned inside of her, a blazing fire that consumed all other thoughts.

Below them, the school came into view, surrounded by a large bubble made out of Light: a shield the Magi had put up to protect the school against Darkness and those who served it. In the darkness of the citywide blackout, it glowed with extra power—the only light all around. The guilt Melanie felt from Lexa flowed in stereo now. A lower, deeper emotional tone came from Conner. He blamed himself for having destroyed the shield a few weeks earlier, thereby allowing Lady Nightwing to get in the night she captured Dr. Timberi.

As they whistled through the shield, Melanie realized that each of the three of them had regrets about that night—a heavy "if only" they carried around.

They landed outside of Madame Cumberland's classroom, resuming their normal forms.

When did you guys figure that streaming-phasing-piggyback thing out? Lexa asked.

About a week ago, Melanie replied. *Right after the funeral. Conner was trying to teach me to stream. And, of course, I couldn't get it. But I figured out that since phasing changes your body's wavelengths, it made me weightless to him.*

Cool! Lexa said. But Melanie heard some hurt in her thoughts as well. During their first adventures as Magi, they'd faced danger and exciting adventures together— the three of them. Now, in addition to her guilt, Lexa felt isolated and left out.

Remembering the cherub's words about fixing the triangle, Melanie sighed. They had a lot of work to do.

CHAPTER 6.

Midnight Meetings

STRUGGLING TO PUSH PAST THE HURT THAT came from knowing Conner and Melanie had been training without her, Lexa shuffled into Madame Cumberland's classroom. Filled in equal measure with posters of France and Madame Cumberland's familiar perfume, it had always been a warm, comfortable place. Tonight, with no power, it was lit by candles, which created an even more inviting feeling, something Lexa welcomed tonight.

Colonel Lee Murrell slumped in a chair by the desk. He looked tired and much older than he had a week ago. His chest heaved up and down, and the bristles of his white hair stuck out at more angles than usual. Madame Cumberland and Mrs. Grant, their English teacher and another of the Magi, stood next to him, both wearing nightgowns, bathrobes, and worried faces. Mrs. Grant always frowned, but tonight her frown went a lot deeper. Lee frowned. Even Madame Cumberland frowned, which almost never happened.

"If this about the lights, I can explain," Conner said.

Mrs. Grant waved her hand, and Lee shook his head. "Are you kidding, Dell? Power lines can get fixed. We got much bigger fish to fry." He gulped something from a Vanderbilt University water bottle Madame Cumberland kept on her desk. "Thank you, Mona," he said.

Madame Cumberland looked at Melanie with concern in her eyes. "Melanie, Lee is exhausted. Could you please Augment him?"

Melanie nodded and ran forward. Taking Lee's leathery hands in her own, she closed her eyes. Pink Light appeared, running from Melanie into Lee. As it did, Lee sat up straighter and looked much less tired and haggard. Augmentation, or the ability to enhance someone's strength and power, was another of Melanie's gifts. Lexa didn't think it was totally fair that Melanie got two gifts.

"Thanks, Melanie," Lee said. "I was weaker than a politician's campaign promise. It's been a long week."

"What's wrong?" Lexa asked.

Lee sighed. "Oh, just about everything. Lexa, I don't have a whole lot of time. I need to get some information. Have you felt anything from Morgan's sigil since the funeral? Anything at all?"

"No. Why?" Lexa asked as foreboding rose like stomach acid inside of her.

Lee rubbed his temples. "About an hour ago, a report came in that Morgan was dead."

That word hung in the air, a dark, ugly scar.

Burning, cold panic filled the room, and Lexa found herself screaming, "No! That's not true. It's a lie!"

After she calmed down, Lee continued.

"Some top-secret source of hers said the Darkhands just killed him. Well, Hortense latched onto that report like a leech on a fat man, and she's saying that Morgan is dead." Hortense was the head of the Adumbrators Office—the Magi intelligence agency—and the equivalent of the CIA and FBI. A difficult, prickly woman, she'd been Dr. Timberi's bitter rival for years.

"What else is there?" Lexa asked. "There's something else you're not telling me." But, deep down, she knew.

"Hortense is ready to call off the search. She's telling people that you know he's dead, but you won't admit it because you can't handle the guilt that comes with it."

Lexa grabbed her ponytail, reeling from what felt like a slap across the face. With a metal glove.

"That's not true." Lexa's voice resonated with a strength that even surprised her a little. "He's definitely alive. I can feel him."

"Lexa, are you sure?" Lee asked.

"Positive. I swear," she said. "It's like his sigil is sleeping or something. But it's alive. I can feel it."

Lee stared at her, his sharp blue eyes shooting into hers. She returned his stare, not blinking as the old solider interrogated her without a word. It seemed to go on longer than science class, but finally, he nodded. "I believe you. That's good enough for me. Now I've got to convince Hortense, and that won't be easy."

"Why?" Melanie asked. "I mean, what does she have to lose by just being extra sure?"

Lee rubbed his temples harder. "Y'all don't understand what an ego that woman has. Recently, just before the funeral, it was time to pick a new Supreme Magistrate.

Hortense wanted that job badly, and she thought she had it in the bag. I mean, she was measuring the office for curtains and picking out paint colors.

"But the Council chose Notzange instead of Hortense." Lee took a drink.

"Notzange's in charge?" Lexa asked. Notzange was the Magus who had trained Madame Cumberland. She'd been kidnapped by Darkhands about the time the Trio had Kindled, and one of their first adventures had involved helping to rescue her.

"Yep," Lee said. "And that was a huge blow to Hortense's pride. She felt publicly humiliated. She's coping with that by throwing around all the weight she has left and exercising every bit of power she can, which means she's not likely to listen to anyone right now or do anything that she thinks shows any weakness."

As Lee paused to take another drink, Madame Cumberland put a comforting arm around Lexa. "I still can't believe she'd be that petty. She and Morgan never liked each other, but to put her own ego ahead of finding him—"

"She's not doing it on purpose," Lee said. "I've never liked Hortense, but she's not a bad person. The Adumbrators get all kinds of reports all the time. This happens to fit what she tends to believe—and, to be fair, there ain't much evidence to the contrary." Lee rubbed his eyes. "Just the word of a thirteen-year-old kid."

"So they'll just abandon him?" Lexa shouted.

"Not if I can convince them otherwise," Lee said. "But it's hard to keep a whole herd of people moving on faith alone. A lot of folks are ready to build a nice memorial, file the report in triplicate, and move on. It's a whole lot easier to cry at his funeral than rip the world apart looking for a needle in a big old haystack." Vivid frustration bloomed in his voice. "And if they can come up with the story of a thirteen-year-old girl who is either lying to avoid blame, or who is having some kind of delusions to protect herself from guilt, then everything's nice and tidy."

Lexa tugged her ponytail hard for a few seconds before replying. The force of long habit pushed her to stick out her chin and launch into a long, indignant monologue. But too much was at stake. She needed to not be a drama queen right now. So she waited until she could control her words.

"I'm not lying. Dr. Timberi's alive. I promise he's alive! I'm not making this up." Her tears smeared the room into a blurry image. "I know it's my fault he got taken, but I would give up my powers if it would bring him back. I would give up my life." She took a deep breath, trying to steady her voice. This crying thing really got in her way. "And if no one else will do anything, then I'll find a way to save him myself."

Madame Cumberland hugged Lexa and patted her hair. "We believe you, Lexa," she said. "And Notzange believes you."

"If Notzange is the Supreme Magistrate, can't she just order Hortense to find him?" Conner asked.

Lee smiled. "Dell, you clearly don't understand how bureaucracies work. Notzange can give orders all day. But if Hortense says she has solid intel that Morgan's dead, the momentum evaporates. People will only go so far on orders—they have to be motivated."

"Lexa, can you talk to Morgan? Contact him?" Mrs. Grant asked.

Lexa shook her head. "No. I've tried. It doesn't work like that. But I can feel his sigil inside of me. He's still alive. It's just asleep. It's been sleeping since the funeral."

"I believe you," Lee said. "I really do. Trying to get the rest of the Magisterium to have the same faith is tricky, but I'll keep trying. Lexa, if you feel anything, if that sigil so much as burps, send me a sigil and let me know right away. Understand?"

"Yes, sir."

"It's late," Mrs. Grant said in a softer-than-usual voice. "You three need to get home. Lexa, keep us posted if anything else happens."

"Yes, ma'am," Lexa said, feeling smaller and more alone than she'd ever felt.

Outside of the classroom, Melanie took her place on Conner's back again, and within seconds, the three of them were streaming back through the night sky.

Oaths and Apologies

As they sailed through the sky, Conner couldn't enjoy the experience of being so close to Melanie. Thinking of the Magisterium giving up on Dr. Timberi turned everything around him to ashes.

An urgent feeling from Lexa interrupted him. She wanted to talk right then. Could they land?

Melanie sent an affirmative reply, so Conner didn't have much of a choice, and he followed Lexa down to the park below. As he and Melanie returned to their normal forms, their emotional link faded.

When they landed, Lexa tossed a ball of yellow Light into the air, creating a lantern that provided the only light in the total darkness. The light illuminated the worried look on her face. She tugged on her ponytail over and over, and even chewed her lip, which she only did during major tests.

"What's wrong, Lexa?" Melanie asked.

"Okay," Lexa said, taking a deep breath. "Please listen,

because I can only say this once. I'm really sorry. Really, really sorry." A tear plunged out of her eye, and Lexa slapped it away like it was a mosquito. "I was a drama queen, and if I hadn't insisted on talking to Dr. Timberi that night, then he wouldn't have been at the school and nothing would have happened." She struggled to keep control of her voice, and Conner squirmed a little, uncomfortable with the raw emotion. Why did girls always want to talk about feelings? Oh well. Maybe it was good to get all of this out.

"It's my fault," she continued, "and I said those horrible things to him. If you want to hate me forever, I totally deserve it. But I would give anything to save Dr. Timberi. Anything. I tried beating myself up, and that didn't bring him back." Her head rose to a defiant angle, with a matching tone in her voice. "So, now it's time to try something else. Hate me if you want, but I'm going to try to save him, and I think that will be more likely if we all work together." She tugged her ponytail one more time. "And also, I know I was a pain last summer. I got jealous and snippy when I shouldn't have. But I'm trying to change, if you'll give me a chance. And, Conner, I'm sorry I believed you were becoming a Darkhand and that I told Melanie you would kill her. I should have trusted you more."

Conner had to respect her honesty and humility. "You're right, Lex," he said after a few seconds of heavy silence. "I am mad at you. I don't really care about the other stuff, but whenever I think about Dr. Timberi, I get mad. And I know that's not fair."

Melanie touched Lexa's arm. "Same here. I've

tried not to blame you, but I have. And Conner's right. That's not fair. You made a small mistake, but you didn't make everything else happen. Anyway, it's kind of my fault."

"What?" Conner asked. Lexa looked shocked.

"I can't stream," Melanie said. "If I had been able to, then we all would have been gone. Dr. Timberi only came back to the school because we were still there, and we were only there because you two refused to leave me when the Darkhands attacked."

Conner opened his heart for the first time. "Well, if I hadn't freaked out with Light and Dark and blown up the shield, Lady Nightwing couldn't have gotten in. I guess all of us are to blame."

Melanie shook her head. "No, we're not. It's Lady Nightwing's fault. Period. I'm sorry, Lexa." She sighed. "I was being unfair, and I'll really work on it."

"Yeah," Conner said. "Me too."

"Since we're doing this," Melanie took a deep breath, "Lexa, I'm sorry Conner and I left you out this summer. We didn't mean to."

Conner felt the weight of both Melanie and Lexa's eyes. Melanie nudged him. "Uh, yeah, me too."

Is that why she was always so mad? he asked in a private thought message to Melanie.

"Apology accepted!" Lexa threw herself into a big hug with Melanie.

After their hug, Melanie looked at Conner. "I'm really sorry about the summer, Conner." She winced. "I shouldn't have believed Lady Nightwing's lies. I pushed you away when you needed me most. I'm so sorry."

"Apology accepted!" In a flash of inspiration, Conner followed Lexa's example and threw himself into a big hug with Melanie.

"I'm sorry too!" Lexa joined their hug as well, which wasn't exactly in Conner's plan.

Conner didn't like talking about feelings, but he had to admit it felt good getting everything out. Everything felt clean and fresh—like the air after a rainstorm.

"Hey, guys," Melanie said in a quiet voice. "Do me a favor. Will you each grab one of my arms and stream?"

"What's up?" Conner asked.

"I'm not sure—maybe nothing. Just do it, please?"

"Sure." Conner linked elbows with her left arm, Lexa with her right. They began to run, and as they did, Conner realized a bright pink comet had formed between him and Lexa.

"No way!" he yelled. "Go, Melanie!"

The pink comet shot past him and Lexa, curving straight up into the sky at a ninety-degree angle, then leveling out and circling the park.

"How is she doing that?" Conner asked. "Remember how long it took us to be able to control it?"

"Maybe because she watched our training and learned from our mistakes?" Lexa asked.

"Oh yeah," Conner said. "Like when a little kid takes a long time to talk and then just starts speaking in complete sentences. Pilaf says that's what he did."

The pink comet turned a loop-de-loop and then landed, fading back into a beaming Melanie. Her smile seemed almost as bright as the comet had been.

"Nice job!" Conner said, grabbing her hands.

"What happened, Mel?" Lexa asked. "Why could you do that all of a sudden?"

"Honestly, I think because we got everything worked out." Melanie grinned. "I spent most of the summer being mad at you, Lexa, and being scared Conner was going to kill me. I think all that stuff weighed me down without realizing it. But when we apologized, I felt so light and happy. I just had a feeling I could stream. And I'd watched you two, so I knew how to do it. That was amazing!"

Melanie jumped up into the air, blurring into a comet again. She took one more spin around the park. Conner had never seen her look quite so giddy.

"Now that we're all friends again, I need to tell you about something," Melanie said. "I mentioned earlier that a cherub came to talk to me."

"Oh yeah! Lee's sigil interrupted us." Lexa said. "What did he say?"

"It was a she, and she said that being mad at each other was like holding on to Darkness, and it meant the Light couldn't help us," Melanie said. Sparrows and stones. That made sense now. "She also said that I was part of a triangle that had to be fixed so we can help Dr. Timberi. I'm pretty sure that triangle is us, the Trio."

"I get the part about holding on to Darkness. But what does that triangle stuff mean?" Conner asked.

Melanie scrunched her nose, sending Conner's heart into some intense hip-hop moves. "Last summer Dr. Timberi told me that our gifts seemed unusually complementary. I'm a Percipient, so I can solve complex problems in my mind. Lexa's a Seer, so she gets dreams and visions and insight from her theelings. Conner, you're superstrong and fast. Our gifts and personalities each represent a dimension of a human being: mind, spirit, and body."

"Whoa," Conner said. "That's deep. So we're like some mystical combination?"

"Yeah, like three parts of one giant soul or something?" Lexa asked.

"He didn't know for sure," Melanie said. "He wanted to think more about it, but then everything happened."

"Maybe that's why his Last Sigil warned us not to fight or let anything separate us," Lexa said.

"Probably," Melanie added.

"We haven't done very well at following that advice," Conner said.

"But now it's going to be different," Lexa said. "It has to be. Guys, listen. Dr. Timberi's sigil told me to find him. Me, not the Magisterium. And he had to know that would include the whole Trio. We need to stop waiting for other people and save him ourselves. If we were captured, he wouldn't sit around waiting for the Magisterium to rescue us. He'd be out tearing the world apart himself."

"True," Melanie said. "But what do we do?"

"Well, I don't know," Lexa said. "But we have to do something. I need to keep trying to contact him and see if we can get any clues."

"I need to learn to control the Darkness," Conner said. "For real. I've just played around with it. I need to get serious about it."

Melanie nodded. "Dr. Timberi thought that could be our secret weapon. But what about me?"

Lexa jumped. "Melanie! I know what you can do—he taught you to Adumbrate, right?"

Adumbration was the art of looking at the shadows given off by the Darkhands and trying to understand what they were doing. It was a complex art that Dr. Timberi had started to teach Melanie.

"Yes, sort of. Just the basics."

"So start Adumbrating and see what you can find. You're so smart you might figure out something no one else does." Lexa smiled. "And when we figure out where he is, we will tear through metal, dig through stone, walk through fire, and swim through floods to save him."

"Yeah!" Conner shouted. "Go team!" He put his hand out in front of him. Melanie put hers on top of his, which is what he'd hoped for. Lexa followed, dropping her hand on Melanie's.

"Go, team! Team Timberi!" Lexa yelled. Then her voice softened. "I think we need to swear an oath to make it for real. An oath to find him, and an oath to stop fighting."

"I agree," Melanie said.

Conner nodded. "I'm in."

"It needs to be the Magi's Oath," Lexa said. "Like he swore that night. Unbreakable. We owe him that much."

Melanie nodded. "Do you remember the words?"

Lexa nodded. "I remember everything about that night. Everything."

Lexa had no drama or self-pity in her voice. Conner would have recognized it. Her simple, sincere statement touched Conner, opening a window into what the last three weeks had been like for Lexa.

Lexa raised her right arm to the square like a witness

in a courtroom, and Conner and Melanie did the same. "Repeat after me: 'I, Alexandra Louise Dell'"—Conner and Melanie said their own names—"'solemnly swear to track down and rescue Dr. Timberi. I also swear not to be petty and fight with anyone. I bind myself to this course with all the power of the Light within me.'"

Yellow light flashed and swirled down Lexa's arm, continuing until it covered her entire body like a streamer. The same thing happened to Conner and Melanie, with red and pink Light, respectively. When the Light covered each of their entire bodies, it flashed, a brilliant three-colored burst that illuminated the entire park before it disappeared.

A solemn silence fell over the park as darkness returned. Even the crickets and frogs seemed to realize something significant and powerful had happened.

CHAPTER 8

GROUNDED

WHEN THEY SOARED OVER HER HOUSE, Melanie peeled off from Conner and Lexa, streaming into her room. More awake and alive than she had ever felt, Melanie circled her room three times, landing on her bed with a flourish. Giggling, she threw up her arms, bowing to the wall like an Olympic gymnast. With a bounce, she jumped to bow to the other side of the room—and came face-to-face with a bright flashlight. When her eyes adjusted, she found herself looking into her mother's very angry glare.

"Melanie Nicole Stephens, where have you been?"

Melanie's exuberance rushed away, vaporized by the icy anger in her mother's eyes. "I can explain—"

"No. You can't." Her mother's voice shook with anger. "There is no possible explanation that will justify you being out of the house after midnight without permission."

"But, Mom—"

"Frank!"

Melanie's hopes sank inside. She was dead.

Her dad wandered into the room, rubbing his eyes. "What's going on, Elise? Melanie, why are you in your regular clothes?"

"Because she just got back."

"What do you mean just got back? From where?"

"I was just about to ask that."

"Melanie Nicole Stephens!" her father bellowed. "Where have you been?"

Dead. Absolutely dead. If they both used her middle name, she was dead.

"I went to the school for a meeting about Dr. Timberi. They're giving up on finding him and so we . . ."

As she spoke, bright purple rose from her dad's neck up into his face. It passed his mouth, nose, and eyes until his entire head had become a purple mask of rage.

"You snuck out of the house for Magi stuff?" he yelled.

"Yes, sir," she whispered.

"Melanie," her mother spoke in a quiet, deadly tone, "you may be a Magi—" Melanie bit back the impulse to correct her mother. *Magus. Magi is plural* "—but you are our daughter. Our *minor* daughter. If this ever happens again—"

"*If* this happens again?" Her dad jumped in. "*If*? How do we know it hasn't? How do we know it doesn't happen every night? I've about it had it with this Magi nonsense!"

"Dad, I—"

He held his hand up, as if shoving her words away. "Not a word, young lady! Not a word! This has gone too far. I was stupid to ever allow it. It's time we put this Magi thing to rest. No more streaming. No more sigils. No more shooting Light!"

"What?"

"I mean it. If I see so much as a spark on your fingers, I'm on the first plane to France, and I'll march right up to the Magisterium and give them a piece of my mind!" He turned and huffed through the door. Melanie's mother shot her one more disappointed look, then followed him.

Give up being a Magus?

Throwing herself down on her pillow, Melanie gave free rein to sobs that shook her entire bed. How could they? They wouldn't even let her explain.

She pounded her pillows with a violence she didn't realize she could generate. For the first time in her life, she decided to ignore and disobey her parents. She would use Lightcraft anyway.

Then she remembered. A few months earlier, Dr. Timberi had warned them that the Light wouldn't follow them if they were disobeying their parents.

A tiny butterfly of hope fluttered in her mind. What if Dr. Timberi had just exaggerated for dramatic effect? Adults did that sometimes.

Melanie held up her hand, opening her gateway. As the gateway opened and Light rushed in, that fragile little butterfly grew stronger.

She raised her hand and fired a sigil.

But nothing came.

She tried again, calling up Light around her fingers.

Nothing.

Not so much as a single pink sparkle. Just like her dad had said.

She hurled a pillow across the room, followed by the loudest, angriest cry she could muster.

"I hate you!" she yelled.

After more shouting, pounding, and many more tears, Melanie lay exhausted on her bed. As fatigue finally overpowered her seething rage and desolate sadness, a thought occurred as she drifted off to sleep. How did her dad know about the Magisterium? Or streaming and sigils? She'd never talked about their training because Magi stuff made him mad. How in the world did he know anything that specific?

· CHAPTER 9 ·

LEXA'S LULLABY

LEXA ROLLED OVER AGAIN, TRYING TO FIND a comfortable position. But she couldn't. Knowing Dr. Timberi might be abandoned by the Magisterium kept her tense and uncomfortable.

As she tossed and turned, one thought looped through her mind: she had to help him. If only they could figure out where he was. If only she could communicate with his sigil.

A theeling jumped into Lexa's mind. If she used the Light to connect to the sigil, would that work?

Opening her gateway, she guided tendrils of Light deep inside her spirit. As her Light found and connected to Dr. Timberi's sigil, the sleeping swan fluttered to life, and his consciousness surged into Lexa's mind.

Dizziness and a feeling of disorientation sent her mind whirling as her consciousness merged with his. For several uncomfortable seconds, she had an acute case of mental double vision. Lexa focused harder and the dizziness and disorientation passed. She became aware of two things. First, a shiny metal ceiling. Second, the aching throb of old pain.

"He's awake," someone said. "Get Lady Nightwing."

Dr. Timberi's thoughts felt muddled, confused by fatigue and pain. But a flash of clarity came, followed by a resolution.

If he said nothing, he could die in peace, knowing he hadn't provided information that could be used to hurt anyone he loved

Faces flashed through his mind. Melanie. Lexa. Conner. And Timothy.

"Tell us about Conner and Lexa Dell, and Melanie Stephens."

Nothing. He would say nothing.

"Why did they Kindle at the same time? Is the Magisterium running an experiment to make people Kindle?"

"Are Madi Stephens and Olaf Larson part of the experiment? What are their powers?"

Nothing.

A door opened and a familiar figure walked into his view. Lexa shivered at the ghastly smirk across Lady Nightwing's pale face. A brilliant and evil Darkhand scientist, she had conducted experiments on kids who were Kindling. She'd tortured Conner in a Shadowbox and had planned a grisly death for him. Merciless and possibly crazy, she had a special hatred for Dr. Timberi.

"Hello, Morgan. I see you are awake now."

Lexa felt his fierce determination to not let her see any weakness. "Hello, Emily."

She laughed. "Oh, a brave face! We'll see how long

that lasts, Morgan. You have no idea what I have planned for you." Her eyes narrowed. "You will die. That is a given."

"I am so glad we could establish that," he said.

"The only variable in this equation concerns how you die. Specifically, how quickly and easily." Lady Nightwing pulled out a syringe. "If you tell me what I want to know, then you can die right now. A quick injection, and poof! No more pain, no more worries. Quick and painless."

Dr. Timberi's chest pounded with hope. That option sounded good. Lady Nightwing could be brutal, and the thought of a quick, easy release appealed to him.

"Or you can fight me. I will win, of course. I will torment your body and soul until you tell me what I want to know. I have a special new toy I've designed—it's almost done, and you can help me test it. It is your choice."

As anxiety and fear pummeled him, Lexa realized just how human Dr. Timberi was. He considered her offer, exploring his options. He could lie. Or give information that didn't matter.

"What is it you want to know?"

"Tell me about your wife's family—"

"No."

He braced himself, knowing that would make her mad.

Lady Nightwing raised her hands. With wild eyes, she sent jagged darts of black fire blasting into him. He bit his lips together, praying that he wouldn't say anything. He clung to silence, the one choice he had left.

Lady Nightwing dropped her hands. "Very well, Morgan. I gave you your choice. As it happens, I'm glad you decided to be stubborn. It provides a rare opportunity to test the new device I've designed on a Magus of your strength. I've had you in a drug-induced coma for three weeks so you could heal up and be strong enough to be useful. If you die right away, that's no use—and no fun, either. Unfortunately, my new toy isn't quite ready. So, for now, take him to the Shadowbox."

Dr. Timberi groaned inside, and Lexa cried out as his fear mingled with her own.

Lexa didn't understand everything the Shadowbox did, but she knew it had almost destroyed Conner, almost made him go crazy. He'd explained that it created a mental and emotional pain beyond description, far worse than any physical suffering he could name.

Although Dr. Timberi focused on keeping his mouth closed, Lexa felt panic rising inside of him. He put on a brave face, but he knew what the Shadowbox could do.

Dr. Timberi! Where are you? she called out. *How can we find you?*

He didn't hear her. Their connection couldn't compete with his surging fear as they locked him in a coffin-like metal box that gave Lexa claustrophobia.

When the doors slammed shut, Lexa couldn't see what exactly happened, but Dr. Timberi's pulse raced, his heart pounded, and a wildfire of terror raged through his spirit.

Desperate to relieve his suffering, Lexa found herself praying and begging and focusing everything she had on helping him—what could she do?

A theeling came, loud and clear, a single word: *Sing.*

Early on in their adventures, when she had been upset and disturbed, Dr. Timberi had sung to her, a song in a strange language that had filled her with Light and peace.

That was his gift—communicating emotion. She didn't have that same gift. And she didn't know that particular song. But still, the theeling came: *Sing!*

Feeling a little silly, Lexa sang the lullaby her mother always sang.

"You came from a land, where all is light,
To a world half-day, and a world half-night.
To guard you by day, you have my love.
And to guard you by night, your friends above."

Dr. Timberi's terror slowed. The panic and pulsing didn't stop or go away, but they grew distant and muffled. His thoughts grew less chaotic and agitated, so she kept singing.

"So sleep, sleep till the darkness ends,
Guarded by your angel friends.
So sleep, sleep, till the darkness ends.
Guarded by your angel friends."

Her song seemed to create a thin shield, like a tent in a bad thunderstorm. It wasn't much, but Lexa hoped it might protect him from the worst of the weather.

After singing the song through several times, she paused. When she stopped, the pain and horror rushed back to him, so she took a deep breath and redoubled her efforts.

After singing it five or six more times, she began to wonder if she could really sing it, over and over, all night long.

Then inspiration struck.

She'd memorized every note and every lyric of every

song from *The Sound of Music* before auditions. Now she sang them all, filling each note with all her energy, concern, and love.

Lexa remembered the picture her dad had shown them earlier: her parents each rocking a baby. The only way to get them to sleep was to rock them all night long.

She would do the same thing for Dr. Timberi, cradling him with her song. She owed him that much.

When her throat got dry, she closed her eyes and imagined her kitchen. Yellow Light flashed, and a large water bottle appeared in her hand. Thank goodness for Translocation—a Magi technique for moving an object instantly from one location to another.

Taking a swallow of water, Lexa sang with all the love and tenderness she imagined in a parent rocking a child to sleep.

Grateful she'd memorized the whole play, Lexa didn't even have to think about it. She knew every line, every song, and could even hum the incidental music. Maybe she hadn't gotten the lead, but now she starred in the most important performance of her life.

At some point during Act Two, the storms inside Dr. Timberi faded, and she decided to try to contact him again.

Dr. Timberi! Can you hear me? It's Lexa, and we're trying to find you. Where are you?

She felt a ragged smile on his face.

Thank you, Lexa, he said in a hoarse, shaky whisper. *Thank you.*

Where are you? Tell me where you are.

His mind struggled to form coherent thoughts.

Gathering the last bit of his energy, he managed a weak whisper, almost more of a breath.

Abyss.

Where is the Abyss? she yelled. *Tell me where you are!*

But he didn't answer. His consciousness faded, and Lexa knew he had passed into a merciful slumber. Lexa sent a sigil to tell Lee about the Abyss. A few minutes after her yellow dolphin sailed off, the rattlesnake appeared to tell her he was working on the clue.

Then, afraid that Dr. Timberi's agony might come back, she continued singing.

At some point, Lexa fell asleep. She thought it was during the third singing of the first act.

CHAPTER 10

PILAF'S NEWS

THE POWER AT MELANIE'S HOUSE HAD BEEN restored the next morning, but her world felt dark. She walked through a cloud all day, refusing to talk to anyone. Finally, at lunchtime, she felt ready, and, using as few words as possible, she explained what had happened. She looked down at her lunch tray, trying to fight the tears as Lexa squealed, "Are you serious, Mel? You can NOT be serious!"

"Hey, Lex," Conner said. "I think a few people at the other end of the lunchroom didn't catch everything you just said."

Melanie looked around. Conner exaggerated, but a lot of people had turned to see what was going on, staring at the corner table the Trio had claimed since they first Kindled.

Kindled.

Melanie started a new round of tears as those memories came rushing back.

The day Conner had lit a bully's gym shorts on fire.

The night the Stalker—Timothy—had shown up at Lexa and Conner's house.

Thinking the teachers were trying to kill them, then discovering they were Magi.

Learning Translocation, going through the Otherwhere, summer at Mockingbird Cottage, and now, finally, at long last, streaming.

For Melanie, it was all gone now.

Melanie took a deep breath, determined not to cry. For once in her life, she wouldn't cry, wouldn't give her parents that power. Forcing her lips to stop quivering, she looked at Lexa. "Yes. I am serious. My parents grounded me from Lightcraft. And now, nothing works."

"That's terrible, Mel!" Lexa said.

"I agree," Melanie said in a tart voice. "That's what I was saying when you started squealing."

Lexa looked like she wanted to say something, but she tugged her ponytail and pushed her lips shut. "I'm sorry, Mel," she said, a few seconds later.

Melanie rubbed her very tired eyes, then did the same thing to her very tired temples. Staying up all night crying did not make for a good day. "I'm sorry too," she said. "I didn't mean to snap."

"What if someone goes to talk to them?" Lexa said. "Maybe Madame Cumberland or Lee?"

"Lexa, last time people talked to Mr. Stephens, he ended up getting us all kicked out of being Magi," Conner said. "Remember that?"

Melanie winced. When the teachers told her parents and the Dells about the Kindling, her dad had freaked out. Dr. Timberi and her dad had shouted at each other, and Lee almost punched her dad after he said some snarky things about Dr. Timberi not having a family and not understanding what it was like to lose people you loved. Knowing Dr. Timberi's history now, Melanie realized why the other Magi had been so horrified by her dad's words.

"It wouldn't help," Melanie said. "It would probably make him madder. My mom's the only one who can calm him down, and she's even more upset than him."

"So what do we do?" Lexa asked.

"I don't know," Melanie said. "I'm hoping after a week or two things will settle down and I can reason with them." Melanie closed her mouth. She could refrain from crying, or she could talk—but not both. And she didn't want to cry anymore.

"Y'all, what's the problem? You look absolutely miserable." Melanie looked up to see Mrs. Grant looking at them. Behind her cardigan sweater and glasses, she wore a sympathetic expression.

"Melanie can't—" Lexa started to blurt but then stopped. It looked like she was in pain, but she shut her mouth and tugged her ponytail. "I should let her tell it."

That shocked Melanie. Lexa Dell voluntarily surrendering the chance to relay dramatic news?

Melanie explained her situation, which prompted a sympathetic murmur from Mrs. Grant. "Oh, Melanie, I'm so sorry." She shook her head. "Now let me ask you one question. You didn't Renounce?"

"I don't think so. What do you mean Renounce?"

"Renunciation is where a Magus swears an oath to

give up his or her powers, and it's final. If you didn't Renounce, this should be temporary. At the very worst, once you are eighteen, your parents won't be able to control your powers." Mrs. Grant looked at her watch. "Oh dear, I need to get those essays graded before next period." As Mrs. Grant trudged off, Pilaf ran over, waving a crisp piece of paper.

"Look!" he said. "Look, you guys! Look!"

Conner grabbed his hand. "Dude. We can't look until you stop waving it."

Pilaf giggled. "Oh yeah." He handed the paper to Conner, who read it.

"Yeah, Pilaf!" Conner said, giving him a fist bump and passing the paper to Melanie.

"That's cool, Pilaf," she said.

The letterhead featured the familiar Magi emblem: a sparkling eight-pointed star circled by a crescent moon. But this Magi emblem sparkled on a shield held by a fierce-looking griffin. Beneath the crest, old-fashioned letters said: *Virtus et Lumen.*

As Melanie, who took French, mouthed the words, Conner, who took Latin, said, "It means 'Power and Light.'"

Beneath that motto, more modern type said, "Magi Services: Office of Assessment and Evaluation."

Addressed to Pilaf, it read:

> *Dear Mr. Larson,*
> *Pursuant to a request from the Supreme Magistrate, we are pleased to invite you to report to our office at the Magisterium. Given accounts of your*

unique abilities, we believe the best course of action is to test you at your earliest possible convenience. Consequently, we have arranged with Mona Cumberland to bring you to our office tomorrow.
Kindest Regards,
Marsha K. Owens, Ph.D.
Interim Director

"I'm finally going to get tested!" Pilaf yelled. "Finally!"

Pilaf could see Light and Dark but couldn't use them. He could hear but couldn't join in head-talk, including private conversations. And his touch could cancel out or neutralize both Light and Dark. No one quite understood Pilaf's powers—what he could do and how, or where they had come from. Melanie knew that, deep down, he hoped that he would Kindle and be able to join the Magi.

"That's awesome, Pilaf," Lexa said with a big smile. "So this Saturday?"

"Yeah, right before my birthday party! How cool is that?"

Melanie looked away. *Don't cry. Don't cry.* Even Pilaf was getting official now. Everyone but her.

"Are you all coming to my party?" Pilaf asked, blinking behind his enormous glasses. "Actually, I'd love to have you at the testing too. I'm a little nervous."

"Oh yeah," Conner said. "Gonna do some serious partying—and testing."

"Yes." Melanie managed to speak without crying.

"I would totally not miss it," Lexa said. She stopped talking as a girl in their grade walked past. "Oh. My. Gosh. Melanie, did you see the way Sarah Jackson just threw herself at Peter Ashworth in art today? Not that I blame her since he's soooo cute. But still—"

"Eeewwww," Melanie said. The change of subject helped her not cry. "Seriously? I didn't see it. I was trying to fix my dog sculpture, which looks more like a road kill pig right now. Wait, I thought Peter liked Annie. They were so cute together."

As Lexa recounted the failed flirtation, Melanie laughed at her descriptions and imitations, and felt a warm glow. Laughing and chatting with Lexa felt good. She'd missed it. Over the summer, she'd had her Magi powers but not her best friend. Now, she'd lost her powers but had her best friend back. She would have preferred to have both. Losing her powers left her feeling empty and barren. But if she had to choose, she would take the friend.

As lunch ended, Conner looked up. "What class do we have next anyway?"

"Study hall," Pilaf said.

"Good," Melanie muttered. "I'm getting so behind on everything."

"The bad news," Pilaf said, "is that Mr. Blinson is in charge of it."

That thought dropped a heavy, wet blanket of gloom over the table.

Mr. Blinson was Dr. Timberi's substitute teacher. No one liked him.

Melanie sprinted away from the lunchroom, anxious to have enough time to get her books out of her locker and get back to study hall. Going to a private school meant lots of homework. The fact that she, Conner, and Lexa were Magi fighting a battle with evil didn't really matter because it was a regular school. A handful of the teachers happened to be Magi, but no one else knew about all of that. So homework still had to be done. And since Dr. Timberi's capture, Melanie had fallen behind.

The study hall they had each Friday afternoon would be a big help, even if it meant extra time with Mr. Blinson.

Holding her books in size order, Melanie walked toward the arts building. As she did, Pilaf joined her. "Hey, Melanie!"

"Hi, Pilaf," she said.

"Can I ask a favor?" he said.

"Sure."

"Can you help me in study hall?"

"Sure. What do you need help with?"

He bobbed his head at a stack of index cards in his hands. "I borrowed some Magi books from Mrs. Grant and made some note cards," he whispered. "I'm trying to study for my Magi tests tomorrow. I don't want to fail."

"Um, are you sure it's that kind of a test?" Melanie asked. "I thought it would be a test of your abilities. Not a written test."

"Maybe." He shrugged. "But I don't want to take any chances."

Stifling a smile, Melanie said, "I'll help you." There went her time to study. But Pilaf was so small and help-less . . . "Oh!" A terrible, sweet-rotten odor filled the air, and Melanie fought the impulse to gag. "What is that smell?"

"The dumpster," Pilaf said. "Mr. Keller told me there was some mix-up with a new company, so it didn't get emptied.

Melanie held her breath and sped up, shivering at the thought of un-emptied garbage sitting in a big metal box warmed by the Tennessee sun. It would be a massive Crock-Pot of germs. She knew you couldn't catch them from just smelling something—but she still sped up.

They walked to the choir room, the location of their assigned study hall. Melanie still struggled every time they walked into the room because it always reminded her of Dr. Timberi. Sitting in his former classroom seemed to mock their sadness, forming a cruel reminder that the world went on even if someone you loved disappeared.

"Have a seat immediately!" Then there was the problem of Dr. Timberi's substitute, Mr. Blinson. A tall, mousy man, who always seemed on the verge of a nervous breakdown.

"I don't want any talking. My predecessor might have been lax, but those days are over." Mr. Blinson bad-mouthed Dr. Timberi constantly, something Melanie disliked.

Yellow Light flashed near Blinson, and he slipped, falling headfirst into the wastebasket. Melanie disliked the way he talked about Dr. Timberi, but it infuriated Lexa, who sat glowering at Mr. Blinson. No one else but Pilaf and the Trio could have seen the Light, but everyone saw him fall and the room erupted in laughter.

"Nice job, Lexa," Pilaf whispered as Mr. Blinson climbed out of the garbage can.

I wish it was the dumpster! Lexa shouted in her thoughts, triggering a furious fit of Pilaf's giggles.

"Enough!" Mr. Blinson yelled. "I want everyone studying."

"Okay, Melanie, are you ready?" Pilaf handed Melanie a massive stack of index cards. "Ask me anything," he said with a grin. "I've been studying since last summer."

"Wait," Lexa asked. "Before you start, I have a science question. What's the difference between luminescence and incandescence?"

"Luminescence is when an object emits light that doesn't result from heat. For example, some fish in the deep sea emit their own light. It's called bioluminescence. Incandescence is when something emits light as a result of heating," Pilaf said without looking at any notes.

"So luminescence means giving off light that comes from inside?" Lexa asked.

"Close enough," Pilaf said. "Okay, Melanie, quiz me."

Melanie picked up the first card. "Explain Light and Dark."

Pilaf scrunched his pale blond, barely-there eyebrows and blinked. "Light is an actual power. It's different than just regular light. Light fills the universe and governs most of the elements. Controlling the Light means you can control almost everything else, except water. Magi are born with the ability to guide the Light. It's almost like the Light is an encrypted Wi-Fi signal and the Magi can connect. Darkness is also a specific power that fights against Light."

A few desks over, Lexa gasped, then jerked upright and froze, staring ahead with wide eyes.

Lexa? Melanie asked. *Lexa, are you okay?* Was she playing a joke on Blinson?

"Ask me another one," Pilaf said.

"Okay, what is Umbra?" Melanie asked, keeping an eye on Lexa.

"Umbra is the organization the Darkhands belong to. Magi call them Darkhands, but their official name is 'Noctivagant,' which means 'One who walks in the Night.' Darkhands use Dark like Magi use Light—"

Lexa screamed, then fell to the floor, crying and writhing in agony.

·CHAPTER 11·

BAD NEWS

LEXA STRUGGLED AS HER CONSCIOUSNESS started turning cartwheels. When the dizziness cleared, she found herself fighting against terrible, muscle-clenching, teeth-grinding pain. As she fought to breathe, she saw through Dr. Timberi's eyes as he stared at the black metal ceiling above.

Between excruciating jolts, he gritted his teeth, determined not to make a sound.

As more pain rolled through him, Lexa realized that she perceived but didn't feel it. In spite of her awareness, the pain didn't hurt her. It reminded Lexa having a tooth drilled once your mouth was numb.

As she became aware of his struggle to keep the cries inside, she realized that instead of the physical sensation, she could feel his mental and emotional responses to the pain.

"Lexa!"

Jumbled voices and the purplish scent of Madame

Cumberland's perfume pulled Lexa back to the class-room, where Conner cradled her head in his lap, while Melanie patted her hands. Pilaf knelt close by, blinking anxious eyes. Madame Cumberland, Mrs. Grant, and Lee all looked down at her with great anxiety on their faces. Everyone else—including Mr. Blinson—had left the classroom.

"Lexa?" Conner asked. "Are you okay?" The obvious anxiety in his voice made her heart smile.

"Yeah, I think so." Her voice croaked like a frog with laryngitis.

"What happened?" Melanie asked.

"It's the same thing that happened last night. My mind merged with Dr. Timberi's. They're hurting him."

Lee kicked a desk, knocking it over and sending it skidding across the room. "Those blankety-blank, skunk-striped, rat-tailed, weasel-eyed snakes! I was afraid of this." Lee punched his hand a few times. "He was one heck of an Adumbrator in his day and sent a whole lot of Dark-hands to one-way tribunals. Umbra lost some of their best operatives because of Morgan."

"Lexa, did you see anything that might give us any clues at all?" Madame Cumberland asked through tears.

"No, ma'am."

"Lexa, I know it's unpleasant, but can you connect again?" Mrs. Grant asked. "Try to talk to him. Get any information he can provide."

Remembering the awareness of his intense pain and terror, Lexa didn't want to connect again. Even if she couldn't feel it directly, it had been an awful experience.

Conner took her hand.

71

Conner, who had given himself up so Melanie's little sister, Madi, could go free. Conner, who had gone into the Shadowbox so Lady Nightwing wouldn't hurt the other kids she had captured.

Lexa closed her eyes, relaxing again, sending Light back inside. Once again the tendrils of yellow Light found the sigil—but this time nothing happened.

She opened her eyes and shook her head. Lee grabbed her shoulders. "What's wrong, Lexa? What's wrong?"

"Lexa, he's not—they didn't—" Madame Cumberland's skin had grown pale and drawn. She and Mrs. Grant hugged each other.

"No," Lexa paused, examining the sigil with the Light. She needed to be sure. "He's alive. I think maybe he passed out or something."

"Okay, I gotta get word back to HQ," Lee said. "Lexa, you keep me posted. Contact me anytime you feel anything at all. I'll catch y'all later!" He jumped up, stretching into a dusty brown comet, which shot out of the building.

"Where is Magisterium headquarters, anyway?" Lexa asked.

"In France," Madame Cumberland said. "A grand old château that dates back to the sixteenth century."

"He'll stream clear to France?"

"Yes. Not everyone can do that, of course. But members of the Phalanx can. It's like a soldier doing a long run with equipment. Very difficult, but they're trained for it."

"Wait!" Melanie said. "Speaking of the Magisterium, we all got a sigil last night."

Madame Cumberland nodded. "Yes. A summons to testify in a tribunal."

"Are we in trouble?" Conner asked.

"No," Madame Cumberland said. "You're witnesses in the trial of Timothy Timberi."

It took Lexa a few seconds to understand whom Madame Cumberland meant. "I'm still not used to calling him that."

"He'll always be the Stalker to me," Conner muttered.

"Since the three of you have been the targets of many of his attacks, you'll be called to testify." The sadness in Madame Cumberland's voice was so massive, it almost had its own gravitational pull. "Now that you've been summoned, a group of Magi called Examiners will come to collect your memories of Timothy."

"Why?" Lexa asked.

"Do you remember the horloge that Morgan showed Melanie how to use this past summer? Well, during the tribunal, a giant horloge in the chamber will broadcast the memories of the witnesses. The Examiners gather those memories."

"How do they do that?" Melanie asked.

"They reach into your minds and collect the memory—extract it, basically."

"Is it painful?" Lexa asked.

"Not exactly painful." Madame Cumberland shook her head and frowned. "But not pleasant. They are very thorough, and having someone sift through your memories can be intrusive. After the emotional exhaustion and sadness of the last few weeks, it may be unpleasant to have someone prodding through your memories of Morgan. I wish it wasn't necessary."

"So once they're inside our heads, they can see all our memories?" Conner asked.

"Yes, although they are supposed to limit themselves to accessing only what they need for the tribunal," Madame Cumberland said. "They'll be looking for anything having to do with Timothy."

A rat of worry began to nibble at Lexa's peace of mind, a rat, with cold teeth, that called all his friends. If the Examiners poked around their memories, they'd find out that Conner could control the Darkness. But Dr. Timberi had specifically warned them not to let the Magisterium know about those powers. Sworn to secrecy, they hadn't even told Madame Cumberland or Lee.

Lexa looked at Conner and Melanie. Worry painted their faces, and she suspected they felt the same fear.

Outside in the hall, the bell rang. "Lexa, are you okay?" Madame Cumberland asked.

"I'm fine," Lexa said.

Mr. Blinson stuck his head in the classroom. "If you are all done using my classroom as a private hospital for Miss Dell, I'd like to pick up a few things." He glared at the students. "Rehearsal starts in five minutes."

"It's not your room," Lexa muttered. "It's Dr. Timberi's."

CHAPTER 12.

How Do You Solve a Problem like Blinson?

SO, DID YOU GUYS GET THE IDEA THAT THOSE *Examiners will figure out that I can use Darkness?* Conner asked. He didn't understand all of the details of what they did, but this possibility worried him.

Yes, Melanie said. *And I don't think that is good. Dr. Timberi warned us not to let the Magisterium find out.*

Conner remembered that conversation. Dr. Timberi worried that if the Magisterium found out, they would basically turn Conner into a living science experiment. A Magi lab rat.

"Oh, snap!" Pilaf said. "I forgot when Lexa passed out. I was supposed to leave early for an orthodontist appointment. Here—I've gotta go." He pulled out three crumpled yellow envelopes from his pocket and handed one to each of the Trio. "Have fun at play practice." Pilaf ran toward the middle school office.

As the Trio trudged to the theater, Conner opened his envelope and laughed.

"What's so funny?" Lexa asked.

"Pilaf's invitation," Conner said, pulling out a card with balloons and candles and "Someone's Having a Birthday!" written in happy-looking letters. "Gotta love Pilaf."

"That's so cute," Melanie said, staring at the invitation. "But where's the party?"

Conner squinted, trying to decipher Pilaf's scrawled handwriting. "I think it's Sky High Sports—you know, that big trampoline place."

"I've never gone there," Lexa said.

"Madi went to a birthday party there last week," Melanie said. "It's this massive building—like a warehouse—and they have trampolines all over the place. You jump or play dodge ball or swing out on a rope over a big pit filled with foam. They even have trampolines on the walls so you can bounce at different angles."

"That sounds fun," Lexa said.

Conner laughed a little louder. "Yeah, it does. Plus, Pilaf's other idea was some kind of Lego-building party. So we lucked out with the bounce place."

"So, this is Saturday, like tomorrow?" Melanie stared at Pilaf's handwriting with no sign of imminent comprehension.

"Yeah," Conner said. "Don't even bother trying to read Pilaf's handwriting. You have to be a guy. And even then, it's pretty bad." Conner dropped his voice. "You're both coming, right? Pilaf only invited the three of us, and he's pretty excited. I want this to be fun for him."

"I'll be there," Melanie replied.

"Me too," Lexa said.

A small weight jumped off Conner's chest. He felt responsible for looking after Pilaf, so he was glad everyone was coming.

Conner's smile faded as they walked into the theater. Lexa unloaded a heavy sigh. "Two hours with Blinson. Depressing."

Everyone shared Lexa's depression. Mr. Blinson had a gift for turning things that should be fun—like play practice—into endless hours of drudgery.

"Yeah," Conner said. "Nice job with the garbage can, though, Lex." He held out his hand for a fist bump.

"Thanks!" Lexa beamed as she pounded his knuckles and Conner smiled back.

Seeing her scream and collapse reminded him that, annoying as she could be, Lexa was his sister. And he loved her.

"Come on, people," Mr. Blinson yelled from the stage. "This is your time you're wasting!" His voice made Conner think of a mouse with a sinus infection. "The sooner we start, the sooner we can finish."

How does he make everything as much fun as a funeral for your pet? Conner asked, drawing a giggle from Melanie and a snicker from Lexa. *Remember when going to play practice was fun?*

Yeah, Lexa said. *Dr. Timberi pushed us hard, but we always laughed at least as much as we worked.*

"Listen, people," Blinson said. "I want Mr. Dell and Miss Stephens onstage, running choreography for 'Sixteen Going on Seventeen.' Nuns, I want you offstage working your vocal parts for the opening. I'll be with you soon."

Conner's bad mood faded a little. Dancing with Melanie sounded like a great way to spend rehearsal.

And it was. Until Lexa started interrupting every few minutes to say, *Ohmygosh! You guys are soooo cute together.*

Lexa's constant commentary seemed to make Melanie tense, so she kept making mistakes, which made her seem even more tense, which led to Blinson getting mad, which made her more tense—so the practice did not end up being the romantic highlight Conner had anticipated.

"Miss Stephens!" Mr. Blinson yelled. "You did one step correctly, and that was probably by accident. What is your problem? Mr. Dell, Miss Stephens, would you please go find a place backstage and run your number? Nuns, onstage now!"

You okay? Conner asked as they walked through the curtains to a quiet corner backstage.

Fine. I just don't like feeling so—on display, Melanie replied.

Isn't that kind of the point of being in a play?

*Well, yes, and it's easy when you're just pretending to be in love with someone. This is, um—*she paused. *It's not quite so pretend.*

Conner's heart jumped into his pounding brain. Had she meant—

"Miss Dell!" Blinson's voice came from the stage. "Miss Dell, kindly focus!"

Conner peeked through the curtains in time to see Lexa grab her head and collapse.

Lexa! Are you okay? He and Melanie ran back onstage and pushed through the crowd gathering around Lexa.

"Sorry," Lexa gasped. "Migraine."

Mr. Blinson tightened his lips. Conner guessed he wanted to say something but realized he'd look like a major jerk if he chewed out a girl who just collapsed. "I've got her, Mr. Blinson," he said. "This happens sometimes. She just needs to lie down."

Conner helped Lexa to her feet. She took a step, staggered, and fell again. He caught her and carried her off-stage, through the curtains and over to an antique couch from *My Fair Lady*.

Lexa, are you okay? Melanie asked.

It's Dr. Timberi, Lexa said between short breaths. *I don't know what they're doing, but it's pretty bad.*

A horrible cry, shout, and scream ripped through Lexa's mind. Because their thoughts were connected, Conner could hear it too.

Lexa gasped and her body went rigid. Next to him, Melanie gasped. Then a plume of burning pink Light jumped out of her chest and rushed into Lexa, who seemed to swallow it like dry ground sucking in the rain. The screaming stopped, and Lexa relaxed.

Mel, what was that? Lexa asked.

It just jumped out, Melanie said, *when I heard the scream. It's the same thing that happened a few weeks ago with Conner and Dr. Timberi. Remote Autonomic Augmentation—*

Wait a minute, Mel! Lexa shouted. *You just did Lightcraft! You Augmented Dr. Timberi and you're headtalking. Do you think your parents ungrounded you?*

Melanie's eyes lit up, shining with excitement. She raised her arm and flicked her fingers.

Nothing happened.

What are you trying to do? Lexa asked.

Shoot a sigil, Melanie sighed. *Nothing. Not even a pink sparkle.* The excitement faded, and her eyes started to sparkle with tears instead of hope.

Just then, Mr. Blinson poked his head through the curtains. "Miss Dell! Perhaps you can tear yourself away from your busy social life and come join the rest of the nuns in rehearsal? Or do you have another migraine? Mr. Dell, Miss Stephens? Is that choreography perfect yet?"

Oh. My. Gosh, Lexa said. *I'm so tired of him. If the Light would let me, I'd totally—I don't know. Do something bad. Turn him into a frog.*

I'd drop him in the dumpster, Melanie said. *Have you smelled it lately?*

"Miss Dell!"

Lexa rolled her eyes and went back onstage.

·CHAPTER 13·

THE FIGHT

"ALL RIGHT," MR. BLINSON SAID, GLARING AT Lexa. "Now that Miss Dell is through with her little drama, let's get back to work. Miss Stephens and Mr. Dell, keep working on your choreography. Captain and Maria, you go offstage right and run the scene on page twenty-two."

Page twenty-two. Lexa turned away as an icy pang of regret stole her breath and then rushed out in the form of hot tears. Page twenty-two. The scene Dr. Timberi had asked them to read at callbacks. For the millionth time, she wished she could go back and change that day. Undo it somehow.

Part of that was because of the guilt. But there was much more than that.

Over the summer, she'd learned about Dr. Timberi's sad past. He had been deliriously in love with his wife, Nicole, and they had a baby boy they both adored. The Darkhands had killed Nicole and taken the child, darkening Dr. Timberi's world forever.

After feeling the pain he still carried, Lexa had made an extra effort to make him smile and laugh and to not feel so alone. She sensed his gratitude and fondness, and over that summer, she knew she had become special to him, like a niece or adopted daughter.

But Lexa had not realized something important. Trying to make someone happy made you special to that person. But it worked in reverse as well. That person became special to you.

Now that Dr. Timberi was gone, Lexa missed him. He'd become so much more than a teacher. A special mentor, a kind and caring friend, like an uncle or a second dad. She missed his laugh, his sarcastic jabs, and the way he knew everything about Lightcraft. She missed the way he pushed them and butted into their lives to tell them when they were not being their best selves—

"Miss Dell!" A thin, nasal voice hacked into her thoughts. "Hello, Miss Dell! We're waiting for you." Mr. Blinson stood glaring at Lexa. "Honestly, I don't understand why Timberi cast you in this role. You wander around in a trance, and your dramatic ability seems limited to causing drama offstage. On the other hand, it's not like Timberi showed any signs of directorial or pedagogical competence in the first place."

Lexa grew aware of yellow sparks crackling in the air around her eyes.

"That's Doctor Timberi." Lexa straightened herself to her full height.

"Oh well, *Doctor* Timberi doesn't seem to realize the theater has continued beyond Broadway 1967. *The*

Sound of Music? It's one big cliché—and that's before you throw in bad acting by kids. Don't even get me started on the shocking lack of precision in the way he allows you to sing."

The yellow sparks flashed brighter and hotter as Lexa glared at Mr. Blinson. "Dr. Timberi felt that the soul of the singer was more important than using the perfect value of sixteenth notes to smack people's knuckles." Her right fingers closed around her left arm, and she squeezed, resisting the urge to punch Blinson.

"And what would you know about music education?" The entire world around Lexa glowed yellow now. Bright, blazing, burning yellow that began to swirl around Mr. Blinson.

"I know that *you* make everything miserable and *he* made learning interesting! You make fun things awful, and he made boring things fun. He got us excited to work, but you just suck all the good out of everything and magnify the misery!"

Conner and Melanie appeared at Lexa's side as the swirls around Blinson grew bigger and brighter.

Lex, Conner said. *Don't lose control.*

"You are a nasty, spoiled little brat—"

"You're not half the teacher he is!" Lexa shouted. The yellow Light near Blinson flashed as streaks of gold spread through it like veins in a leaf. "You pompous, preening jackanapes!"

Crackling with power, Lexa glared at Blinson. The veins of gold Light grew brighter. "What's wrong, you toadying ignoramus? Does the cat have your cowardly, craven, contemptible tongue?"

Blinson huffed and stammered. "Your attitude shows a shocking lack of respect—"

"Respect is freely given when it is honestly earned." Lexa felt her voice thunder through the theater, roaring the way Dr. Timberi's did when he got angry. "But what would you know of that? You pinch-toed, prune-lipped, emotionally parsimonious, arrogant, limited, foul-breathed, condescending, nose-breathing, popped pimple of an infectious little worm? Artless, beslubbering canker-blossom! Toad-spotted skainsmate! Spleeny, qualling, lumpish, mammering, pribbling, ill-nurtured, flap-mouthed measle!"

The yellow-gold Light churned and rumbled, growing in volume and intensity. The stage lights flickered, and the air buzzed with electric energy.

Blinson blinked and huffed some more. "You are a nasty, talentless little beast. Timberi is nothing more than a charismatic faker—a total fraud, and I will make sure your headmaster and everyone in this learning community knows it!"

"Go away!" Lexa yelled. A surge of emotion rushed through her, and once again the lights flickered, this time going out completely, leaving the theater in total blackness just before Lexa shoved Blinson and yelled, "Just go away!" As Lexa's hands shot forward, the swirls of Light near Blinson flashed even brighter in the darkness, and he flew backwards a few feet.

Full of fury, Lexa pulled her hands back, ready to lash out with another volley of Light.

Lex, I don't think that's a good idea, Conner said. He and Melanie each grabbed one of Lexa's arms to hold her back, but as soon as they touched Lexa, the power inside of her swelled and grew, multiplying until she thought she might burst.

A massive tidal wave of yellow, pink, and red Light exploded out of Lexa and rolled across the stage, sizzling and hissing.

Lighting the darkness of the theater, the multi-colored Light hit Blinson with a flash so bright that it forced Lexa's eyes closed. For a few seconds, she felt an immense weight push down on her, as if she was trying to carry an elephant or an SUV. She heard Conner and Melanie gasp as well—and then it ended.

When Lexa opened her eyes again, the theater was dark, but Conner, Melanie, and Lexa all glowed with their respective colors of Light. That Light revealed Melanie's face as it flickered between shock and panic. *Lexa! You blew up the teacher!*

Lexa stared back at Melanie, feeling a little shocked and panicked herself. *You guys helped! It wasn't just me!*

Madame Cumberland appeared in a silver comet as Mrs. Grant emerged from a blue comet right behind her. Lee and four members of the Twilight Phalanx were only a heartbeat behind, appearing in ferocious-looking battle stances. Apparently deciding there was no battle, they relaxed a little. More comets came as the other Magi who taught at the school joined them: Mr. Miller, Mrs. Sharpe, Mrs. Davis, Mr. Duffy, and Coach Jackson.

Madame Cumberland looked at the Trio. *Great Caesar's Ghost! What in the world just happened?*

The whole school shook! Mrs. Grant said. *Maybe the whole city.*

Feeling very small and vulnerable, Lexa squeaked out a few thoughts. *Um, Mr. Blinson said rude things about Dr. Timberi and . . . I'm not sure what happened. I just meant to maybe zap him a little, but this huge wave came out of me and—I don't know what happened then.*

Had she killed Blinson? She didn't like him, but she didn't mean to really hurt him. Just make him stop. Lexa wrapped her arms around herself and huddled against the wall.

Did the other students see anything? Mrs. Sharpe asked. She always took charge in situations like this.

Lexa couldn't put words together. Melanie jumped in. *No—the lights went out while we were yelling at each other. There was a lot of Light, but they couldn't have seen that, right?*

That's a relief, at least, Mrs. Grant thought with a heavy sigh. *A public disappearance would have been difficult to explain.*

Mrs. Sharpe held out her hand. *I'll get the others out of here. Let me get a flashlight—I've got one in my car.* Cream-colored Light flashed in her hand and Lexa saw a flashlight appear. Translocation was definitely one of the more convenient tricks they'd learned.

By now the other students had started to talk, yell, and generally make massive amounts of noise.

"Everyone calm down!" Mrs. Sharpe shouted, clicking her flashlight on. "Just follow me out to the lobby and call or text your parents. Let them know rehearsal is over." She escorted the other students out of the theater.

"Mr. Blinson?" Madame Cumberland called. No answer.

"Mr. Blinson?" The other Magi all started calling him as well, and soon they'd fanned out, searching the theater and the classrooms nearby.

"I didn't mean to hurt him," Lexa repeated as panic fluttered up from her stomach to her throat. Would she get in trouble? Had she broken a Magi law? Would she end up in a tribunal?

No one said anything for a few seconds. The adult Magi came back from the search, giving each other long, worried looks. Threads of Light darted back and forth between their heads, which indicated they were having private thought conversations.

After several of those conversations, Madame Cumberland said, "Why don't I drive you three home? It's been a very difficult day—well, really a difficult few weeks for us all."

No one spoke as they walked to Madame Cumberland's car. The entire way, Lexa had visions of herself in leg irons and shackles, standing in front of a room full of Magi judges in black robes and wigs. What terrible punishments would come her way now? Execution?

How did Magi execute prisoners anyway? Lexa pulled her seat belt on and clicked it shut. Was that what they did when you got a lethal injection? Strap you to a chair? Did they still behead people in the Magi world? Or, even worse, could they take her powers away somehow? Kick her out of the Magi?

"Now, why don't you tell me what happened back there," Madame Cumberland said.

"Mr. Blinson made me really mad," Lexa said with a mouth as dry as sandpaper. "He was bad-mouthing Dr.

Timberi, and I started arguing with him. Words just started jumping out of my mouth."

"Lexa," Melanie said, "when you were saying that stuff, I saw gold Light mixed in with yours. And the things you said—that sounded a lot like Dr. Timberi."

"What did you call him again?" Conner asked.

"Pompous, preening jackanapes," Lexa said, then paused. "What's a jackanapes anyway?"

"An impudent, conceited fellow," Madame Cumberland said.

"Well, that's Blinson, for sure," Conner said. "But Melanie's right. Those words had to be from Dr. Timberi. I mean, last time we argued you called me a stupid, freaking jerk. That's a big difference from 'pompous, whatever, whatever.'"

"Lexa, were you communicating directly with Morgan?" Madame Cumberland asked, turning around from the driver's seat to look at Lexa with hopeful eyes.

"No, ma'am. It just kind of jumped out of me. Like a burp. I didn't have any control."

"Hmmmmm," Madame Cumberland said, tapping her fingers on the steering wheel. "Lexa, I wonder if having Morgan's sigil inside of you makes you say what Morgan would say in the same situation. There is certainly some kind of connection."

Mrs. Grant's sigil—a blue ballet dancer—appeared, pirouetting in the air near Madame Cumberland. "We found Mr. Blinson."

The car went silent for a few seconds. "Where was he?" Lexa asked. "Is he . . . alive?" She gulped down against the knot in her throat.

"He was in the dumpster," the ballerina said, and Lexa thought she might have smirked for a second. "He's fine. I think once he burns his clothes and showers for several weeks he might return to normal." The ballerina faded.

Everyone laughed for a few minutes, breaking the tension.

"Wait," Melanie said. "Does that mean Lexa Translocated Mr. Blinson?"

Madame Cumberland shook her head. "It's supposed to be impossible to Translocate a human. It's theoretically possible, but it would require more power than any single Magus could possibly have."

"Then what happened?" Lexa asked.

Madame Cumberland looked through the rearview mirror and smiled. "I have no idea. You all need to remember that there's a lot about Lightcraft we don't understand."

CHALLENGE FROM THE CHERUBIM

AFTER MADAME CUMBERLAND DROPPED everyone off, Conner went to get a snack and then start his homework. While he did that, Lexa marched straight to their mom and told her everything that had happened that day.

Their mom took it all reasonably well, and, before long, the Trio were all ignoring their homework and discussing the incident. No one understood what had happened—and everyone was especially confused about Melanie and how her powers seemed to work sometimes, but not others.

Did you guys see your Light mixed in with mine? Lexa asked in a private message to Conner and Melanie.

Yes, Melanie said.

Yeah, Conner added.

And I felt something, Melanie continued. *Something really heavy pushing down on me.*

Like you were trying to bench press a school bus? Conner asked.

Exactly, Melanie said.

Me too, Conner agreed.

So what does that mean? Lexa asked. *All of us were doing something, right? I mean, together. I've never felt that much power. I know it wasn't just me.*

Was it because me and Melanie grabbed you? Do you think Melanie Augmented you? Conner asked. *I mean, that's what an Augmentor does, right? Make other people's powers stronger?*

Maybe. Lexa paused, and Conner could hear her trying to think about it. *But it felt way stronger than that. Plus, I saw red Light there, so you were involved somehow too. Anyway, I've never felt that much power before. It was amazing. And a little scary.*

Yeah, well, you think it was scary for you, Conner said. *Imagine how Blinson felt. By the way, don't forget Pilaf's birthday party tomorrow. He's so excited he can hardly stand it.*

I'm not sure my parents will let me come, Melanie said. *They grounded me from Magi stuff and everything else.*

The next morning, as Conner paced back and forth in front of the window, a car pulled up in the driveway. Conner's mom walked out to chat with Mrs. Stephens, while Melanie jumped out of the car and ran up to the house.

They let you come! Conner said, wondering if a hug would be too much. He hesitated, but then started to open his arms. She didn't notice, so he dropped them and settled on a fist bump instead. Not quite what he'd had in mind.

Yeah, Melanie said, *they weren't going to, but your mom*

talked them into it. They felt bad ruining Pilaf's party. She dropped her thoughts to an even quieter level. *I didn't mention that part of the day included a trip through the Otherwhere to the Magisterium in France.*

As Conner laughed, Lexa came down the stairs and hugged Melanie. Conner promised himself to be faster next time.

Before Conner could join the hug, Madame Cumberland drove up. Pilaf jumped out of the back seat before the car had come to a complete stop. He quivered and shivered, and Conner thought he might pop from excitement.

After a few polite comments to Conner's mom, Madame Cumberland opened a portal through the Otherwhere, and everyone followed her inside. As they stood in the space between four arches, blinding, blazing Light shot out, surrounding each of them. The cherubim always inspected the souls of those who wanted to pass through the Otherwhere.

We know you, Conner Dell. A strong, resonant voice filled Conner's mind.

You were very brave, Conner Dell. Another voice, also strong, but softer somehow. Conner thought it must be a female. *You accepted the task we gave you and took Light into the Darkness. And now you are healed.*

Thank you, Conner said. *I mean, thanks for sending the Lucents to heal me. Dr. Timberi thought you did that because I obeyed your request to go to the Darkhand base.*

Morgan Timberi was correct, the second voice said. *By following our request, you bonded yourself to our protection.*

In that case, why didn't you do it sooner? Conner asked. *It was a pretty crummy summer. You could have made it a lot better by doing that sooner.*

Because you needed to learn important things, as did your friends. Things you will need to know. Things you will know more powerfully because you discovered them for yourselves, the first voice said.

Wait, what important things? Do you mean that I'm a bridge between Light and Dark? Is that the thing I had to learn?

That is an important component, the first voice said.

So there's more?

Yes, the second voice said.

Just a guess, Conner replied. *I'll bet you aren't going to tell me.*

Can a parent in your world tell an infant how to walk? the first voice asked.

No, not really. They could try, but the baby has to figure it out by trying. Okay, I get it. It just seems like you could make things a lot easier by—

It is not our task to make things easy for you, nor to do that which you can do for yourself, the second voice said. *We have our own work to do, Conner Dell. Our own battles to fight in the war against Darkness. Why should we do your work as well? We do only that which no one else can do.*

The lights around him started to fade.

Wait! Do you know where Dr. Timberi is?

In a place of terrible Darkness. He needs you to find him. But to do that, you will need a soul of rare strength: a heart, mind, and spirit united.

Where is he? Can you tell me where he is?

That is your mission, Conner Dell. It belongs to you and your friends. If we revealed his location, it would rob you.

The strength and knowledge you will need to complete the task will be developed along the way.

The lights retreated back inside the arch.

Conner looked at Lexa and Melanie. *Did they tell you anything about Dr. Timberi?*

Just that it was our job, Melanie said.

Yeah, that's what they told me, Lexa said.

Same, Conner said.

That left a heavy feeling in the air, and no one said anything else the rest of the way.

CHAPTER 15.

THE CHÂTEAU DE LA LUMIÈRE

FIRST IN LINE, MELANIE STEPPED OUT OF the Otherwhere, right up to a pair of tall iron gates. The Magi crest had been worked into the curves of the black metal bars.

Are you okay, Mel? Lexa asked.

Yeah, fine. Thanks. In reality, she was puzzled. She'd stayed up all night trying to figure out why she had been able to use some powers but not others. And, to her frustration, the cherubim hadn't given her any answers when she'd asked. Unanswered questions always irritated Melanie, chafing at her brain.

A few steps behind, Madame Cumberland sighed, her face painted with a happy, wistful smile. "Welcome to the Château de la Lumière." She waved her hands and her street clothes faded, replaced by shimmering, silver Magi robes. Next, her sigil appeared: a silver rosebush that twined up the gates, burst into bloom, and then vanished with a flash.

Two guards in hooded gray capes appeared, each carrying a long staff that glowed with changing colors of Light, shifting like rainbows at high speed. The guards said nothing but ran their staffs up and down and around each person in the group—it reminded Melanie of portable scanners at an airport security gate.

The guards nodded at each other, then pounded the ground with the bottom of their staffs. The gate swung open, and Madame Cumberland led them up a long gravel walk lined with stately old trees. As gravel crunched under their feet, they walked past beds of flowers, bushes carved into elaborate topiaries, sparkling fountains, and jewel-toned peacocks. Melanie recognized the same deep and powerful sense of peace that she felt at Mockingbird Cottage.

The peace provided the silence Melanie needed to think. She could have sworn that the cherub who had visited her the other night had been the cherub who inspected her soul a few minutes ago. Melanie had never noticed if they encountered the same cherub more than once. And, once again, the cherub had asked her about the password for Dr. Timberi's key. She almost asked the others what they thought about this, but right then the trees stopped, revealing a magnificent old building soaring up from a rich green lawn. Row after row of tall windows dotted the creamy white walls, and graceful turrets and towers crowned the shining blue-gray roof.

"It was built in the sixteenth century," said Madame Cumberland. "The owner died childless and left it as a gift for the Sodality."

They entered through massive wooden doors and found

the building empty. "Not many people work on a Saturday," Madame Cumberland said. She led them through hallways with high, vaulted ceilings and past rows of windows overlooking a misty lake. The hall turned, and they came to a polished door with a sign that said, "Office of Assessment and Evaluation."

"Mona? Is that you?" A rich, mahogany voice came behind them and everyone turned around. A tall African woman glided down the hall. Like other adult Magi, she wore colored robes. But hers seemed to be woven of living rainbows, shifting and changing color each time she moved.

"Notzange!" Lexa called out.

Madame Cumberland dropped into a curtsey. "Your Eminence," she said. As she stood, the woman pulled her into a warm embrace.

Lee followed a few steps behind, and he smiled at the Trio and Pilaf.

You four might want to bow or curtsey, he said. *Last time you saw her, she was just plain old Notzange. But she's had a big promotion since then. Meet Her Eminence, the Supreme Magistrate.*

Melanie watched as Lexa dropped into an elaborate curtsey, polished over years of curtain calls.

"Hello, Lexa." The elegant tones and accent of Notzange's voice matched her regal bearing. "Hello, Conner, Melanie." Notzange nodded and smiled at each of them.

"Who's that?" Pilaf probably meant to whisper, but it came out louder than would have been preferable.

The Supreme Magistrate smiled at him. "My name is Notzange Kimburu. I had the honor of training Madame

Cumberland many years ago, and I became acquainted with these three last April when I was captured by the Darkhands. They helped to find and rescue me."

"Her Eminence was recently installed as the Supreme Magistrate," Madame Cumberland said with pride. "That's like being the President or the Pope, or both, perhaps."

Notzange walked to Pilaf now, smiling down at his pale, blinking face. His eyes seemed even wider than normal behind his glasses. "You must be Olaf."

"Yes, ma'am. But everyone just calls me Pilaf. It's a nickname I got in second grade."

Notzange smiled. "I understand you have shown some interesting symptoms lately leading to questions about whether you are a Magus."

"Yes, ma'am. That's why we're here today. I'm being tested."

"Pilaf," Madame Cumberland said, "Her Eminence is the only Magus alive who can tell in advance if someone will Kindle. It's a very rare gift, and she'd like to test you."

"Really?" Pilaf's voice got so excited, the last syllable was nothing but a squeal.

"I am sorry I did not come when your abilities were first manifest. It has been a very busy few months. But we will rectify that now." Notzange put her long, gnarled fingers on Pilaf's head, holding them there for what seemed like a very long time. When she removed them, she frowned in a thoughtful way. "You will not Kindle, Pilaf."

Water rose in Pilaf's eyes, filling the space behind his giant glasses until his eyes seemed to be swimming in twin goldfish bowls. He forced the brightest, most artificial smile Melanie had ever seen and said, "Yeah, I didn't think I would." He smiled harder. "I was just curious. I knew I wouldn't. I wouldn't really want to be a Magi anyway—"

Notzange put her fingers under his chin and lifted his face. "My dear, your gift is unique, even singular. I feel something inside of you. Great power. You are special, Pilaf. Very special. Guard your gift well."

A giant grin cracked Pilaf's face, a smile so real and big Melanie thought the corners of his mouth might meet at the back of his head.

"With your permission, I would still like you to go through the testing process so we can find out a little more about your abilities, Pilaf," Notzange said.

"Sure!"

"Thank you. Now, if you will excuse me, I must return to my office as I have a great deal of work to do. Good-bye."

She hugged Madame Cumberland again and then left.

"Any word on Morgan?" Madame Cumberland asked Lee.

He frowned. "No. 'Fraid not. Notzange's working everyone pretty hard, but I think Hortense's people have basically given up. They don't believe he's alive. I'm pushing all I can, though. You never know what might turn up. We'll keep searching." His words sounded far more hopeful than his voice. "Speaking of that, I need to go follow up on some leads. Happy birthday, Pilaf."

"Thanks!" Pilaf replied as Lee hugged Madame Cumberland and left.

Fighting back tears, Madame Cumberland knocked on the door.

A moment later, a middle-aged Chinese woman in

a white coat opened the door. "Yes?" She looked a bit confused.

"Olaf Larson is here," Madame Cumberland said, nudging Pilaf forward.

The woman in the white coat blinked.

"The Supreme Magistrate wanted him tested?" Madame Cumberland added.

"Oh, yes!" The woman smiled. "Sorry, I forgot." She looked at Pilaf. "You can come back."

"Can everyone else come too?"

"Certainly," she said with a smile. She looked at everyone. "I'm Dr. Seo, by the way." Dr. Seo led them into a room that looked like a combination doctor's office and pre-school playroom. When they got there, Dr. Seo seemed a little startled that they were behind her. She introduced herself again.

"PhD or MD?" Pilaf asked.

"Both." Dr. Seo smiled. "Kind of a nerd. I really liked school."

"Me too!" Pilaf yelled. "I love school! Well, except for lunch and physical education and breaks between classes."

Basically everything that makes school semibearable for everyone else, Conner thought.

"So I guess you go by 'Pilaf'?" Dr. Seo asked, looking at some papers.

"Yes, ma'am," Pilaf said.

"Very well, Pilaf. Now, let me go over your case history very quickly. No family history of Lightcraft or involvement with the Magi?"

"No, ma'am."

"And when did you first experience Photoperception?"

"Excuse me?"

"Photoperception is the ability to see Lightcraft being used around you."

"Last April. One day, I noticed that Conner and Melanie and Lexa were all sort of glowing. And so were some of our teachers. Later on I started to see layers of Darkness covering some people."

Dr. Seo cupped her right hand and held it out in front of her, creating a circle made of purple Light. "Can you see this?"

"Yes, it's a circle."

She went through various shapes out of Light, everything from hexagons to a dodecahedron, all of which Pilaf accurately named.

Dr. Seo nodded and scribbled some notes. "But you've never actually used or manipulated the Light in any way?"

"No, ma'am."

"Interesting. Now, tell me about what happened over the summer."

"I started to be able to absorb Light. Or Darkness. Either one. Basically, I neutralize it."

"Interesting." Dr. Seo drew blood, listened to his heart, and did an MRI of his brain. She had him repeat head-talking conversations and asked him to analyze Light from different colors of the spectrum. She scanned his irises, then hooked him up to something like an EKG.

Each time she started a new test, Dr. Seo explained what she was testing for and asked permission. Each time, Pilaf yelled, "Cool!" and jumped into the test with complete excitement.

Melanie, on the other hand, grew more and more uneasy. Watching all these tests reminded her of the danger Conner faced. What if the Examiners found out he could use Darkness? He'd be hooked up to machines all day long, and no one would ask his permission. The thought scratched at the back of her mind over and over.

After the last test, Dr. Seo walked them over to a computer and tapped a few keys. Pilaf's brain scans filled monitor.

"These are scans from the functional MRI we did. It allows us to observe the brain during various activities. When Magi experience photoperception, this area of the brain—the visual cortex—is quite active. Now, Pilaf, when you see the Light, your visual cortex is active, like we'd expect to see in a Magus. However, unlike other Magi, this area—the fusiform cortex—is also very active, suggesting a more complex response. There's additional activity in your amygdala, which suggests a deep emotional response as well."

"Can you translate that for the rest of us?" Conner asked.

Dr. Seo blinked a few times and looked slightly confused. With all the blinking, Melanie wondered if the doctor might be distantly related to Pilaf. "When Pilaf sees Light, his brain uses about three times the area of a normal Magus, so we would assume that he can see far more than the average Magus. I suspect that's why he can also see Darkness. However, this part of the brain, the part that is associated with *doing* Lightcraft, shows no activity at all." Dr. Seo paused.

"That's all academic, though. Here's some important, more practical information. It appears that Pilaf processes the Light in almost the same way that the body would process rays from the sun, and that worries me."

"Why?" Pilaf asked.

"When sunlight touches your skin, your body produces Vitamin D. That's good, but too much can be a problem. Vitamin D is fat soluble, which means it doesn't pass easily through your body. It's stored inside of your fat cells and too much can actually be toxic. Of course, we're talking very high levels.

"Pilaf, it appears your body absorbs and processes Light as if it was a very concentrated dose of sunlight. Your blood tests show high doses of a chemical related to Vitamin D. So be cautious, Pilaf. Magi metabolize Light very easily, but you don't seem to share this trait. So think of the Light being like the sun. It can be harmless and even beneficial, but extreme or prolonged exposure could cause some problems for you." Dr. Seo frowned. "But that's not what worries me the most."

"What does?" Pilaf asked.

"Based on the way your body metabolizes Light, I am ninety percent sure that Darkness is physically toxic for you. According to your history, the first time you ingested Darkness, you sneezed and got a rash. The last time, you ended up vomiting. I worry that large doses or prolonged exposure could cause liver or kidney damage or worse down the road. I really need to emphasize that, Pilaf. Neutralizing too much Darkness could kill you."

Gnats of worry swarmed Melanie. In an attempt to save Conner, Pilaf had neutralized massive amounts of

Darkness a few weeks ago. How much had already accu-
mulated inside of him? Had it already started damaging
him, or was it lurking there, waiting for more to come so
it could start gnawing Pilaf's internal organs?

Dr. Seo checked her notes again. "What I don't understand is how you developed these powers. You don't have
a family history. And what you can do is so rare as to be
historically unique." She nibbled on the end of a pencil.
"This has to be tied in somehow to your friends' Kindling.
It happened around the same time, right?"

"Yes, ma'am," Pilaf answered.

"That's another mystery I'd like to figure out," Dr. Seo
said. "A triple Kindling is extremely rare. This has all got
to be related somehow." She nibbled a little harder at the
pencil. "No one ever tested you three, right?"

"No, ma'am," Melanie said. And now, no one could.

Dr. Seo nodded. "I wonder . . ." Her voice trailed off,
and she pulled out a cart with a machine on it. "This is
a modified spectrophotometer, which measures various
properties of wavelength. It has a few modifications so
that it can sense the unique Light signatures of individual
Magi." She plugged the machine into her laptop.

"Could you do me a favor, you three?" she asked.
"When I ask you, please shoot a sigil into this slot in the
machine. We'll go in alphabetical order. Conner, you first."

Conner shot a bright red German shepherd at the
machine, which beeped and sent some graphs onto the
laptop.

"Okay. Lexa, you next, please?"

Lexa's bright yellow dolphin jumped into the machine,
setting off a new round of beeps and graphs on the monitor.

"And Melanie," Dr. Seo said.

"I can't," Melanie said in a small voice.

"Her parents grounded her," Madame Cumberland jumped in.

"Oh, okay. I suspect that doesn't matter anyway." Dr. Seo nodded and tapped some keys. "Oh, wow," she said. "Wow."

"What is it?" Melanie asked, wondering why it didn't matter that she didn't shoot a sigil.

"Look at these Light signatures." Dr. Seo pointed to the monitor, which showed three images—one red, one yellow, and one a pale, milky blue. They reminded Melanie of the snowflakes she'd made as a child by cutting away parts of a folded piece of paper. "The red and yellow are Conner and Lexa's Light signatures. The blue one is from Light that Pilaf radiated during one of the tests. If you look at the core in the middle, the patterns are almost identical." Dr. Seo tapped a key and everything disappeared except for the part in the middle of each image. Even with untrained eyes, Melanie saw the identical pattern at the center of the Light signatures. Swirling and loopy, it could have been an elegant, intricate piece of lace.

"What does that mean?" She felt so alone.

"Conner, Lexa, and Pilaf have the same core Light Signature. We would expect that for Conner and Lexa since we usually see the same patterns in families. My children would have the same basic core as me, although if their father were a Magus, they would inherit some of his pattern as well. It's closely linked to genetics. But none of you are related to Pilaf, right?"

"No, ma'am," Lexa said.

Dr. Seo blinked a few times. "Strange. Maybe since Conner and Lexa are twins, their combined Kindling was so strong that it sparked Melanie's Kindling and also triggered Pilaf's powers. That would make sense." She nodded her head and started scrawling more notes. "I need to study this a little more. Thank you for coming by."

That is so cool! Lexa said as Madame Cumberland took them back through the Otherwhere. *Mel, it's like we're twin Magi or something—or triplets. Even better!*

Melanie didn't reply, so after several attempts at conversation, Lexa gave up, which was what Melanie most wanted at that moment. She didn't trust herself to talk—or think—to anyone.

Of course! Of course Lexa and Conner had started this. She, on the other hand, had just happened to be there at the right time: an innocent bystander swept up in Lexa's Kindling like a car being carried away by a flood. She was starting to feel like the debris in Lexa's raging flood of life.

Even if she did get her powers back, what did she have to look forward to? A life of living in Lexa's shadow?

CHAPTER 16.

SKIRMISH AT
SKY HIGH SPORTS

ARE YOU OKAY? CONNER ASKED MELANIE.
She seemed upset about something.

Just tired, she said. Clearly she didn't want to talk. Or did she? Conner wondered if there was a rule about how many times you were supposed to keep asking when a girl said she was fine but obviously wasn't. He'd have to check with Lexa about that.

They walked in silence through the Otherwere until Madame Cumberland opened a portal and let them out in the parking lot at Sky High Sports.

"My instructions were to bring you here," she said. "Your mother will come get you in two hours. Happy birthday, Pilaf!"

"Thanks!" His smile was as contagious as a cold in a kindergarten classroom, and he quivered with what Conner assumed was excitement.

Madame Cumberland left, and they went in and stood at the counter while a grumpy employee wrapped a wristband around everyone's wrists. Leaving her earbuds in, the employee nudged the volume down on her iPod enough to shout, "You've got two hours." She nudged the volume back up.

"There's no one here," Melanie said as they walked into the massive jumping area.

"Yeah, my mom tends to go overboard on a lot of things," Pilaf said. "She rented the whole place. I told her not to, but she did anyway."

"Cool!" Lexa said, and Conner had to agree.

Raised decks running along the two long sides of the rectangular building contained different jumping activities: a foam pit, a dodgeball court, and a tennis court-sized trampoline for serious jumping. Across the room, additional jumping areas had been put up for toddlers, younger children, and birthday parties.

Melanie sat down on a bench near the plastic shoe cubby and worked at untying her shoes. She didn't make eye contact, and since she hadn't said a word since leaving the Magisterium, Conner decided to give her some space.

"Last one to the foam pit's a rotten egg!" Pilaf ran up the ramp as fast his skinny legs could go with Conner running behind, fast enough to look convincing but not fast enough to beat Pilaf.

Pilaf got there first, swinging out on a large, knotted rope. He shrieked something that sounded like Tarzan on helium, then let go of the rope and dropped, disappearing beneath a colored sea of soft foam blocks. A minute later a tremor spread through the foam, and Pilaf resurfaced, laughing and shouting, "That was awesome!"

Conner grabbed the rope, ran across the platform,

and sailed out into the air over the pit, managing a quick flip before he disappeared in the foam.

"That was awesome, Conner!" Pilaf yelled when Conner climbed out.

"My turn!" Lexa yelled. Streaming, she grabbed the rope and propelled herself across the foam pit and up into the air. When she reached the middle of the pit, she stopped streaming, then turned a double backflip before plummeting down and disappearing beneath the foam blocks.

"Nice, Lex!" Conner yelled as he and Pilaf cheered and burst into applause. Conner heard a loud clap—but when the smell of sulfur pinched his nostrils, he realized it was an explosion.

As more explosions rocked the room, Conner grabbed Pilaf and dropped to the floor. He looked up in time to see a stream of black flames screaming through the air where his belly button had been a fraction of a second earlier.

Is everyone okay? he asked.

The smoke that already filled the air made it difficult to see anything.

"I'm right behind you!" Pilaf shouted, louder than necessary.

Another blast of black fire spurred him to movement. *Come on, Pilaf!* Staying on his stomach, he army-crawled several yards to a picnic table, which he knocked over and used as a makeshift shelter.

The table shook as a blob of Darkness hammered into it, blowing the top half into toothpicks.

Melanie, where are you?

Behind the shoe cubby on the main floor, she said.

Okay, I'll be right over. Conner didn't normally worry

about Melanie in fights since she had become an amazing fighter. But without her powers, he worried. A lot.

More bursts of Darkness came now.

We need to get you somewhere safe, buddy, Conner said.

I'm still in the foam pit. I had a theeling that told me to stay here, Lexa said. *Pilaf, come hide with me.*

Pilaf turned bright, bright red, and Conner had to choke down the laugh trying to come out.

Another burst of black fire blew the rest of the table into splinters.

Hang on. Let me create a distraction, Conner said. *I don't want them to notice where you go.*

Conner jumped out from behind the table and organized an Illumination in his hands—a big, red fire hose made out of Light. Imagining the hose squirting at full capacity, he sent a powerful spray of red Light all around. Some of the red Light hit one of the cyclones, sending it spinning in reverse.

Now, Pilaf!

Pilaf scurried across the deck and dove into the foam pit. As he did, some of Conner's tension faded. Lexa could protect Pilaf. Now he just had to figure out how to keep Melanie safe.

Black fire crashed into the shoe cubby, melting it into a stinky, smoldering lump as Melanie rolled away.

Yeeee-haaaaaaaw! A dusty brown comet shot into the air, then stopped, and Lee appeared in the air, cradling a double-barreled shotgun made out of Light. He peppered the air with Light-ammo for a few seconds, becoming a comet again in time to avoid hitting the floor.

As Lee's comet streamed toward the ceiling, two more

comets appeared on each side of him—emerald green and aqua. The green comet belonged to Lee's second-in-command, Lieutenant Miranda Grimaldi. The aqua comet belonged to a guy named Brighton, the buffest Magus Conner had ever seen.

Dropping into a steep dive, the three comets blasted toward the source of the explosions and fire—the special birthday party area.

Five black cyclones spun out from hiding, whirling away from the blazing comets.

Conner streamed down the ramp to the shoe rack, hoping to get Melanie to the safety of the foam pit. As he streamed, a hailstorm of Darkness filled the air with shrapnel-like shards. He dodged them, but a sharp cry below pounded an icy nail through his heart. Melanie fell backward, grasping her shoulder.

Melanie! He landed at her side. *Are you okay?*

I'm fine, she gasped. *It was just a little Darkness.* Three or four scorches had burned through the shoulder and arm of her shirt. Worse, her face had turned a pale, pasty color.

We need to get you into the foam pit, he said, scooping her up in his arms. As she made contact with him, power surged inside Conner, like someone had cranked the volume way up on his ability to use the Light.

Are you Augumenting me?

I think, she said. *I'm not sure. It just happens.*

Conner picked a Darkhand cyclone and made the shape of a pistol with his pointer finger and thumb. He flicked his wrist, and an enormous torrent of red Light tinged with pink rushed out and slammed into the cyclone, dropping it to the floor.

Yeah, you're definitely Augmenting me. No way I could do that on my own. Concentrated blasts of Darkness interrupted them, and Conner ran up the ramp.

He couldn't stream with Melanie, but he ran as fast as he could. By the time they reached the deck, the pale white of her skin had turned to an ashy gray.

As they came to the edge of the foam pit, two of the cyclones landed on the other side, shooting twin streams of black fire at Melanie.

"Noooooo!" Conner dropped Melanie into the pit, jumping between her and the incoming fire. As the flames rushed closer, the heat grew intense. He threw his arms wide open. "Go away!" he yelled. The streams of flame jerked and quivered but followed the motion of his arms, shooting away to his right and left.

Lee's comet appeared, taking the cyclones by surprise, knocking them each about twenty yards away. The cyclone faded, revealing a Darkhand motionless on the ground.

DELL! Lee's voice cut into his mind as the dusty-colored comet flew by. *What in the world did you just do?*

I made the Darkness go away.

That's what I thought. You do that on purpose?

Uh, sort of.

Five explosions interrupted their conversation. Conner looked over to see five more cyclones appear in the air.

Lee laughed in his mind. *These poor yahoos don't know when they're licked! Dell, we'll talk about this soon. Can you keep Melanie and Pilaf safe?*

Yes, sir.

Lee streamed across the room, joining the aqua comet in playing bumper cars with three tornadoes.

Conner!

Lexa's thoughts pulled his attention to the foam pit, where he saw Lexa's eyes peeking out from under a few blocks.

What's wrong, Lex?

Nothing, she said. *I have an idea. Can you get out of the way for a sec—go chase some tornadoes or something?*

Sure. He'd learned to trust Lexa's theelings.

Mel, Lexa said, *can you Augment me?*

I can try, Melanie replied. Her thoughts sounded weak and shaky, which filled Conner with a terrible fear.

Are you okay? he asked. His thoughts flapped around like a wounded moth, sounding far more vulnerable than he liked.

I'm fine, she replied. *I promise. I'm just tired and a little dizzy. Don't worry about me. Just get away so Lexa can do her plan.*

With reluctance, Conner streamed away, leaving the foam pit open.

Pilaf's head popped up through some of the blocks. "Hey poopy-face Darkhands!" he shouted. "Nanny-nanny-boo-boo! Can't get me!"

Five of the eight remaining tornadoes rushed for the pit, gunning for Pilaf.

As they whirled closer, the foam shook and trembled, and Conner sensed huge quantities of Light boiling down inside the pit, hidden by the top layer of blocks. Pilaf kept taunting the Darkhands, and as they spun nearer, the blocks shook like popcorn seeds getting ready to pop.

When the Darkhands reached the edge of the pit,

Lexa jumped up through the foam, thrusting her arms up and flinging them forward.

As she did, the whole pit exploded. Foam blocks glowing with pinkish-yellow Light filled the air, pelting Darkhands all over the place. Four cyclones went down, dropped by dozens of the Light-infused blocks.

Nice job, Lex, Conner thought. No wonder her theelings told her to stay in the pit. With a perfect sneak attack, she had the Darkhands on the run.

Time to end this. Focusing on one of the tornadoes, Conner extended his left arm and called the shadows inside of it. The shadows tried to come to him, but something tugged back, like a big fish on the end of a fishing line. Conner concentrated harder. A few globs of Darkness peeled away from the cyclone, but nothing else happened. He focused harder, feeling the Darkness resist his efforts. It pulled away, but as it did, he comprehended the structure of the Darkness swirling around the man inside.

Reaching out with his mind, Conner found a small gap in the spinning shadows. He grabbed at that gap and held on. The cyclone kept spinning, but Conner held on. The result was like unwrapping a mummy. Conner pulled layer after layer of shadows away, until the cyclone unraveled and the man inside fell to the ground.

More comets shot in now, Madame Cumberland in silver and Mrs. Grant in blue. The combined Magi made short work of the remaining Darkhands.

The buff Magus named Brighton treated Melanie's injuries. It turned out he was the medic for the Twilight Phalanx. "She'll be fine," he said to Conner. "Nothing serious."

"Nice shooting everyone!" Lee said. "Grimaldi, call HQ and get them to send a clean-up crew. The rest of you, let's get outta here. Dell, you and me need to have a little powwow. Let's meet back at Mona's room."

"What about Pilaf?" Conner asked. "And Melanie?"

"Don't worry about them," Madame Cumberland said. "Norma Sharpe streamed home to get her car. She doesn't live far, and she should be here any minute. She'll drive them to the school. I'll wait here until she comes."

When everyone arrived at the school, Lee called them into a huddle.

"Okay, Dell, we just saw you do some pretty crazy stuff. What's going on?"

Conner looked at Melanie and Lexa. He didn't dare risk a private thought conversation. The other Magi would know he was talking and might get suspicious.

Dr. Timberi had sworn them to secrecy about his new abilities. No one knew but the Trio, Pilaf, and Dr. Timberi.

"What is it?" Lee said. "I've known you three jackrabbits long enough to tell that something's itching your collective craw. Y'all look guiltier than a dirty hound dog at a French poodle show."

Conner looked at Melanie and Lexa again, hoping they'd understand his unspoken question.

Melanie and Lexa nodded. Conner thought he knew what they meant. If he couldn't trust Lee and Madame Cumberland, then nothing mattered because he couldn't trust anyone at all.

"Well, Dr. Timberi swore us to secrecy, but it's probably okay to tell you—"

"Wait!" Mrs. Grant yelled. "Did you swear the Magi's Oath?"

"No," Conner said. "We just promised."

"Oh, good." Mrs. Grant let out a long sigh.

"Why?"

"Because if you break the Magi's Oath, you'll die," Madame Cumberland said. "Or possibly lose your powers."

"That's good to know," Conner said. *I was already planning on keeping the oath we swore in the park the other night,* he added in a private message to Melanie and Lexa. *But it's probably good to remember that dying thing.*

Yeah, Lexa said. *Good point. But you better start talking. I think they're getting suspicious since we're having a private conversation.*

Conner nodded and looked at the adults. "When Lady Nightwing put me in the Shadowbox, I was wearing a necklace the cherubim gave me. So I took Light into the gateway of Darkness, which ended up causing some kind of reaction no one understands. Basically, it turned me into a border between Light and Darkness. I can use both of them. Dr. Timberi thinks that it's a really big deal. But we're not sure exactly what to do with it. I've been trying to control shadows, and I'm okay at that. But beyond doing some pretty cool shadow puppets, I don't know what else to do."

Lee let out a low whistle. "Jehoshaphat's saddle sores! That's some secret." He shook his head and chuckled. "Morgan's a tricky old dog."

"What do you mean?" Lexa asked.

"I'm guessing this all came out the night that Conner blew up the shield at school, right?"

Conner nodded.

"During that fight, we all saw Conner channel Light and Dark. But Morgan filed a report with the Magisterium and told us all about the phantumbras attacking and the Lucents. He sort of implied the Darkness just followed the phantumbras. Didn't say a word about being a bridge between Light and Dark. Gave us lots to think about while keeping us away from what he didn't want us to see. Classic misdirection." Lee grinned. "Classic Morgan. He always wrote his own rules."

"Did Morgan say why he wanted you to keep this quiet?" Madame Cumberland asked.

Melanie nodded. "Yes, ma'am. He was afraid if the Darkhands found out, they would never stop until they got Conner. And he thought that it was more likely for word to spread as more people knew."

"Plus he doesn't trust the Magisterium," Lexa said. "At all. He worried they might basically make Conner a prisoner or a lab rat or both."

"Morgan was right on all counts," Lee said. "You were right not to tell anyone—especially the Magisterium."

"Is the Magisterium bad?" Lexa asked.

"No." Lee shrugged. "In fact, the Magisterium has some fantastic people. But collectively, the organization is hidebound, wrongheaded, and just plain stupid—but completely convinced it possesses a unique blend of wisdom and virtue. It's the nature of bureaucracies to fuss about things that ain't important and forget about things that really matter. Magisterium's no different."

"Conner, did you say you had been practicing?" Madame Cumberland asked.

"Yes, ma'am."

"But only with regular shadows, right?" Lee added.

"Yes, sir. I worked on real Darkness the night Dr. Timberi got taken and then today. But I don't have many chances."

"Regular shadows ain't gonna teach you much. They're about as close to Darkness as a lizard is to a crocodile. We need to get you some practice controlling hundred-and-ninety proof, grade-triple-A, industrial-strength Darkness." Lee's eyes lit up like taillights at rush hour. "Dell, I think you need to come along with the Phalanx on some patrols. Get in some skirmishes."

"Are you serious?" Conner and Melanie both yelled at the same time—although Conner noticed their tones were quite different.

"That would be dangerous!" Melanie said.

"Yep," Lee said. "It is. When you became Magi, your world got dangerous. That boat's already sailed, Stephens. It's hard to fight evil safely. Think about what happened today. You came to a birthday party—and got ambushed. That's happened to you since you Kindled. It's happened at school, at Disney World, and at an ice cream place—to name a few examples.

"I promise that Conner will be in a noncombat role. He'll be at least as safe as he is every day, probably safer," Lee said, sending Conner's excitement plummeting. That didn't sound as exciting.

"Safer?" Melanie asked.

"You bet," Lee said. "He'll be safer because the whole

Phalanx will be protecting him. Look, Stephens, if we wanna beat the bad guys and hopefully help Morgan, we need to use every weapon we have."

"What about the other people in the Phalanx?" It didn't appear that Melanie planned to surrender. "Won't they find out that Conner can do this? Will they tell the Magisterium?"

Lee nodded. "Fair question, Stephens. They won't tell anyone. I'll make them swear the Magi's Oath." Melanie opened her mouth to say something else, but Madame Cumberland interrupted her.

"Oh no," Madame Cumberland said. "Oh no!"

"What's wrong, Mona?" Mrs. Grant asked.

"The Examiners are coming to evaluate everyone's memories. When they explore Conner's, they'll surely come across what he can do with Darkness. And then the Magisterium will know."

Lee said some words that earned him a sharp look from Mrs. Grant.

Conner didn't care. He didn't want to become a lab rat.

NEUTRALIZATION

SUNDAY, AFTER A LONG, DEEP SLEEP, LEXA woke up to her mom telling her to get ready for church, where she and Conner got more sleep. Afterward, Lexa streamed over to Melanie's house, where she found Melanie sitting on the bed, flicking her hands over and over.

"Any luck?" Lexa asked.

"Still nothing," Melanie said with trembling lips. "Nothing at all."

"But you can still head-talk," Lexa said. "Plus you Augmented me."

"I know," Melanie said, pounding a pillow. "And it's almost as frustrating to not understand what's going on as it is to lose my powers." She flung the pillow across the room. The pain in her friend's voice scraped at Lexa's heart. Lexa would prefer to lose an arm or leg—or even her life—before her powers.

Hey Lex, Conner's voice came into her thoughts. *Where are you?*

I'm at Mel's, Lexa said.

Oh, hi, Melanie! Lexa sensed Conner's voice opening a connection in Melanie's head as well, so now it became a three-way conversation. *Pilaf's coming over. He's got an idea he wants to talk about with all of us.*

Sure! Melanie practically yelled. Lexa knew Melanie's decision had almost nothing to do with Pilaf, and for a few seconds, she felt jealous. She'd come to try to comfort Melanie, but as soon as Conner—*Stop!* She told herself. *Just stop now.* Lexa yanked her ponytail. She would not do this.

She decided to think it was cute that Melanie liked to be with Conner. And to be glad it was her brother and not some jerk she hated.

We'll be right there, Lexa said with a smile in her voice that she almost felt.

"I guess I'll just ride my bike," Melanie said, and Lexa sensed the deep sadness, the sense of loss that echoed inside of Melanie's emptiness. "Thanks to my parents I can't stream." She hit another pillow. Then she pulled a face and did an ugly imitation of her parents. "No more streaming. No more sigils. No more shooting Light!" Melanie's face changed. The sorrow and rage turned into triumph. "That's it, Lexa! That's it!"

"What's it?"

"That's what my dad said. His exact words. That's why I can head-talk and phase and Augment—he didn't forbid me from doing those things! The things he specifically said are the things I can't do."

Lexa nodded. It made sense. But that answered one question and raised another. "How did your dad even know what all that stuff is called? That seems really specific for him."

Melanie's eyes narrowed a bit. "I know. I wondered that too, and I haven't figured it out yet, but I will. Okay, let's go."

They got Melanie's bike out of the garage, and Melanie began pedaling toward the Dell's house. An idea jumped into Lexa's mind. "Hold on, Mel," she said. She grabbed the back of Melanie's seat and started to run. Within three or four steps, she blurred into a yellow comet—propelling Melanie's bike down the sidewalk at superspeed.

Melanie laughed as they shot past pedestrians and passed cars with no problem. With Lexa's propulsion, they arrived at the Dells' in just a few minutes. They walked into the house and found Pilaf waiting with Conner in the living room.

"What's up?" Lexa asked.

Pilaf took a breath. "I have an idea, but I need your help. I've been thinking about how the Examiners are coming and how we can't let them find out about Conner." He looked at Lexa and Melanie. "I think if you two swear the Magi's Oath not to reveal anything about Conner, then the Examiners probably can't access anything that would break that oath. Since the Light enforces those oaths, I don't think the Light will let them access anything that will compromise that."

That made Lexa's head spin, but Melanie nodded. "That makes sense, Pilaf. Nice job."

Pilaf beamed.

"But what about Conner?" Lexa asked. "Will it work for him to swear the Oath?"

"I wouldn't count on it," Pilaf said. "I think since it's his memory and his secret it will be harder to hide. But I have an idea. If I'm with Conner when they do their thing, I can use my neutralizing powers to interfere with the Light if they get too close."

Melanie scrunched her nose. "But can you do that, Pilaf? I mean, won't they notice you're interfering?"

"That's what I need your help with. I was thinking that I can probably learn how to control it—like turn it up or down."

"It would totally make sense!" Lexa said. "Before we started training, we couldn't control our Lightcraft. But now we do it without even trying."

"I think I see where you're going with this, Pilaf," Melanie said. She wrinkled her nose again and closed her eyes. Pink Light flashed and a pair of dish-washing gloves appeared in the air, hovering for a second before they fell to the floor.

"Hah!" Melanie yelled in triumph. "I can still do Translocation! My dad's not as smart as he thought he was." She grabbed the gloves and extended her arms toward Pilaf. "Pilaf, can you please put these on? Wait, maybe just one. Keep your right hand uncovered."

"Sure." He pulled it on with a snapping sound that made Lexa cringe since it reminded her of doing the dishes.

"Okay," Melanie said. "Lexa, can you make some Light appear in your hand?"

A ball of yellow Light appeared just above Lexa's fingers. Melanie continued her instructions. "Touch Lexa's hand, Pilaf." Pilaf blushed, then reached out. When the tip of his finger tapped Lexa's skin, the Light disappeared, and she gasped from shock as the energy dissipated.

"Are you okay?" Pilaf asked.

"Fine," Lexa said. "It just closed my gateway really suddenly. I couldn't even connect to the Light." The suddenness of it had left her breathless.

Melanie nodded. "Okay, Pilaf, do that again but use the rubber glove instead."

They repeated the procedure, but this time, when Pilaf's gloved fingertip touched Lexa's hand, nothing happened.

"So we know that the rubber insulates," Melanie said. "Now, let's see if you can control it. Try it with the ungloved hand."

Pilaf reached out and seemed to be trying to touch Lexa with even less skin than before. Still, it only took the tiniest bit of contact to make Lexa's Light disappear. Once again, Lexa felt exhausted and empty as Pilaf's touch cut her off from the Light. What a terrible feeling!

Pilaf set his jaw and concentrated. He blinked faster and faster, accelerating until Lexa thought she felt a breeze. She wanted to direct the breeze back at Pilaf, because beads of sweat had popped out all over his pasty-white forehead.

About the time Pilaf's eyelids hit hummingbird-wing speed, a small spark appeared in Lexa's hand. The spark grew larger and larger, lurching and gasping to greater size. As the spark grew, so did Lexa's inner strength. She felt stronger and more powerful.

Pilaf's jaw got so tight Lexa worried he might dislocate it. But with a little more practice, he got to the point he could disrupt the Light by degrees, making it get bigger or smaller in mostly-smooth increments.

"Hey, I just had an idea," Pilaf said, pulling his hand away from Lexa. He took a couple of deep breaths, as if he'd been doing wind sprints. Lexa could tell Pilaf's mind was spinning because his eyes began to blink again. "If I can cancel out your Light in small doses, I wonder if I can cancel myself out completely."

"What?" Conner asked.

"I mean, what if I can balance Light and Dark so that I'm basically not in the equation at all?"

Melanie nodded. "You mean so that you were totally neutral. Not charged either way."

Pilaf nodded. "Exactly."

"That might be cool," Conner said. "But why would it matter?"

"Because then you could carry him when you stream," Melanie said. "It would sort of be like me phasing. He wouldn't weigh anything as far as the Light and Dark were concerned."

Lexa gasped, and the room spun out of control. At first she thought she might be weak from having her Light cancelled out. But then her vision got hazy as an awareness of pain overwhelmed all her other senses. Once again, she couldn't actually feel it, but she could feel someone feeling it.

"Morgan, you really are going to have to give up at some point."

The prison came back into view, and once more Lexa had the strange sensation of seeing with two pairs of mind's eyes.

The cold, sneering face of Lady Nightwing appeared, and Dr. Timberi clung to his determination to not speak.

But the determination felt different to Lexa. Weaker. Like ice growing thin and brittle.

She couldn't blame him. The raging pain grew so great that it almost pierced whatever barrier kept his consciousness separate from hers.

Focusing all her effort, Lexa started to sing.

Mel! she yelled in her head. *Mel! He needs help.*

As she sang, Dr. Timberi relaxed. Lexa didn't know if it blocked the pain or if it just soothed him, but she felt a shift in his mind. Just then, a flash of pink Light nearly blinded her. She felt it swoosh into her and then disappear.

As Melanie's Light reached his sigil, Dr. Timberi's mind grew warm, and the pain faded away.

Mel, it's working! Keep going.

As Lexa sang harder, Melanie touched Lexa's arm, sending a flood of pink Light rushing inside to join Lexa's song.

And then Conner joined the circle, putting his arms around both of them.

It felt like someone had cranked up the volume on powerful speakers. A river of energy became a flood, swelling into a tidal wave of power. It rushed through Lexa's spirit, pouring into Dr. Timberi's sigil.

He raised a weak hand and pointed it at Lady Nightwing.

An immense explosion of Light filled Lexa's range of vision. A woman's shrill scream rattled in her ears—and then the connection faded.

CHAPTER 18

THE EXAMINERS

"WHAT JUST HAPPENED?" MELANIE ASKED, looking at Lexa. "I felt something, but I don't know what it was."

Lexa shook her head. "I don't know for sure. But I think maybe Dr. Timberi used our Light to shoot Lady Nightwing!"

"He shot her?" Melanie's tension rushed out, tripping on the relief rushing in, and they ended up tangled together in a loud burst of laughter. It sounded a little maniacal, but it beat crying.

"You guys," Lexa said, "that was really powerful. Like amazing. I felt all of our Light together inside of me before it went into Dr. Timberi's sigil. I've never felt anything like that—" She stopped. "Except when I zapped Blinson."

Melanie's mental whiteboard jumped to life with a jolt of energy so strong it made her shake. The complex symbols covering the board hummed and whirred, buzzing as they rearranged themselves, forming an equation, and—boom! It all clicked into place.

"Oh my gosh!" she said. "I think I just figured something out. Something really cool. When Lexa zapped Blinson, remember what was happening?"

"Yeah," Conner said. "Me and you were trying to grab Lexa so she didn't—" He stopped and shook his head. "Whoa. That's deep."

Melanie nodded, relishing the adrenaline that coursed through her when an idea excited her or a new problem got solved. Trying to keep her voice calm, she said, "Exactly. We were touching her. Which is what we were doing a few moments ago. Both times there was an incredibly powerful reaction."

"I thought it was because you were Augmenting her," Conner said.

"I think it's more," Melanie said. She grabbed Lexa's hand. "Do a sigil, Lex."

Lexa raised her own hand and shot a sigil. A large, yellow dolphin appeared with a slight pinkish tint. It looked much brighter and more vivid than Lexa's normal sigil.

"Now join us, Conner," Melanie said, extending her other hand to him. The excitement of a new discovery crackled in the air. Or was it the excitement of Conner holding her hand?

Conner grabbed Melanie's fingers, then touched Lexa's arm with his other hand. Lexa shot a blast of Light that stole Melanie's vision for a few seconds and shook the room. Instead of Lexa's normal yellow, this Light looked like a sunrise—yellow, pink, and red blended, but not blurred, together. After their vision cleared, they stared at each other for a few seconds, blinking like Pilaf in full thinking mode.

"Whoa," Conner said. "Intense. So when we're touching, it's like extra strength?"

Melanie nodded. "I think it's even more than that. Remember what Dr. Timberi said last summer? He said our gifts are complementary. Conner's strength and speed represent the physical aspect of a human. Lexa's gifts as a Seer represent the spirit, and my gifts are more mental, so they represent the mind."

"So when I said we were like one mystical person the other day, I was actually right?" Conner asked.

Melanie nodded. "I think so. I think when we combine our powers we're like one combined human soul—except that it's more powerful than normal because that soul is made up of three different people, with all of our own energy and strength. So it's not just three, it's actually three to the third power." She paused. "I think."

Lexa jumped up. "Oh! Plus, you're an Augmentor, Mel, so it's even more than triple strength. Our strength just gets bigger and bigger."

"Like an echo chamber," Pilaf said. "It just keeps rebounding all around you three, amplifying constantly. This is really big, you guys. Really, really big."

"That must be why Lexa could Translocate Blinson," Conner said. "Right? Normally you can't Translocate humans like that."

"Do you think other Magi can link their powers like this?" Lexa asked.

"No," Melanie said. "I don't think so. If they could,

wouldn't they do it more? I've never seen anyone combine or link their powers in all the battles we've been in. I think this is really different, really special. Something Dr. Timberi was starting to figure out."

Shivers seemed to run through the room. Melanie couldn't stop thinking about the possibilities.

"So what do we do now?" Lexa asked.

"We keep it quiet," Melanie said. "And we practice and experiment. And then we'll find Dr. Timberi. If Lady Nightwing's still alive, we'll grab hands and blast her twisted soul into, uh, into . . ."

"Into sub-atomic particles that will make quarks look like mountains," Pilaf said, glaring and punching his right hand into his left.

Melanie's mind raced all that night, trying to grasp the full implications of their discovery. More than anything, she wanted to talk it out with Dr. Timberi. How many problems had they solved that way together? She smiled, remembering those talks.

They were each a body, mind, and spirit. So each of them could be represented by a three. And then you took the three of them and combined them. But it wouldn't be three times three, it would be three cubed—three times three times three. Right? Plus whatever extra value her Augmenting powers gave them, multiplied by Conner's superstrength. Or was it the other way around? Pilaf's theory that it created a feedback loop of some kind sounded correct. She wondered if there were any theoretical limits to what they could do. Was it possible for humans to channel that much power? What other variables might be at play?

She puzzled over these questions Sunday night, the next day during school, over supper, and for the entire time she should have been doing homework. Focusing on these thoughts, Melanie faintly heard the doorbell ring but didn't think much of it until she heard her father yelling.

"I don't care if you work for the Easter Bunny and the Tooth Fairy at the same time! You aren't dragging Melanie into this!"

Hearing her name, she ran out of her room, down the hall, and descended the stairs three at a time.

Two people stood at the door—a man and a woman in black suits, each holding out some kind of a badge in a leather case. Her father blocked their entry, standing in front of them, close enough to be considered quite aggressive, and Melanie's mom stood behind him, brandishing her marble rolling pin.

"Uh, Dad?" Melanie asked. "What's going on?"

"Are you Melanie Stephens?" The woman looked up at her.

"Yes."

The woman raised her hand and shot a column of grayish Light at Melanie. The Light scanned her, then vanished. The woman nodded. "Identify confirmed."

"I said stop!" her dad roared. "I've already forbidden her from—"

Melanie panicked. If he said something large and sweeping, it might take her remaining powers away, and she wouldn't be able to do anything.

"Dad!" she shouted, trying to distract him before he

could say that he'd forbidden her from all Magi activity ever again.

"Melanie, let me handle this."

"Sir," the man's tone dripped with irritation masked as patience, "we simply wish to extract some of your daughter's memories. She is a key witness in the trial of a notorious Darkhand."

"What?" her father asked. "Melanie—a witness?"

"The trial of Timothy Timberi starts next week, sir. And we have a great deal of work—"

"Wait," her dad said. "What did you say? Whose trial?"

"Dr. Timberi's son," Melanie said with a sinking feeling. Now it was all over. Anything to do with Dr. Timberi set her dad off like a bottle rocket. He'd really freak out. "You don't know this, but he was married and had a son. His wife's name was Nicole. The Darkhands killed her and kidnapped his son when he was a little boy."

Her dad stared at her, blinking and shaking his head for several seconds.

What was up with her dad? Did he feel guilty for being a jerk now that Dr. Timberi was gone?

"He's on trial? Timothy?"

"Yes, Dad."

Her dad said nothing, this time for several minutes, and thick silence wrapped the room. Not the empty silence that comes from a lack of emotion or thought. Rather, a thick, highly charged silence that seemed to come from emotion too great for words.

"Melanie," her father said, "can your testimony—your memories—help him?"

"Maybe." Melanie stared at her father in complete

confusion. Had she walked into some crazy, upside-down world?

Her dad looked at the Examiners. "Go ahead," he said, stepping aside. "Do what you need to do. Melanie, you have my permission."

Melanie sensed him weakening and saw a unique opportunity. She took a deep breath, afraid to make him mad. At the same time—no risk, no reward. "What if I need to go to the tribunal? What if I need to use Lightcraft?"

"Do what you need to do. Help Timothy. You have my permission." He walked out of the room, followed by Melanie's mom, who looked confused—something Melanie could relate to. As her parents walked out and the Examiners walked in, Melanie wondered what had happened to the real Frank Stephens.

CHAPTER 19.

PILAF'S EXPERIMENT

CONNER WATCHED AS HIS PARENTS exchanged suspicious looks. "You're sure this won't hurt them?" Conner's dad asked the Examiners.

"Positive," the man said.

"Okay, but we're staying in the room," his dad added.

"That will be fine, sir," the man said.

"Um, can Pilaf stay too?" Conner asked. Everyone looked at him. "I, uh, I'm a little nervous. It helps when he's here." He felt himself blush. That was a dumb excuse. No one would believe him. Actually, he really hoped no one would believe him.

"Conner's just being nice," Pilaf said. "I'm extremely curious about how this works and I wanted to watch, so Conner said he'd work it out for me."

Thanks, Pilaf, Conner said.

"Certainly," the man said. "We'll start with Alexandra."

"Lexa. Please." Lexa dropped herself down on a chair. The woman opened their briefcase and pulled out a series of flat hoops, each of which fit inside the other. She shot a sigil—an orange bloodhound—and the hoops jumped up, spinning around and around an invisible axis, in constant orbits, each at different angles.

Conner recognized an horloge—a device Magi used to record and analyze Light. Dr. Timberi had taught Melanie how to use one over the summer, so it seemed familiar and welcoming to Conner.

The woman ran a cable of the orange Light from the horloge to Lexa's temple. She and the man both put their hands on Lexa's head and closed their eyes. Orange Light flashed where the woman's fingers met Lexa's hair, followed by olive-brown Light from the man. They kept their eyes closed for several minutes before removing their hands. Then they each shot a sigil into the horloge.

"Could you please send your sigil as well? Thank you," the woman said. "We have secured your memories in the horloge. Now for Conner."

Are you sure this is going to work? Conner asked Pilaf as he sat down in the chair. Pilaf sat next to him and shrugged.

When the Examiners put their hands on his head, it felt like their fingers continued down, pushing into his brain. It didn't hurt, but Conner felt strange as they looked at his thoughts like a librarian thumbing through the pages in a book. As they examined his memories involving the Stalker, they got close to the time he'd heard shadows talking at Dauphin Island. He tapped Pilaf's shoe and Pilaf poked his back.

"Did you just lose connection?" the woman asked the man.

"Yes. Did you?"

"Yes. Odd."

Pilaf removed his finger, and they went back to the memories. This time they almost found the memory of Conner going full-postal penumbra, floating in the air and sucking up Light and Dark all around him. He tapped Pilaf's foot again, and Pilaf jabbed his finger into Conner's back.

"Sorry," Conner said, feeling their stares as the connection ended. "I think I blacked out after that last memory."

After a few more minutes and one more of Pilaf's interventions, the Examiners stopped.

"Thank you for your time," the woman said after Conner had sent his sigil into the horloge.

"The tribunal will be held this coming Friday. More information will be sent to you."

After the Examiners left, a bright pink comet shot into the living room, resolving into Melanie. Conner's parents jumped a bit but didn't freak out in any embarrassing ways.

"Mel! You streamed?" Lexa squealed.

"Yes!" Melanie practically danced as she talked. Nearly everything came out as a laugh. "My dad let me have my powers back!"

Everyone cheered, and then Conner said, "So what are we hanging out here for? Let's go celebrate! Come on!"

The snap of rubber pulled his attention away from Melanie to Pilaf, who was pulling on the latex dish-washing gloves.

"I'm ready," Pilaf said with a big grin. "Can I come too?"

"Totally, Pilaf," Conner said. "Hop on my back and let's see how your cancelling-out thing works."

They blasted out of the house—red, yellow, and pink comets. And clinging with yellow gloves to Conner's back, a perfect zero between Light and Dark, Pilaf giggled the whole time, cheering as if he rode a roller coaster.

Filling the darkening sky with Light, they flew together. Conner's whole soul seemed to grin.

Melanie had her powers back. Pilaf was learning to use his powers. Conner was going to go hang with the Twilight Phalanx. And they were basically the most powerful Magi ever. He didn't understand everything about Melanie's mathematical formula. But he understood it enough to know they were epically powerful. Mostly, everyone was friends again.

Watch out, Darkhands, Conner thought. *The Four Musketeers are back in business. Dr. Timberi, we'll find you!*

· CHAPTER 20 ·

THE DOG THAT DIDN'T BARK

WEDNESDAY NIGHT, MELANIE INVITED everyone over to her house to study. They hadn't done much of that lately, and Melanie decided they needed to keep their grades up even with everything going on. They would graduate from Marion Academy that year, which meant applying to private high schools in the next few months.

Melanie looked back at her homework and groaned. Literature was not her thing. She didn't like open-ended, not-a-wrong answer situations. She liked math, with clear right and wrong answers. No doubt or ambiguity.

Dell! A brown rattlesnake sigil appeared in the air in front of Conner. *Dell! You there?* Lee's voice shook with energy.

"Yes, sir!" Conner said, jumping up.

We got a lead on Morgan! the rattlesnake said. *We're taking off right now. Why don't you come join us? Meet you at your school athletic field.*

"Yes, sir!" Conner said, saluting. He grabbed his books. "I'm going to go let Mom and Dad know," he said. "See you later!" Without waiting for anyone to say anything, he blasted out of the room as a bright red comet.

"Lee, wait!" Lexa said.

What's wrong, Dell?

"What's the lead? Did you figure out what the Abyss was?"

No word on the Abyss. But we have a good lead and I'm hopeful. Hortense's folks have been looking for any place that shows increased Dark activity. We found a place where a lot has been going on.

"Okay," Lexa said. "Keep us posted!"

Will do! The snake faded.

Fighting a twinge of jealousy that Conner got to go *do* something (and several twinges of worry for Conner's safety), Melanie forced herself to focus on the English essay question again. "Discuss the significance of Sherlock Holmes solving a case based on the lack of something happening as opposed to the presence of evidence."

Grabbing her pen, Melanie began to write: "In 'Silver Blaze,' Sherlock Holmes realized that a dog did not bark during the night when a crime occurred. Most people didn't notice this, but Holmes thought it was strange. Normally, you'd expect a dog to bark, so the fact that the dog didn't bark led him to the conclusion that nothing unusual happened. That meant the crime must have been committed by someone the dog knew. So the absence of evidence—"

Melanie stopped as symbols spun all across the whiteboard in her mind.

Over the summer, when he was teaching her to Adumbrate, Dr. Timberi got more worried when the Darkhands didn't seem to be doing anything. The fact that he couldn't see their action always bothered him.

It wasn't exactly the same thing, but it was similar. The idea that a negative, or lack of something, could actually be hiding an important clue.

Hiding a clue.

A few more symbols spun to life on the whiteboard, humming and buzzing now.

After kidnapping the Trio and Pilaf last spring, some Darkhands had locked them in a supply closet, waiting for Lady Nightwing to come. One of the Darkhands had said, ". . . let Lady Nightwing know we have them. Call her—no Noctigavation. Don't make any adumbrations for the Magi to pick up."

As the whiteboard jumped and buzzed to life, Melanie shouted, "That's it!"

"What's it, Mel?" Lexa asked.

"The Magisterium's wrong! I know how to find Dr. Timberi," she said. "I know how they're hiding him."

"Where?" Lexa jumped out of her chair.

"Well, I don't know exactly where, but I know how to find it. We need to find a place where there is no Dark activity—a place where there *was* Darkness, but where it stopped recently. A place no dogs are barking."

"What?"

"Never mind the dogs. But do you see what I mean? They wouldn't want to risk doing anything to draw attention to wherever they are keeping him."

Understanding flashed in Lexa's eyes. "You mean like

when they had us locked up and they used the phone to communicate so they wouldn't draw attention with adumbrations."

"Exactly."

"Oh, wow! It seems so obvious! I can't believe we didn't think of that! "

Of course, Melanie thought. Difficult questions always seemed obvious—after she figured them out. "And yet no one did think of it. Except me."

"Oh, sorry—I didn't mean that the way it sounded," Lexa said. "Seriously. I'm sorry. I meant that you're amazing for figuring that out when no one else did."

Melanie looked at Lexa more closely. Lexa Dell just apologized? Straight off with no arguments or self-justification? Wow.

"It's okay," Melanie said, softening toward Lexa. "And it doesn't really matter. The important thing is that we find some place that's had a dramatic stop in Dark activity and get there."

"But how do we do that?"

Melanie paused. "I don't know." An idea hit her. "Yes, I do! Come on—we have to get to Mockingbird Cottage!"

Pilaf pulled on his rubber gloves and Lexa carried him piggyback. It took only a few minutes for the three of them to stream over to Mockingbird Cottage. The entire way, Melanie kept saying silent prayers of gratitude that she'd finally learned to stream. It made life so much easier. Not to mention she didn't feel like such a loser Magus.

As they landed on the front lawn, the peace that always covered Mockingbird Cottage washed over

Melanie immediately. No wonder the Magi called it a Sanctuary.

"What are we doing here?" Lexa asked.

"I need the horloge Dr. Timberi used during the summer, Lexa. He said it was hooked up to the network the Adumbrators use so he could get information about anywhere in the world."

"Can you use the horloge?"

"I think so. He taught me enough last summer that I think I can figure it out." Melanie led them around the side of the house to the back deck. The table was still there, as was Dr. Timberi's favorite chair. But no horloge.

Melanie indulged in an exasperated sigh. "This was where it was last time I saw it," she said.

"Wait," Lexa said. "This is the thing with all the hoops that spun around?"

"Yes." Melanie felt her irritation seep into her words. "Just a sec."

Lexa knocked on the door, which brought Sadie, the caretaker. After greeting everyone, Sadie let Lexa walk into the house, leaving Melanie and Pilaf alone in the yard. It hadn't been cool enough for the trees to start turning colors yet. But that would start anytime now. The yard and all the trees had the ragged look common to plants at the end of the summer in Nashville: tired and worn out, ready for fall and winter to bring them rest.

Lexa walked out of the door, carrying a flat wooden box. She opened it, revealing seven metal hoops fitting inside each other in descending order of circumference.

"That's it," Melanie said. "Where did you find it?"

"Last summer I spent a lot of time up in the garret,"

Lexa said. "While you and Conner were kind of, uh, hanging out together." Melanie appreciated Lexa's discretion. "Anyways, I was up there one day, and Dr. Timberi came and grabbed this from a cabinet there."

"Nice job, Lex," Melanie said. "Really nice job. I never would have found this." She took the hoops out of the box and put them on the table. "I think the Examiners did it by shooting a sigil—"

Melanie shot her pink unicorn at the hoops, which jumped up and began to spin, each on its own invisible axis. A wave of dizziness crashed over Melanie as flashes of Light and clouds of Darkness spun in her mind.

She broke the connection with the horloge and stepped back.

"Are you okay?" Lexa asked. "You look kind of green."

"Yeah, I'm fine. Just a little dizzy. It's really overwhelming. Every time I used this, Dr. Timberi was already controlling it. I just followed his instructions. I think each of the hoops does something different, so I have to figure out which hoop measures Light and Darkness."

Melanie sent another sigil, this time focusing on the largest of the hoops. It seemed like a good place to start. As soon as her sigil entered the orbit of the outside hoop, a clear image formed in her mind. Light and Dark each filled approximately half the space, bumping and pushing up against each other. Conner had compared it to two cocky guys shoving each other as they get ready to fight. Constantly moving, constantly poking and prodding, Light and Dark tried to push into the other's territory. Sometimes the Light seemed stronger, pushing forward and displacing the Darkness.

Other times, the Darkness surged, rushing in where the Light had been earlier. Neither seemed to get a permanent advantage.

Okay, that must be like the view of the whole universe or something. Melanie changed her focus to the next hoop, but it didn't show anything.

Concentrating on the third hoop, Melanie saw an image of Nashville created entirely from shadows and light in an infinite number of shades and varieties. All of Nashville, represented through Light and Dark.

Okay, well, that gave her something to work with. First of all, she had to establish whether or not this thing could go backwards and give her a comparison of the past and present. An experiment occurred to her. Guiding the horloge with her thoughts, she zoomed in on Marion Academy. As she suspected, the shield around the school showed up, a large bubble of Light surrounding Marion Academy.

Go back a month, she thought. The image shifted, disappearing and then reforming, this time with no bubble of Light. Perfect. Since Conner had accidentally disabled the shield during a big battle, this demonstrated that the horloge could show the past.

Triumph and excitement rushed through Melanie. She could do this! It might take a few minutes, but she could totally get enough data to locate Dr. Timberi. A few minutes of observation, some analysis, and a sigil to Lee— Dr. Timberi would be back by suppertime tomorrow!

All she needed was a more global view—smaller than the universe but bigger than Nashville. Melanie instructed the horloge to zoom out, which it did. Before long, she saw the areas surrounding Nashville—and then it stopped. It didn't zoom out any farther and nothing she tried made it. When she pushed it harder, it went blank—then back to the cosmic, universal view.

Her excitement faded, replaced by a bitter disappointment.

That second hoop must be the part that displayed the world. But it wasn't hooked up to whatever network was required.

She withdrew her mind from the horloge.

"What did you find out?" Lexa asked.

It took Melanie a minute or two to push through the sense of failure and disappointment she felt. She had been so close! Forcing her voice to remain even, she said, "I found out that it goes back in time—which is good. The problem is that I can't see a view of the world. It shows a local view and something I think is the universe. I guess it doesn't have the sensory ability to pick up the whole world on its own. It probably has to be connected to the network Dr. Timberi talked about. He said the Adumbrators got information from all over the world so they could see everywhere."

"How can you see the whole universe but not the world? The world's smaller."

Melanie frowned. "I don't know. Maybe because it takes less precision? It might be easier to sense the huge, giant cosmic amounts of Light and Dark than it is to get detailed, specific information about specific locations. It's the difference between seeing how bright or dark the sky is versus looking at planets through a powerful telescope."

"So what do we do?"

"I don't know!" Melanie hit the table with her fist. She had been so close! The horloge shook and collapsed, the hoops falling down and laying still.

"Maybe Lee can talk to people at the Magisterium and get us connected?" Lexa said.

"We can ask, but it's not likely to happen if Hortense is in charge," Melanie said.

"Oh well," Lexa said. "Maybe that lead will turn out to be right and the Phalanx is rescuing Dr. Timberi right now!"

But even as she spoke, Melanie knew that was too optimistic. A heavy silence pulled down everyone's previously high spirits.

Fighting a temptation to hurl the stupid thing across the yard, Melanie put the horloge rings back in the case. "I wonder how Conner's doing."

THE BATTLE

CONNER WONDERED HOW LONG THEY'D been streaming. The Phalanx streamed in a circular formation that created a whirlpool effect, allowing them to stream faster, longer, and farther than normal. It allowed head-talking, but it also removed any ability to process time. It could have been twenty minutes or two hours later when Lee's thoughts came into Conner's head.

We're almost to our target. We don't have a whole lot of intel, but if we're right about what they've got there, this could get uglier than two rabid skunks in a swimming pool. So expect the worse. Once we get there, Grimaldi will have command. Grimaldi?

Lieutenant Miranda Grimaldi joined the conversation next. *When we arrive, Colonel Murrell will go inside and, hopefully, do a quick extraction. Our job is to create a diversion, so your orders are to cause as much noise as possible and keep the enemy busy.*

If the extraction is unsuccessful, the situation will

escalate. In that case, the diversion ends and we fight to win. At that point, it will be a free-fire zone, so terminate with extreme prejudice. During the battle, Dell is to be protected at all costs.

Dell, your orders are to figure out how to use the Darkness. You are not to engage the enemy.

We stream the rest of the way in Phalanx formation, then peel off once we're there. Questions? Okay then, let's go!

The Phalanx members peeled off, landing in some kind of rocky desert area. As Light exploded all around, soldiers in black uniforms ran out of a bunker while a few Darkhands materialized from clouds of smoke. A few seconds later, the battle became fierce.

Dell, take shelter behind those rocks and start working on the Darkness, Grimaldi ordered. *I'm serious. Don't waste your time or endanger yourself fighting.*

Conner obeyed, streaming over to the big rock formation she'd indicated.

Grimaldi jumped into the thick of battle, slashing with a glowing silver staff. She swung it to her right, dropping a really big, mean-looking lady to the ground. Then she spun, blurring into a one-hundred-and-eighty degree turn and taking out two guys with jabs to the chest and blows to the knees.

Dell!

Miranda's urgent voice pulled Conner's attention away from the fight and he looked up in time to see a jet of black fire shooting toward him.

As the flames rushed closer, Miranda jumped into the air. *Focus, Dell!* she said. *Figure out how to control this stuff. I'll distract them.* She jumped over the flames to the left, then turned a back handspring, sailing over and landing to the right of the fire. She went back and forth like that, vaulting over the flames while sending large blasts of emerald-green Light in the direction of their origin.

Conner focused on the fire, reaching out to it with his mind. It reminded him of a pillowcase stuffed with hundreds of angry wasps. He ordered it to stop and felt that tug again, as if it was struggling somehow. The struggle seemed to slow the fire, but it still blasted at him, so he ducked. The flames crashed into the rocks above him, leaving a smoking gap about the size of a cantaloupe.

Darkness–1, Dell–0. Epic fail. He looked around and saw Brighton, the buff Phalanx soldier, a few yards away. Someone had thrown a blob of Darkness at his back.

Conner stretched his arm out and called to the shadows. *Stop!* he shouted. The Darkness slowed down, stopping for a second or two, but then pulled itself toward Brighton again, almost like it was being dragged or pushed along.

Using as much energy as he could this time, Conner stretched both arms out and yelled again, *Stop!*

The Darkness struggled visibly, and Conner felt a conflict inside of it. The blob lurched forward, but part of it didn't move, so the Darkness tore itself apart, splitting into dozens of shadowy fragments that fell to the ground and skittered away.

As the shadows disappeared, black sparks crackled in the air, then fell down, burning spots into the rock beneath before they also vanished.

Conner exhaled, realizing he'd been holding his breath for the last few moments. As he inhaled he saw black flames headed for Grimaldi, so he reached out and ordered the fire away. The flames sped up, burning hotter and bigger than before. Conner concentrated harder, and the darkness pulled back like a shark on a fishing line. Conner set his teeth and concentrated even harder. He didn't plan to let this one get away.

While struggling back and forth, Conner probed the flames with his mind. The fire felt like wasps in a pillowcase. Lots of wasps. Thinking about that image, an idea jumped into Conner's mind. What if someone opened the pillowcase?

Straining every mental muscle, he tried to find an opening, a way to grab the flames, but they moved too quickly. After a few more mental tugs, the flames won, rushing straight for Grimaldi.

Miranda dropped to the ground and rolled away, so the flames did no harm. But while she was down, a Darkhand tried to sneak up on her from behind.

Behind you! Conner shouted.

Miranda used her staff to leap up and whirl around toward the woman. As she whirled, a massive emerald green mace appeared in her hand. The momentum of her turn sent the mace's glowing ball of Light crashing into the woman with tremendous force. As the woman fell to the ground, Miranda slapped the silver staff across her own left hand, changing it into a crossbow, which she used to attack four Darkhands.

Thanks, Dell, she said.

Lee's voice boomed into his mind, and Conner assumed all the others heard it. *I'm back. Stop the diversion movement and attack.* Cold anger burned in his voice. *Wipe the rocks with these buzzards.*

Lee burst out of the bunker, semistreaming and dragging someone in a lab coat through the air by the scruff of his neck. Conner knew firsthand how hard it was to stream with human cargo, so that alone was impressive.

Dusty Light glowed around the prisoner, and Lee swung him by the ankle several times before throwing him into a small knot of other bad guys.

Lee held his hands like a gunfighter in a cowboy movie. Illuminated pistols appeared in his hands and he hit a Darkhand with bullets of Light. As the man fell to the ground, Lee blew the barrel of each of the Light-pistols, then jumped as a bolt of black fire winged the heels of his cowboy boots. He flipped, landed, and twirled his hand above his head. An Illuminated lariat appeared and sailed through the air, straight for another Darkhand. She saw it coming and dodged. Anticipating her motion, Lee clapped his hands and his rattlesnake sigil appeared, coiled and rattling. It lunged forward and sank its fangs into the woman's leg—filling her with potent Light. She fell to the ground.

When another Darkhand came, Lee streamed into a comet and then stopped, fading back into human form just in time to give the guy a serious jet-propelled headbutt. The Darkhand went flying, and Lee turned into a comet again, blasting into another bad guy.

As the last Darkhand fell, Conner stepped out from behind the rocks. His jaw ached, and he realized he'd been clenching it the entire time. He didn't think he'd ever seen a battle as fierce as this.

Grimaldi looked at Lee with an obvious question in her eyes.

Lee kicked a rock, sending it flying, and then pounded his hand with a clenched fist. *Nothing at all,* he said. *Let me talk with that skunk over there.* He pointed to one of the few conscious Darkhands: the guy in the lab coat he'd brought out earlier.

A stream of Light shot out of Lee's finger and hit the man in the chest. The man gasped as small bolts of brown lightning flashed all across his body.

As the lightning crackled, the man glowed and floated into the air. Lee didn't seem too concerned about making his journey smooth.

What's he doing? Conner asked Grimaldi. He'd never seen this before. In all the fights he'd been involved in, they dropped the bad guys and then left. He never really thought about what happened after.

This won't hurt him, Dell, Lee said. *Scares the chicken scratch out of 'em, though. Especially if they're not trained Darkhands.*

Lee rotated his finger, and the man rotated too, following Lee's motion. As the man rolled upside down, Conner thought about a hamster in one of those exercise balls that just keeps rolling and rolling.

Lee flicked his finger up, and the man bounced at least thirty feet in the air. When Lee pulled his finger back in, the man plummeted toward the ground.

As the man screamed, Lee's finger shot out, arresting the man's movement and freezing him three or four feet above the ground.

"Talk," Lee said. "Talk real fast. My patience is plum tuckered out. Where'd they take the prisoner?"

"There was a prisoner here, but they moved him. I

don't know any details. This is usually just a listening post."

"You wanna tell me where they took him, or are you in the mood for some cliff diving with no water?"

"The Abyss. That's all I know, I swear! I don't know anything else."

Lee set the man down. "I believe you, which is good news for you. Someone cuff this weasel scat." He kicked another rock. "Get the rest of these bottom-feeders cuffed and contained and call a clean-up crew. I want them taken to HQ for interrogation, and I want to know about anything they say. Knock-knock jokes, defiant speeches—anything at all. And I want one of you there the whole time. Do not leave this operation to any bureaucrat."

The Phalanx saluted and got busy, handcuffing the unconscious Darkhands and containing them in bubbles of Light. Unsure what to do, Conner stood still and tried to stay out of the way.

Any luck with your mission, Dell? Miranda asked.

A little. I can't always control the Darkness, but I think I figured out how to neutralize it. I just need more practice—

An explosion interrupted Conner, and he looked over his shoulder. As Lee glared at the building, brown Light appeared, sizzling in the air around him. Tension jumped out all over his face, and for a minute Conner worried he might be having a heart attack.

Lee punched the air and another explosion ripped through the bunker. And another. Punch after punch, and explosion after explosion. The bunker collapsed in a cloud of rock dust and Lee's signature Light.

"I'm sorry, Morgan," Lee whispered. "I let you down."

CHAPTER 22

ALL THROUGH THE NIGHT

LEXA HEARD CONNER STREAM INTO THEIR home, appearing downstairs where he talked to their parents for a few minutes. Unable to wait the amount of time it would take Conner to walk up to his room, Lexa streamed downstairs, stopping just a centimeter away from crashing into him. "Did you find Doc—" She stopped. Conner's expression answered her question.

"Are you okay?" She regretted not asking that first.

"Yeah." He nodded. "Just tired. Really, really tired."

"So how was it?"

"Intense. These were serious fighters."

"Did you figure out anything about the Darkness?"

He paused and frowned. "Well, sort of, but not really."

"What?"

"I need to think about it for a little. Lex, I'm sorry, but I'm seriously wiped out right now. I can barely think, let alone talk."

She opened her mouth to squeal in protest, but a

thought stopped her. *Lexa,* she told herself, *he said he doesn't want to talk. Don't be a pain.*

Lexa thought the effort it took to bite back her questions might tear her apart.

In fact, it seemed to cause her literal, physical pain. The room oozed around her in waves, and she couldn't catch her breath. Pain everywhere, elephants of pain on her chest, squeezing her breath away. Hot coals of pain in her head, burning her vision away.

The pain wracked Lexa in so many ways that she didn't realize what was happening until Lady Nightwing's cold eyes filled her mind's eye.

Lexa grabbed Conner's hand. *Get Mel! Hurry.* She started to sing, but as Lady Nightwing talked, a theeling told her to listen. Hoping to hear something important, Lexa listened while she hummed, trying to catch every word.

"Now you see what my new toy can do," Lady Nightwing wheezed. She limped and leaned on a cane. Her face had been scarred to the point that Lexa almost didn't recognize her. Most of her hair had fallen out, and what was left had faded from ebony black to ashy gray. "That's twice now you've almost killed me, and that must be paid back with interest." She took a deep breath, and her lungs rattled like a baby's toy. "I will admit that you continue to surprise me. Light cannot exist down here. It should be impossible for you to use it. And yet you did. I don't know how you managed that, Morgan. But I will find out. For now, I have an idea." She held out a black box. "I bioengineered these sometime back but never used them. You give me a perfect chance." She opened the box, and a dozen or so black dots crawled across the white lining inside. "Ticks, Morgan. Like you might get in the woods on a hike. But these have some improvements. They suck blood, but that's not what they live on." She laughed, but it came out as a gnarled cackle. "They eat Light. Suck it right out of your soul. So after a few days, whatever Light you still have will be gone." She shook the box over Dr. Timberi, who responded with a wave of nausea.

What's going on? Melanie streamed into the room and Lexa grabbed her hand.

Hurry, guys! Send another blast!

Their combined Light rushed through Lexa. She felt Conner's sheer power, amplified by Melanie's Augmentation, blending with the fire of her own soul. It jumped into Dr. Timberi's sigil—and then terrible, terrible pain raged through Lexa, threatening to tear her body away from her soul. The pain robbed her legs of strength, and as she collapsed, she heard screams and realized it wasn't Lady Nightwing screaming this time. It was Dr. Timberi.

Stop, Lexa gasped. *Stop!*

Conner and Melanie's Light faded, and the connection to Dr. Timberi slammed shut.

Wait! she yelled. *Dr. Timberi, come back!*

"What happened?" Conner asked.

"I don't know—when we sent that Light, it hurt him somehow. Really bad."

"I'll bet she put a Refraction collar on him," Conner said. "That makes sense if he almost killed her last time. They put one on me when they kidnapped me at Disney World. If you open your gateway and use the Light, it somehow bends the energy and turns it into pain. I've never felt anything like it before."

"So when we sent all that Light into him, we were basically hurting him?" Melanie asked. Her lips began to quiver.

"What was happening?" Conner asked. "I mean, what else?"

"Ticks," Lexa said, feeling cold, slimy squiggles all over her skin. "Light-sucking ticks. She figured out that he has Light even though he shouldn't. I don't think she knows it's us, though. She said something I think might be important. She said, 'Light cannot exist down here. It should be impossible for you to use it.'"

"Underwater," Melanie said, getting excited. "The Abyss. Of course. It's underwater. Light doesn't exist underwater."

"Where, though?" Conner said. "I mean, isn't most of the Earth made of water?"

Melanie pounded her hand into her fist, releasing a groan of frustration that grew into something just short of a scream. "I could find it! I know I could. If I could just get access to the Adumbrator's network on the horloge. All I need to do is find some place where there has been a sudden decline in Dark activity—somewhere near water."

"But if they're torturing him, then that's Darkness," Lexa said. "So wouldn't it show up as increased Darkness?"

"No," Melanie said. "Not if it's underwater. If it's far enough down, then the water would insulate and hide it. Trust me on this. I *know* I'm right. I just need that information. I sent a sigil to Lee, after your battle, and he said he'd try to get me hooked up. Bad news, though— Hortense controls that information."

"Yeah, really bad news," Lexa said.

"We're going there Friday, right?" Conner asked. "To the Magisterium, I mean. We can talk to Hortense, and if she says no, we'll talk to Notzange."

"I hope he makes it that long," Lexa said. "Guys, I need to go. I need to sing to him. That won't set the collar off. Maybe he can't use the Light. But he can still feel love and peace. And he really needs it. Lady Nightwing said something about a new toy she'd made, and it was hurting him so badly."

Lexa went to her room and made herself comfortable. Reaching inside for the sigil, she started to sing. Bit by bit, she felt the connection open—like a stubborn door being pushed open inch by inch.

As pain rushed through the connection, Lexa focused on her song. Like a gentle rain on a wildfire, her song seemed to have only a small effect. But Lexa hoped that as long as she sang, the fire would fade a little at least.

The door to her room opened, and she looked up.

Conner walked in, carrying a case of bottled water and their grandmother's hymnbook from the piano in the front room.

He opened a water bottle and put it next to her. "In case you get thirsty," he said. Then he opened the hymnbook. "In case you run out of stuff to sing. I know he likes show tunes, but this was all I could find."

Lexa didn't want to risk breaking the connection with Dr. Timberi to talk or even think. So she just reached out, squeezed Conner's hand, and smiled.

He squeezed and smiled back. "I'm proud of you, Lex."

Then he clapped his hands and Translocated several two-liters of Mountain Dew. Lexa looked at him with a question in her eyes. "We're going to be up all night, right? Gotta have a little help."

When Lexa's voice got tired, Conner joined in. Together they sang for the rest of the night.

CHAPTER 23

THE TRIAL
OF TIMOTHY TIMBERI

FRIDAY, AFTER SCHOOL, MELANIE CARRIED her luggage down to the front room, followed by her little sister, Madi. She still worried that her dad might change his mind.

"It's not fair that you get to go to France and not me," Madi said. "I saw Dark things too." Since their adventures began, Madi had seen a lot of Light and Dark, things that she shouldn't have been able to see because she hadn't Kindled.

"That's enough, Madi," her mom said. She looked at Melanie, smoothed her hair, and then pulled her into a tight hug. "Be careful."

"It's just a trial, Mom. It's not dangerous."

"I didn't think sending to you to seventh grade last year was dangerous. Or going to Disney World for vacation," her mom said. "But the danger seems to come anyway."

"All ready?" Her dad walked into the room as well. He still unusually quiet and had a distant look in his eyes.

"Yes, Dad." Melanie hugged him. "Thank you for letting me go."

"Just help him if you can," he replied. Then, in a whisper, he added, "And don't think too badly of me."

That seemed a little odd. Melanie really didn't understand her dad lately. She hugged him extra tight for a few more seconds, then stepped away. "I'll see you all Sunday night!"

She looked at her luggage and closed her eyes. Holding out her hands, she imagined the Dell's living room, and all the bags vanished with a pink flash, Translocated in a second or two.

Melanie gave Madi a final hug, took some running steps, faded into a comet, and arrived at the Dell's several minutes after that.

Conner, Lexa, and Pilaf—with rubber gloves and floral-print suitcase in tow—all stood there waiting for her, as well as Madame Cumberland, who was smiling as always.

"Hello, Melanie," she said. "If you all are ready, it's time to go." Madame Cumberland turned a key in front of her, and the air parted like curtains as the Shroud opened.

After the cherubim's interrogation, they walked through the long corridor of the Otherwhere while Lexa peppered Madame Cumberland with questions about the tribunal.

"Does Timothy have a lawyer?"

"Yes, Timothy's Advocate will make sure he is treated fairly. But a Magi tribunal is different than the sort of trial you see on TV. There are not many procedural rules. In fact, it's more like a debate than a modern trial. The Tribunal Magistrate will make sure everyone who wishes to speak is heard."

"Is there a jury?" Melanie asked.

"No, Melanie. The Tribunal Magistrate has two associate magistrates, and the three of them will come to a verdict. No one knows who those three will be, though. As Supreme Magistrate, Notzange will appoint someone. In a high-profile case like this, it is a closely held secret."

Madame Cumberland stopped and opened the Shroud, leading them out of the Otherwhere and up to the ornate gates of the Château de Lumière. With a wave of her hands, shimmering, silver robes appeared as her street clothes faded. Once again, her sigil summoned two guards who scanned them and then allowed them inside the gates.

As they walked up the path to the château, Conner looked at Madame Cumberland. "So, if they find him guilty, are there special Magi prisons or something?"

"Yes, there are Magi prisons," Madame Cumberland said. "But that is not the only option. If he's convicted, then the three magistrates will recommend a sentence: imprisonment, execution, or Renunciation.

"What's Renunciation?" Melanie asked.

"It's where the accused person uses his or her own powers to cut himself off from the Light or Dark for good."

"That's awful!" Lexa said. "I think I'd rather die."

"Yes," Madame Cumberland said. "That's not an uncommon response. In fact, many convicted prisoners over the years have chosen execution instead of Renunciation."

They walked through the front doors and into a lobby crammed full of people. The entire château seemed stuffed with Magi—a sharp contrast to the empty halls they'd encountered on their last visit. "Why are these people here?" Lexa muttered. "Shouldn't they be out looking for Dr. Timberi? This is such a waste of time!"

"Lexa, they can't just keep him in jail forever," Madame Cumberland said. "That would be unjust. A fast and fair tribunal is a Magi tradition."

"Well, still . . . ," Lexa muttered a few more things beneath her breath.

Madame Cumberland checked them in at the front desk. She spoke in rapid French, so Melanie only understood a few words. The desk clerk gave Madame Cumberland three keys, and Madame Cumberland led them down the hallways, which bustled and hummed with people today.

"Since you all are witnesses, they've provided lovely rooms," Madame Cumberland said. "One for the boys, one for the girls, and—"

"Mona! Mona, is that you?" A cheerful woman with silvery-blonde hair pulled Madame Cumberland into a hug.

"Hello, Cassie," Madame Cumberland replied.

"It's been so long," Cassie said, beaming at the students. She smiled at each one of them in turn, Melanie, Conner, Lexa, and Pilaf—then her head snapped back to Melanie. "Oh my!" she said. "Oh my goodness, you look just like—"

"Cassie, I hope we'll have a chance to catch up," Madame Cumberland interrupted with a big smile and a loud voice. "But, for now, I hope you'll excuse me. I need to get everyone down to their seats. They're witnesses, you know."

"Oh, of course they are," Cassie said. "It's really quite touching, when you think about—"

"It's so nice to see you again, Cassie!" Madame Cumberland jumped in again and shooed Melanie and the others away.

Lexa looked at Melanie and sent her a private thought message. *Is it just me, or did that lady seem to know something about you? Have you ever seen her before?*

It wasn't just you, and no, I've never seen her before, Melanie said. *Something's up.*

But she didn't have a chance to ask Madame Cumberland because person after person kept coming up to greet her. In fact, it took them longer to get past all of Madame Cumberland's friends and admirers than it had taken them to get to France. They finally reached the bottom of the staircase, stopping at an enormous pair of wooden doors. Two more of the cloaked guards stood there, and once more they scanned everyone with their long silver staffs. When the guards finished, the doors opened and Madame Cumberland led everyone in.

"Welcome to the assembly room," Madame Cumberland said in an almost reverent whisper.

An enormous ellipse, the assembly room was made mostly of tan marble. A semi-circular series of ascending platforms filled one end of the ellipse. Each platform was fronted by a low wall of dark, polished wood and contained a number of chairs.

"That's where the senior Magi sit," Madame

Cumberland said. "They're the Council of Magi who actually make up the Magisterium."

In front of the platforms, an enormous horloge rotated in a slow, steady pattern. It looked at least as tall as Melanie. A small witness stand sat on the floor next to the horloge.

A massive silver Magi emblem—a crescent moon circling an eight-pointed star—glittered in the floor in the middle of the room.

"Look!" Conner pointed to the other end of the elliptical room. A platform sloped into two very long ramps that curved all the way down to the marble floor. Rows of benches lined the floor between the ramps.

The air shimmered above the platform, and a comet blasted through, following the curve of one of the ramps. It slowed down, fading into a human by the time the ramp met the floor. Another comet shot in, using the same process on the other side of the ramp, also fading into a human taking brisk steps. More and more comets appeared, crisscrossing each other on the central platform and using the ramps to decelerate.

"Cool," Conner said.

As Madame Cumberland led them to the benches between the streaming ramps, Melanie looked around the enormous assembly room, which was filling now with a rainbow of Magi in different colored robes. Nearly all of them wore hats—turbans or hoods or flat caps that looked like they belonged in the Middle Ages. Madame Cumberland put on a veil that hung down the back of her head and blended in to her flowing, silver robes.

"On formal occasions, most full-fledged Magi wear head coverings," she said.

Lee sauntered in, waved, walked to the tiered platforms across the room, and sat down. A few minutes later, Hortense swept up onto the raised platforms as well. She gave Lee a curt nod before settling in a chair a few seats past him.

"What's she doing here?" Lexa said. "She should be out looking for Dr. Timberi!"

"Hortense is part of the Magisterium, Lexa," Madame Cumberland said, "and this is a high-profile tribunal."

"It's a waste of time!" Lexa said. "Why does Timothy even need a trial? Everyone know's he's guilty. Think of all the things he tried to do just to us! We don't need a trial to prove that."

"Everyone is entitled to a fair trial, Lexa." Madame Cumberland didn't smile.

Lexa shrugged. "Well, I just hope they hurry and find him guilty. I don't want to sound mean, and I don't like the idea of him being executed, but he needs to be in jail for the rest of his life."

Madame Cumberland didn't say anything, but her mouth got very tight.

After all Timothy had done, Melanie agreed with Lexa. Timothy was dangerous. Did Madame Cumberland disagree with that? She'd fought battles with him, for heaven's sake! Or did the fact that she had known Timothy as a baby prevent her from seeing just how dangerous he was?

"I agree," Conner said. "He definitely needs to be in jail. Forever."

"Will you all excuse me?" Madame Cumberland said. "I need to take care of something." She walked away.

As the room continued to fill, the hum of conversations grew louder until a series of sharp raps on the floor called everyone's attention to the platforms across the room.

The highest platform had its own set of doors, and as those doors opened, everyone stood. A man in flowing robes and a long judge's wig walked in. A woman in a similar robe and wig followed him.

And then a little buzz ran around the room. Without a wig and wearing the same colorful robes she wore earlier, Notzange walked in.

From the conversations around her, Melanie gathered that the Supreme Magistrate did not usually preside at tribunals.

Notzange took her seat, and the two other magistrates did the same.

Once seated, Notzange rapped the table in front of her with a golden orb about the size of a large apple.

"This tribunal will come to order. We meet today by order and authority of the Magisterium of the Sodality of the Midnight Stars to consider the case of Timothy Timberi."

Once again, she pounded the table in front of her. "Summon the accused."

Six hooded guards in long gray robes stepped forward, encircling the Magi emblem in the floor. They each carried a carved wooden staff, which they pounded on the marble floor three times. As the sharp raps echoed through the chamber, the emblem sparkled, then erupted in flames that shot up and twined together, creating a pillar that reached to the high ceiling. As the column of flames rotated, a bubble of clear Light appeared in the center of the column. It grew bigger until a human body appeared inside of it, floating inside the revolving column of fire.

Melanie let out a little cry. "Will the fire hurt him?" she asked in a breathless voice.

"No." Melanie looked up. Mrs. Grant had just arrived, breathless and looking harried. She straightened her blue robes and sat down by Melanie. "He'll be just fine unless he tries to escape."

"State your name for the tribunal," Notzange said.

"Timothy." The word seemed unfamiliar to him—as if he were speaking a long-forgotten language. "Timothy Timberi," he said in a soft voice.

It sounded strange to hear him use any name at all, but especially that last name. Melanie fought a choking sensation in her throat.

Notzange nodded, and the female magistrate next to her pulled out a scroll and read, "Timothy Timberi, you are charged with knowing congress with agents of the Dark; of kidnapping, attempted murder, and of willingly working Darkness Most Foul. If you are found guilty, you might forfeit your freedom, your powers, or, possibly, your life."

"I don't have a life," Timothy said in a soft voice. "Only an existence."

"Be that as it may," the woman said, "do you understand that you are on trial, potentially for your life?"

"I understand that the Magi will imprison or kill me. Which, ironically, is exactly what the Umbra tried to do when they found out I wanted to leave them and join the Magi."

Another murmur ran through the courtroom.

"The tribunal will be silent," Notzange said. "Timothy Timberi, you are accused of willingly working Darkness Most Foul and committing various and sundry crimes, known and unknown. How do you plead?"

He scowled and shrugged. "Does it matter? You all have made your minds up already."

"Does the accused have an Advocate?" Notzange asked.

"Yes, Your Eminence."

Melanie's head whipped back over her shoulder as Madame Cumberland appeared on one of the streaming ramps. "I request recognition as his Advocate."

Notzange smiled and inclined her head. "The tribunal recognizes Mona Cumberland. You may come forward."

Madame Cumberland walked down to the floor, stopping between the chairs occupied by the Council and the spinning column of Light. She looked up at Timothy, rotating in the air above her head, and gave him a warm smile. As far as Melanie could see, he didn't even look back at her.

"The Prosecutor will come forward," Notzange said.

A tall, regal man stood up, wearing flowing gray robes and a flat cap. He nodded to the platforms of magistrates. "Your Eminence, members of the Council, and honored guests. The crimes of the Accused are many and severe. These crimes call for vigorous and decisive action to remove him as a threat to the world. In recent months, he has participated in some of Umbra's most reprehensible plots. In his relatively short career as a Noctivagant, he has been responsible for an unusually high number of actions.

"At the direction of Emily Jacoway, the infamous Lady

Nightwing, the prisoner hunted new Adepts with a vigor that went far beyond duty. He is known to have kidnapped at least four of the children upon whom Jacoway experimented in her barbaric effort to harness the power of Kindling. A complete account of his crimes would take weeks. We can provide clear and convincing proof by focusing on his most recent assignments, which involved attempts to subvert, kidnap, and even kill the Adepts who attracted the Sodality's attention with a triple Kindling a few months ago."

The Prosecutor gestured to the horloge, which began to accelerate. As it spun, small rays of Light shot up, creating something like a 3-D jumbotron in the area above the whirling hoops. The Light shimmered, forming a picture of the cafeteria at Marion Academy.

"That's my memory," Lexa whispered.

The tribunal watched Lexa's memory of Dr. Timberi fighting Timothy several months earlier. At the time, Melanie had not noticed the pain in Dr. Timberi's face. But now, knowing the situation, it seemed obvious that fighting his son to protect his students caused him terrible internal agony.

Lexa's memory focused on the moment Dr. Timberi had to choose between protecting Lexa and Melanie or shielding himself. He protected them, providing an opening to Timothy, who threw shadow knives into his father's unprotected back.

"I love you," Dr. Timberi gasped as the knives hit. He fell to the floor.

At the time, Melanie had assumed he'd been expressing his affection for the Trio. And maybe he had been.

But now, it looked like he'd been speaking primarily to his son.

The horloge faded, leaving a heavy, brooding silence over the room. "That is the prisoner who stands before you: a man so consumed by Darkness that he would destroy his own father by hitting him in the back.

"That the prisoner is guilty of working Darkness is beyond doubt. We will also prove that his existence constitutes real and grave danger to those who follow the Light. "

He paused, probably to let his words sink in. Then he said, "The prosecution calls Alexandra Louise Dell."

TESTIMONY

AS LEXA WALKED DOWN THE AISLE TO THE witness stand, she passed Timothy and looked up at him.

He looked different. Last time she'd seen him, his long, greasy hair oozed over the pale, almost gray skin of his face, and his beetle-black eyes boiled with hatred. Since then, someone had cut his hair, and instead of an old black coat, he wore light gray robes. But his face had changed the most. The anger and hate were gone, but nothing had replaced them, and he looked blank and worn out. Something about the emptiness stabbed at Lexa's heart.

Lexa slipped into the witness chair.

"You are Alexandra Louise Dell?" Notzange asked.

Lexa flinched at her formal name. "Just Lexa, ma'am. Please."

The Supreme Magistrate nodded. "Very well. Lexa, I shall ask you to swear the Magi's oath. It will use your own power to bind you to tell the truth. Do you understand and agree to that?"

"Yes, ma'am."

"Very well." Notzange waved her hand, and an immense, ancient book floated through the air, hovering in front of Lexa. The thick parchment pages flipped open as if someone was fingering through them. When they stopped, Lexa spoke the words written in large, ornate calligraphy.

"I, Alexandra Louise Dell, do solemnly bind myself to tell the complete truth in this tribunal. I do so with all my power, of my own choice, and with sincere intent."

As she finished the words, yellow Light coiled around her, spiraling up and down before vanishing with a flash.

"Lexa." The Prosecutor stood near the witness box. "That was your memory we just watched in the horloge. Is that correct?"

"Yes, sir," Lexa said.

"Let me make certain I understand. In your memory, Timothy attempted to kill his father. Is that correct?"

"Yes, sir. Timothy was using Darkness to eat at Dr. Timberi's soul. He said he wanted Dr. Timberi to hear our screams while he killed us. The only reason it didn't happen is that we fought him off."

"Was this the first encounter you had with the Accused?"

"No, sir." Lexa repeated their history with Timothy—the way he'd shown up in their neighborhood and killed all the dogs, the way he'd tried to kidnap them, and how he'd attacked them twice.

Timothy didn't argue or even look up as Lexa accused him of attempted kidnapping and attempted murder.

"Thank you, Lexa," the Prosecutor said.

"Does the Advocate have any questions?" Notzange asked.

"Not at this time," Madame Cumberland said. "But I reserve the right to call her back if needed."

"So noted. Lexa, you are dismissed," Notzange said. "Next witness, please."

"The Prosecution calls Melanie Nicole Stephens."

Lexa happened to be walking past Timothy as they called out Melanie's name, so she saw his head snap up. A sudden light in his eyes pushed away a little of the deadness. He stared at Melanie with an intensity Lexa did not understand.

Melanie took the stand and read the oath from the book.

"I, Melanie Nicole Stephens, do solemnly bind myself to tell the complete truth in this tribunal. I do so with all my power, of my own choice, and with sincere intent."

The Prosecutor showed one of Melanie's memories: the night the Darkhands attacked at the mall. Melanie's memory ended with the Stalker shooting Darkness at Mrs. Grant's unprotected back while Lady Nightwing threw knives at the same target.

Sitting next to Lexa, Mrs. Grant clicked her tongue and sniffed.

The Prosecutor looked at Melanie and smiled. "Melanie, it is so wonderful to meet you after all this time."

Confusion washed across Melanie's face as she looked at the Prosecutor. "Thank you. It's nice to meet you too."

"Melanie, in the memory we just saw, it appears Timothy tried to ambush Carol Grant, a member of the Sodality. Is that accurate?"

"Yes, sir. He shot Darkness at her back."

"No, I didn't." Timothy spoke for the first time since he'd been charged.

Lexa sucked her breath in at the same time everyone else in the courtroom did too, creating a fairly loud collective gasp.

"Excuse me?" the Prosecutor said.

"I was trying to save her from the knives Lady Nightwing threw," Timothy said. "I didn't dare use Light because there were too many Darkhands there. If they had seen me use Light, I would have tipped my hand that I was trying to leave. So I shot Darkness at the knives and stopped them from hitting her."

"May we watch that memory again?" Madame Cumberland asked.

Notzange nodded and the horloge showed Melanie's memory again. Lexa had to admit that Timothy's explanation was possible. The darkness did hit the knives, not Mrs. Grant. She couldn't be sure, but it seemed possible.

"You expect us to believe that you were really trying to save her?" the Prosecutor asked.

"What you choose to believe is beyond my control," Timothy said. "I didn't argue with anything up until now because everything you said was true. I did those things. I know I'll die. I've accepted that. But I don't want to die for things I didn't do."

It took Notzange eight seconds to quiet the courtroom down after that. Lexa counted. "That is a lovely story," the Prosecutor said. "And conveniently, it cannot be proved or disproved. However, I don't believe there are any other examples where the Accused demonstrated this touching compassion for Magi. In light of that—"

"That's not true." Somehow Timothy's quiet voice managed to echo through the room. "Melanie, a few months ago, you were at your school, being chased by a girl who was shooting black fire at you. Do you remember?"

Lexa remembered that night. It had been when they first realized Conner could control Darkness.

Melanie frowned, and Lexa could almost see the whiteboard moving in her brain. "Well, we were running to get away from her, and you shot some kind of strange Light. It hit her and she fell down."

"May we see that?" Madame Cumberland asked, and the horloge broadcast Melanie's memory. It happened exactly as Melanie described.

"It appears to me that he was shooting at Melanie and the unfortunate girl ran into it," the Prosecutor said.

Madame Cumberland gave him her biggest smile. "How interesting. I thought it seemed clear that Timothy figured out that girl's trajectory and shot accordingly. I'll also note that it's not Darkness he's shooting. That would be two occasions where Timothy tried to help one of the Magi."

"Three," Melanie said.

"Excuse me?" the Prosecutor and Madame Cumberland both spoke at the same time.

"The night Dr. Timberi got taken, we were fighting with Lady Nightwing and some Darkhands. At one point, Lady Nightwing threw some knives at Dr. Timberi's back. Before they could hit him, some strange, greenish Light appeared and knocked them down. That saved his life. I remember wondering who had done that—" Melanie stopped. Her chin quivered, and Lexa recognized the warning signs of tears. But Melanie gulped, set her jaw, and managed not to cry—although her voice got very tight. "It wasn't me, Conner, or Lexa. And Timothy was there right after that."

"Thank you, Melanie," the Prosecutor said, jumping in. "Your Eminence, this speculation is irrelevant. The Accused has admitted to working Darkness. These minor ambiguities make no real difference." He looked up at Timothy. "You do admit to doing all the things that the first witness described, correct?"

Timothy frowned but met the Prosecutor's gaze. "Yes."

"Madame Advocate," Notzange said, "do you have any further questions for this witness?"

"Not at this time, but I reserve the right to call her again," Madame Cumberland said. "Your Eminence, may I please confer with you?"

"Yes, by all means," Notzange said. "Melanie, you may step down. If the Advocate and Prosecutor will please step forward, we will confer."

Melanie walked back to the benches. Once again, Lexa noticed Timothy staring at her.

Save him.

Lexa looked up to see who had spoken. But nobody was looking at her.

SAVE HIM. A great big theeling shook her by the shoulders, knocking logical thought away and leaving her stunned. Save Timothy?

It went against everything she had experienced, everything she thought she knew. It didn't make sense, couldn't be right.

And yet . . . her theelings had never led her astray.

As Melanie sat down, she sent Lexa a private thought message. *Are you okay, Lexa? You seem a little . . . dazed or something.*

We need to save him.

That's what my dad said too, Melanie replied.

We need to talk to Timothy, Lexa said, including Conner in the thought as well.

"Are you ser—" Conner caught his yell as everyone around stared at them.

Are you serious? he repeated.

Yes, I'm serious. It's important. I have a theeling. We have to save him.

But he tried to kill us! Conner shouted. *He was going to carve us up like jack-o'-lanterns.*

I'm just telling you what my theeling says.

Notzange pounded the orb. "In light of the latest testimony, the Advocate has requested additional time to speak with the Accused. We will adjourn now for one hour's time." She pounded the orb again and stood, as did everyone else in the room. She turned and left the bench, followed by the two other magistrates.

As they left, the guards in the gray capes hit the floor with their staffs. The pillar of fire and Timothy both vanished.

"Well, that was dramatic," Mrs. Grant said. "Mona hasn't been able to get Timothy to talk this whole time. Even after she volunteered to be his Advocate two weeks ago, he hasn't said a word to her."

"So does Madame Cumberland think he's guilty?" Pilaf asked.

Mrs. Grant shrugged. "That's a complicated question,

Mr. Larson. Everyone knows he's been a Darkhand, and technically, that's all they need to prove in order to convict him. But Mona feels sure there are some extenuating circumstances. No one else wanted to be his Advocate, and Mona couldn't just abandon him. I think she's hoping to sway the magistrates to go with imprisonment instead of death or Renunciation."

"Can we see him?" Lexa asked. "We need to talk with Timothy. I have a theeling."

Mrs. Grant sighed as if the weight of Lexa's request had squeezed the air out of her. "I don't know about that. It's pretty high security around him—but maybe Mona can manage something." She pulled out a red pen from somewhere inside of her robes and waved it in the air. Her sigil—a blue ballerina—pirouetted through the air before vanishing.

A few minutes later, a silver rosebush burst into bloom in front of them and Madame Cumberland's voice said, "I think that would be fine. I'll notify the guards."

Mrs. Grant sighed again, even heavier. "I guess I'd better take you to the dungeons, then. It's quite a walk, so we'd better get started now."

So what are we going to say once we get there? Conner asked. *Hi, I'm Conner Dell—you tried to chop me into sushi after you killed my neighbor's dog a few months ago. It's so nice to finally meet you . . .*

Lexa rolled her eyes—physically and mentally. *I don't know. But we have to talk to him. I just know we do.*

FACE-TO-FACE

MRS. GRANT LED THEM DOWN STAIRCASES that seemed as endless to Conner as Latin class. He felt pretty sure they'd use up most of the hour getting to Timothy's cell.

"Mrs. Grant," he asked, "why don't we just stream?"

"Oh my goodness!" she said in great horror. "Can you imagine how dangerous it would be if a building full of Magi streamed? The collisions would be terrible. Streaming is strictly forbidden inside unless there's an emergency. Here we are." The staircase ended at a massive metal door. Mrs. Grant waved her pen, and her ballerina sigil sailed through the door. A few seconds later, some of those guards in the gray capes opened it and scanned them with the long silver staffs again.

The guards led them down a long hall, their progress interrupted often by metal gates that opened only when the guards shot a sigil at them. A barrier made entirely of Light filled the hall behind each of the gates. Heavy wooden doors reinforced by metal bands lined each side of the hallway. At the end of the hallway, a column of fire burned in front of a door wrapped with extra metal bands and also covered with a web of bright white Light.

They walked through the fire, which felt like stepping into a really warm bathtub. The guard rapped the end of his staff against different parts of the door in some kind of elaborate pattern. The fire faded and the door swung open. "Go ahead," he said.

"Y'all go on," Mrs. Grant said with a sigh. "I haven't had time to make any arrangements for a room or anything. I hope they have something left." She turned and followed the guard back out through the door, which slammed shut after they passed through. A web of Light crisscrossed across the back of the door as well.

They stood at the bottom of some stone steps that led up to a raised second level.

"Timothy, you must help me help you!" Madame Cumberland's voice came from the level above them, frustrated, tense, and desperate—something Conner had never heard before. "Timothy, please!"

Climbing the stairs brought them up to the main level of the cell, where Timothy sat slouched on a small bed. Madame Cumberland sat on a chair, nearly knee to knee with him. Timothy shifted, turning away from her. As he moved, the air shimmered and crackled, revealing a nearly transparent bubble of Light that encased him.

Madame Cumberland threw up her hands and stood up, walking away from him in obvious agitation.

Are you okay? Melanie asked.

No! Madame Cumberland came the closest Conner

had ever seen her get to snapping. *He won't say a word. Stubborn and willful child!*

The room became so tense that Conner thought he could have plucked the air and made it vibrate like a guitar string.

As Timothy saw the Four Musketeers, the tension in the room increased, tightening the string even more. Conner assumed that everyone else was also remembering all the times Timothy had tried to kill them. That made it awkward.

"I love you, Timothy!" Lexa blurted out, breaking the silence.

Timothy looked up, staring at her like everyone else in the room.

Lexa's face flashed between confusion and embarrassment.

"Excuse me?" Timothy asked.

"I'm sorry—I didn't mean to say that. It just sort of jumped out." Lexa's eyes expanded and she jumped up and down. "Oh my gosh!" she squealed. "Timothy, that was a message from your dad! His sigil's inside of me and—"

Timothy jumped up, crossing the room to Lexa in three strides. "What did you say?"

"Your dad's sigil is inside of me, so sometimes I blurt out things that he would say if he was here. That was what your dad would say. It's like a message from his soul!"

"My father's alive?" Timothy's dead face came back to life, lighting up like a big city after a blackout.

"Well, yes," Lexa said, sounding a little confused.

"Are you sure?" He ran his fingers through his hair, and

Conner thought he would have grabbed Lexa and shaken her if the bubble of Light hadn't stopped him. "Where is he right—"

Shafts of Light shot down from the ceiling, surrounding Timothy. "Wait!" he yelled, "I need to find—

The shafts of Light blurred and blended into each other, forming a bubble around Timothy. A circular opening appeared in the ceiling above him, and a roaring column of fire burst up from the floor where he stood. The fire shot through the opening in the ceiling, carrying him with it and ending their conversation.

"Did he not know Dr. Timberi was alive?" Melanie asked.

Madame Cumberland blinked and didn't say anything for a few seconds. She looked stunned. "I just assumed he did, but he's been in prison ever since you brought him back after the fight. He wasn't at Morgan's Remembrance when Lexa told us all Morgan was alive. We all believed the Darkhands had killed Morgan until Lexa told us differently. Timothy must have thought the same thing. Oh my," she said in a soft voice. "That poor boy. No wonder he hasn't cared about anything. He thinks his father is dead and that it's his fault. I can't imagine how he must feel."

I can. Lexa's thought fluttered by, a tiny whisper so soft that Conner guessed no one else heard her.

Back in the assembly room, something seemed different. People seemed to be watching and waiting for something. Conner looked around, trying to figure out what it was. Nothing had changed except for one thing: Timothy.

Timothy stood tall and straight, and as he rotated in the column of fire, his eyes scanned the crowd, meeting and matching people's gazes. New energy crackled out from him. He reminded Conner of a panther getting ready to pounce on his prey.

Conner's breath caught, and he had to fight some unexpected tears. Something about Timothy reminded him of the way Dr. Timberi looked right before he jumped into a fight. Timothy was definitely his father's son. And it stung.

Conner had mixed feelings about helping Timothy. Actually, his feelings were not mixed at all. If Timothy felt guilty for Dr. Timberi being gone, there was a good reason for that.

The Magistrates entered and took their places, and Notzange pounded her orb. "The tribunal will come to order."

"Your Eminence?" Timothy said.

"Yes? Do you have something to say?" Notzange said.

"I do, Your Eminence. I wish to make a defense."

"You may proceed," Notzange said.

Timothy nodded. "Thank you." He stared at the crowd. "I can't—and won't—deny the things I've done. But I think it's only fair you understand everything, including how I came to be here today. I'd like to tell you my story."

CHAPTER 26

TIMOTHY'S STORY

MELANIE LEANED FORWARD—ALONG WITH everyone else in the now-silent room.

"You may proceed," Notzange said.

Timothy raised his hands, and a stream of the strange Light rushed out. A sickly greenish color, it looked like bleached Darkness, something neither Light nor Dark. Whatever it was, it poured into the horloge, which whirled to life. A moment later, Timothy's memories filled the room.

A child's bedroom. Bright colors and toys. Laughter and music. Then smoke and explosions and fire obscured everything. Shouts. A woman crying. And then nothing. Blankness that finally faded, revealing a large room full of beds. A woman in a white uniform.

"Timothy, can you hear me?"

"Where am I?" a young child's voice said. "Where's my mommy?"

"Timothy, I have some bad news for you. I'll need you

to be very brave," the woman said. "Your mother is dead. She's gone. And your father killed her."

As everyone gasped, the memory faded, dissolved into searing pain that filled the room.

"That is one of my earliest memories," Timothy said. "It was the beginning of a process designed to convince me that my mother was an angel and my father was a devil. All through my life, I have been told about my mother. Umbra gave me pictures of her. When I was a child, we celebrated her birthday. There was an empty chair at the dinner table for her. Two things were repeated over and over: my mother was an angel and my father had killed her. I was told that Umbra had saved me, that my father had wanted to kill me too."

Melanie couldn't think of a more terrible thing to tell a child, and she couldn't think of anything less true about Dr. Timberi.

"I remember thinking that if I didn't cry, no one could hurt me. If I didn't feel, I wouldn't be sad. So one of the first things I did was to seal my emotions off.

"I was sent to an orphanage school. A lot of it's a blur now, but one thing I do remember is that we constantly talked about how evil the Magi were. I remember one math problem that went something like this: if ten Magi attack us, and we kill seven of them, how many will be left?"

Indignant mutters flitted around the room, although they faded before Notzange could hit the table with her orb.

He sent more of the strange Light/Dark hybrid at the horloge, which broadcast memories of a shabby, gray building. Children in tattered clothes ran wild through a dining hall of some kind. Older children pushed and shoved younger kids, stealing their food and tormenting them in every possible way.

A sharp slap on the table in the dining hall got everyone's attention. An old woman with a pinched face had smacked the table with her cane. In one hand she held a snappish, yappy dog that nipped at a few stray fingers. As she began yelling at the children, the memory faded out and Timothy continued.

"My teacher was a bitter old woman who enjoyed devising the worst possible punishment for each child. She had tried a few punishments on me, but they didn't seem to work. I closed my feelings off, so she never got any response. She told me the next time I did something wrong, she'd beat me until I cried.

"She had that obnoxious little dog that she carried everywhere. It would walk up and down the aisles of the classroom and nip at you if you weren't careful. We all hated it.

"One night, the older kids poisoned the teacher's dog and then put the poison in my drawer. The teacher flew into a rage. She grabbed her cane and told me she'd beat me to death. I believed her."

The horloge revolved again. They saw the woman's face, disfigured by a beast-like rage that frightened Melanie even at this distance. The woman shrieked and yelled, raising the cane and bringing it down at Timothy's head.

He dodged the blow, but she raised it again.

This time, driven by adrenaline-fueled instinct, Timothy raised his hands. Amber Light exploded out of his hands and knocked the woman over.

Amid shouts and chaos, the door slammed open and a man ran in.

Timothy's memories faded, and he began talking again.

"I was sure I was going to be in trouble when the headmaster ran in. I got ready to shoot him, but he smiled. 'You have nothing to fear,' he said. 'I'm not going to punish you. If she was too weak to fight back, that is her problem. But I want to find out more about you.' He took me under his wing and got me extra training.

"I spent my older childhood and adolescence being taught to use Darkness. It's very similar to using the Light. If you can use Light, you can use Darkness. But it's different enough that it takes practice and training. I was taught to hate Magi and especially my father. They repeated over and over that he had killed my mother. And then, when I got older, they put me in the Shadowbox. Often."

Melanie struggled with her tears. She couldn't imagine what Timothy's life had been like. What would she have become if she had been kidnapped, brainwashed, mistreated, and then put in the Shadowbox over and over?

Her stomach tightened as she remembered what Conner had told her about his experience there. She couldn't imagine the impact that multiple times in the Shadowbox would have, the way it would twist someone's mind and soul.

For the first time ever, her heart went out to Timothy.

"The Shadowbox warped me," Timothy said. "It turned me into a Darkhand, and I embraced it willingly. I hated Magi, especially my father. I wanted to become powerful and go fight a great evil.

"Then I met Lady Nightwing, and she became my world. I worshipped her. She fueled the fire of my zeal to fight the Magi, and I wanted to impress her, to win her praise.

"So everything I've been accused of is true—up until fight with my father in the school cafeteria. That changed everything."

"Timothy," Madame Cumberland said, "can you explain what happened there?"

Timothy nodded. "I can try, but it wasn't a linear, logical process." He frowned a little, and Melanie felt a sharp tug at her heart. Dr. Timberi frowned like that when he started to explain something complicated.

"After the cafeteria fight, I was seriously weakened. I spent a lot of time recovering. And during that time, I started to think.

"I realized how much my dad loved these kids. He sacrificed himself to save them with no hesitation. If he had really killed my mother, if he was a murderer, why would he sacrifice himself? I could also tell that these kids loved him. If he were a bad person, why would they love him?

"As I thought about those things, something else occurred to me. As my shadow-knives pounded into his back, my father said, 'I love you.' That shocked me. How could he say that to me? After all I'd done to the Magi, how could he think that, let alone say it?" Raw emotion simmered in Timothy's voice, and he paused.

"The power of my father's love cut through everything I'd been told. I knew, somehow, that my father loved me, and I realized I had almost killed him. I began to question everything I'd been told. As my convictions grew weaker, something happened that tipped the balance."

"What was that?" Madame Cumberland asked.

"I mentioned that all my life, Umbra had really built up my mom's memory. They did that to turn me against my father, but because of their efforts, she was very real to me. She was always in my heart, and in a twisted way, I sincerely believed that everything I did was done to avenge her." He paused. "Umbra made a huge mistake. One day, someone left some files out. When I read them, I found out that Melanie Stephens was my cousin. My mother's blood runs through her veins. And I had tried to kill her."

CHAPTER 27

FAMILY SECRETS

MELANIE WAITED FOR THE OUTRAGED gasps as people responded to such an obvious, outrageous lie. But no buzz came. Instead, Timothy continued. "When I saw those files, something snapped in my head. Melanie looks a lot like my mother. And I realized I'd almost killed her at Umbra's orders. When I realized how close I'd come to killing my mother's niece, everything Umbra ever told me fell apart. I started to see things clearly, as they really were. And once that happened, I decided to leave Umbra."

Why had the room become silent? It should be echoing the loud chaos tearing through Melanie's mind and heart right now.

Where was the noise?

Mrs. Grant patted Melanie on the back. *I'm sorry you had to hear it like this. We were afraid this might come out.*

Melanie didn't know what to say. Her mind whirred

around without clicking, like a lock unable to find the right combination.

When they had first Kindled, when it had all begun, Melanie's neat, well-ordered life whirled out of control. Now it happened again, but on a more fundamental, far more intimate level.

Her family—which meant her—was not what she thought. Not even close. Suddenly, she felt surrounded by secrets. What else did she not know? What other family secrets lurked out there, waiting to be sprung on her? Timothy was her cousin? Timothy Timberi, the Stalker, was her cousin? That meant—she took a deep breath—Dr. Timberi was her uncle. His dead wife—her aunt.

No one Melanie knew seemed to be who or what she thought. Her teacher was her uncle. Her mortal enemy was her cousin. And her father was not an only child. Even her own name was not what it seemed: Melanie Nicole Stephens. She carried the name of a dead aunt she'd never even known existed.

And what about everyone who knew and didn't tell her? That seemed to be the entire Magi world, including those she knew and trusted most. She pulled away from Mrs. Grant, moving as far as the bench would allow her.

From her place on the floor, Madame Cumberland caught Melanie's eye and smiled that sympathetic smile. For a few seconds, Melanie wanted to fling herself into Madame Cumberland's comforting hug and soft voice. But she resisted. Madame Cumberland had also kept the secret. That made her partly responsible for Melanie's shattered trust.

Melanie ran out, not caring that she stepped all over people's feet getting out of her bench. Driven by a sense of hurt, betrayal, and profound loneliness, Melanie ran with no purpose except to get away from everyone who had betrayed her. She ran until a dead end stopped her, and she paused in front of an ancient-looking tapestry. With nowhere else to go, she sat down on a bench and cried, mourning for the death of her world as she had known it, mourning for the trust that had died along with that world. And, mourning for a dead aunt, a namesake she would never know.

What had Dr. Timberi—Uncle Morgan—been thinking all those years? How could he do this to her? After all they'd been through, all the time they'd spent together, had it never occurred to him to say, "Oh, by the way, Melanie, I'm your long-lost uncle"?

Looking back, she did remember all the times he'd glowed with pride as she figured out a difficult concept or answered a complex question. No wonder he seemed to take a special pride in her success.

But couldn't he have said something?

"'Bout done with the waterworks, Stephens?"

She looked up. Lee stood nearby. The complete lack of either sympathy or harshness in his voice caught her off guard. "Take all the time you need," he said in a matter-of-fact tone. "No rush. But we need to talk, and I ain't competing with all that." He gestured to the tears running down her face. Dusty tan Light appeared in his hand, followed by a bandana, which he handed to her.

"Now, Stephens, let me just guess. You probably feel angry and hurt and betrayed and confused, don't you?

More bent out of shape than a tuba that got hit by a tractor. Am I right?"

"Yes, sir."

"Thought so. Well, that's too bad. And I don't mean to sound harsh. But you gotta get over it."

That wasn't what she was expecting to hear.

"It's unfortunate you heard about it like that, Stephens, but that's the way it had to be."

"Why?" Her voice rose to a level of anger she'd rarely used with an adult. Except when she'd yelled at her parents the other night. "Why did it have to be that way?"

"Because your dad's a puffed-up, big-mouthed blowhard who loves you a lot."

It took Melanie a few seconds to realize she didn't have any idea what he meant. "Excuse me?"

"Okay, let me tell you what happened. Then you tell me what you would have done different. Mind if I set down?"

Melanie scooted over.

"Nicole was your dad's sister. From all I heard, he loved her dearly. I knew Nicole back when she was working for the Adumbrators. Morgan and I were roommates when they dated and fell in love. Once those two got hitched, they had me over all the time. Nicole got worried I wasn't eating. Oh, could she cook!"

Lee smiled, the warm and sincere glow of happy memories. "Nicole was something else, I'll tell you. Smart as a whip, and just all-around amazing—you ever know someone who was just about perfect at anything they did? That was her. Tracking down Darkhands or rustling up a perfect pot roast—I'm telling you, she could do just about anything better than anyone else.

"She loved her kid brother—your daddy. I hadn't met him yet, but she talked about him a lot. That was pre-email, but they wrote each other all the time.

"When Nicole died, he was devastated. And unfortunately, he and Morgan had a falling out. They got going one night and both said some pretty harsh things, I guess. He blamed Morgan, and Morgan lashed right back at him. Long story short, they became bitter enemies. Morgan went his way, your daddy went his, and they thought that was the end of it.

"Well, your daddy met your mama, and you were born years later. He remembered his sister in your name. Incidentally, I don't think your mama knew any of this. I got the idea even she really didn't know anything."

"But why?" Melanie shouted. "Why the big secret?"

"Stephens, you're a smart kid. Think about it from your daddy's point of view.

"He's not a Magus, so he didn't understand much about the Magi world—only that his big sister and nephew got killed by some shadowy group. He worried that the same people might come after the rest of Nicole's family, and that terrified him. Morgan assured him that Umbra wouldn't come after your family, tried to explain that they only cared about Magi.

"But memories of his dead sister haunted your daddy, and he didn't want to take any chances. He figured secrecy was the best protection. So he made Morgan swear the Magi's Oath not to tell you, and he asked everyone else to keep it quiet. We had to respect that, Melanie.

"From your daddy's point of view, everything's going fine. Years pass, and you end up in a school where Morgan teaches. He may not like that you're around Morgan, but he can live with it because the Oath compels Morgan to keep it secret. And then, all of a sudden—"

Melanie jumped as a jolt of understanding shocked her. "We Kindled."

"Yep. Must have scared your daddy to death. Remember, the Magus your daddy really loved most died. And then he finds out you've Kindled and that you were attacked."

"Wait a minute," Melanie said. "I remember that day. My dad said something about how Dr. Timberi didn't have a family to worry about."

"Yep, he did," Lee said. "And if you remember, I about punched him. Knowing Morgan's history, that was just plain mean. Like I said, I don't like your father. But tell me what you would have done differently if you were your daddy or Morgan. The only catch is that you have to act only on the information they had. No hindsight allowed."

Melanie paused. She didn't like what her father had done. But she understood it. And, in the same situation, with the same information he had, she might have done the same thing. And Dr. Timberi had no choice.

The anger faded, leaving her feeling deflated, tired, and sad, but no longer angry.

Understanding began to illuminate the dark corners of Melanie's mind and heart.

"Now, I have a little message for you." Lee wiggled his fingers, and a small, carved box appeared in them. "You remember how Last Sigils work? Basically, a sigil left with instructions to give a message to someone? Well, Morgan left a sigil for you. He figured the day would come that you'd hear this story, and he wanted to be able to talk to you when it did. Being Morgan, he planned ahead just in case he wasn't around."

Lee handed the box to Melanie. "I'm gonna back off a bit and let you have a few quiet moments alone."

His footsteps echoed down the stone halls as Melanie stared at the box. It looked a little like the Reliquary in which Dr. Timberi's Last Sigil had been stored.

She paused. For some reason, the thought of opening it made her nervous. Perhaps because once she did, this new revelation would be permanent and real. Her life would never be the same again.

With trembling fingers, she opened the box. A gold swan soared out. Pale and shaky, like a TV with bad reception, it looked weaker than his sigils usually were.

The swan smiled, and Dr. Timberi's voice filled the corridor.

"Hello, Melanie. If you get this, then you have learned about our family's secret. I hope you are not unduly upset. I know that discovering secrets can be very upsetting and unsettling.

"Because of that, I want to explain my part in keeping the secret. Simply put, your father's wishes placed me under a solemn obligation not to say anything to you, although it nearly killed me! It was so difficult to teach you each day, knowing you were my niece, yet not being able to say anything. But I had sworn that Magi's Oath.

"When you tried out for your first play, I was so proud, and I enjoyed working with you and getting to know you better. You were everything I would have hoped for in a niece. Being around you was enjoyable in its own right, but it also helped me feel closer to Nicole. Of course you know about her by now. She was beautiful and wonderful and brilliant and full of life. I see those qualities in you.

"But I came to love you, not merely because you reminded me of her and not merely because I was your uncle. I came to love you because you are such a wonderful person. I cannot describe the pride I feel when you pose a complex question about Lightcraft—and then demonstrate a keen mind by reasoning your way to the answer.

"Forgive me, Melanie, for not telling you. And forgive your father. Personally, I think he was wrong to shelter you from your Magi connections. But I understand his intentions.

"Your father and I have never liked each other, Melanie. To be honest, I've always found him to be extremely unpleasant. I don't understand how either you or Nicole could be related to him. But he loves you. He's a good man and a good father who was trying to protect his little girl. Perfection should never be the enemy of the good.

"As for me, I am delighted to finally be able to discuss this openly and express my tremendous affection and pride."

The sigil faded out, leaving Melanie crying quietly as Lee came back.

"Good night! Every time Morgan leaves one of these things, people start carrying on! All right, wipe those tears away, Stephens. We gotta figure out a way to free your Uncle Morgan."

CHAPTER 28

THE KINDLING EXPLAINED

CONNER SQUIRMED ON THE BENCH. HE realized that it had been built hundreds of years ago, but since then, people had invented cushions and all kinds of wonderful things. Down on the floor, Madame Cumberland had a triumphant glow as she asked Timothy about his efforts to leave Umbra.

"Why were you at Dauphin Island?" Madame Cumberland asked.

"I was trying to get in touch with my father. I wanted to leave Umbra and didn't know how. I thought he could help me."

"Your father wasn't there," the Prosecutor said.

"I know." Timothy had an edge in his voice. "My father was recovering after our battle. He'd gone to a Sanctuary—which meant there was no way I could contact him directly. I thought the best way to get in touch with him without raising suspicion was through the kids. Our intelligence was tracking them, and I knew where they were.

I decided to go that night and talk with Conner and ask him to take a message to my dad."

"And is that what happened?" Madame Cumberland asked.

"No. Conner saw me. But right then, the Twilight Phalanx showed up. I didn't want to mess with them, so I phased and made myself invisible."

"You expect us to believe you can use the Light?" the Prosecutor asked. "Phasing is a Magi technique.

"Yes. I did phase. I can also stream."

"And how did you learn to stream?"

"I taught myself. It's not all that different from what Darkhands do when they become cyclones."

The Prosecutor snorted. "It is difficult to believe that, as a practicing Darkhand, you picked up on the essentials of Lightcraft."

"And yet many things happen that are difficult to believe," Timothy replied, garnishing his words with extra snark.

Lexa stood up. "Your Honor, I object!"

Lexa! Conner said. *What are you doing?*

Too late. The entire assembly room swivelled their necks to stare at Lexa. Conner slouched down on the bench, hoping no one would notice he happened to be related to the crazy girl yelling out.

"Excuse me?" Notzange stared at Lexa.

"I mean, I don't object, but I have something to say. May I please speak?" Lexa curtsied.

"You have already been examined," the Prosecutor said.

"With respect, Your Eminence, I did reserve the right to recall her," Madame Cumberland said with a gentle bow.

"Very well. You may speak, Lexa."

"Thank you. Um, so, at Dauphin Island Conner said he saw Timothy. No one believed him at the time, but it turned out to be true. Anyways, the Adumbrators did these scans and they found a Light signature that no one recognized. When they scanned it, it was a close match to Dr. Timberi. Wouldn't that sort of fit with what Timothy's saying? That he was using the Light at that point?

"And also, couldn't you just have him do some Lightcraft now and compare the Light signatures to whatever they scanned at Dauphin Island?"

At that moment, Lee and Melanie walked back into the room. Melanie had been crying—but she looked happy now.

A loud laugh burst out of Lee's mouth. "'Atta girl, Lexa."

Notzange pounded the metal ball. "Silence, please. Is that all, Lexa?"

Lexa tugged on her ponytail. "Well, since you asked, no. Not to be rude, but I totally don't understand why the whole Magisterium is sitting here having a trial for Timothy when his dad is out there somewhere being tortured by the Darkhands," Lexa said. "It's almost like no one really cares enough to actually do something—"

The metal ball hit the surface in front of the Magistrate with a sharp crack that split the air all through the chamber.

"You are out of order, Lexa. That will be enough."

"Yes, ma'am." Lexa dropped her head. "It's just that I miss Dr. Timberi so much and I'm really worried about him." Her voice quivered and her jaw shook. That expression happened to be one of Lexa's specialities. She pulled it with her parents or other unsuspecting adults all the time. Conner looked over at her—and realized that Lexa was not playing a role. The tears and emotion were all genuine. "Anyways, I just wish we could find him. Melanie has a really good theory about where he might be, but she needs some information from the Adumbrators office and it just seems like no one cares."

"Madame Director Benet?" Notzange looked at Hortense in her seat down below the Magistrate's bench.

Hortense's mouth looked like she'd guzzled lemonade and discovered it was really lemon juice. "Yes, Your Eminence?"

"There must have been a misunderstanding. I am certain that your office would not mind sharing this information with Melanie or listening to her theory?"

Hortense tightened her lips. "We would be happy to discuss whatever Miss Stephens needs." Conner didn't think that her words had a lot of sincerity in them.

"I thought so," Notzange said. "Now, Lexa, please sit down."

"Your Eminence," Madame Cumberland said, "what of Lexa's first point—the unidentified Light signature at Dauphin Island? Can that scan be retrieved?"

Notzange looked at Hortense again.

Hortense nodded, then flicked her wrist. Her crisp movement brought a flash of fuchsia Light, and a hedgehog sigil scurried away. "I have asked my staff to feed the scans in question into the horloge, Your Eminence."

"Thank you, Madame Director," Notzange said.

A moment later, the horloge flashed and projected a

Light signature into the room. A pale green color, as if regular green had become really sick.

"Whoa!" Conner muttered. The swirling, interlocked lace pattern of the Light was unmistakable. Anyone could recognize the same pattern that had showed up in Conner, Lexa, and Pilaf's Light signatures.

"This is the Light signature that we retrieved from Dauphin Island," Hortense said. "At the time, the closest match was to Morgan Timberi." Another Light signature appeared, bright gold. It shared some similarities with Timothy, but only around the edges. "You can see that there are some similarities between the two, although they are not exact matches.

"Our database automatically compares the signatures of living Magi—not those who are dead. Based on what we know now, my staff went back through the records and pulled up the Light signature that belonged to Nicole Timberi, Timothy's mother." A peach Light signature flashed, composed of lacy loops and swirls.

Conner's pulse sped up. Nicole's Light signature matched the unknown sample—and also matched the pattern in his and Lexa's Light signatures.

Notzange nodded. "Timothy, if you can produce Light with this same signature, I think it will establish that you did, indeed, work Lightcraft at Dauphin Island. And, in my mind, that would provide strong evidence of the fact that you have tried to leave Umbra. Can you organize a sigil?"

Timothy frowned. "No. I can't. I haven't learned how to do that yet. I can Phase and stream and shoot Light. But I can't do a sigil."

"Very well," Notzange said. "Can you provide some Light for us? Dr. Seo—I see you are here. Would you kindly analyze some Light from Timothy and provide us with the Light signature?"

Dr. Seo stood up. "Yes, Your Eminence."

"We would like to expedite this tribunal along. How much time will you need?"

"Ten or fifteen minutes should be sufficient."

"Thank you. This tribunal will recess for that test to be performed; however, I will ask that everyone remain seated so we can reconvene as soon as Dr. Seo has finished."

As Timothy and the column of fire disappeared, Dr. Seo hurried out of the room, and Lee and Melanie made their way to the group.

Pilaf looked at everyone. His eyes began to blink, indicating deep thought. "Dr. Seo thought maybe Conner and Lexa Kindling at the same time was strong enough to make Melanie Kindle and make me do . . . whatever I do. Conner, Lexa, and me all have Light signatures that are almost identical to Nicole Timberi. So the Dells couldn't have made Melanie Kindle, right? I mean, it wouldn't go backwards like that."

"Wait a minute," Lee said. "Stephens, do you mean to tell me you haven't figured that out yet?"

Melanie stared at him. "What do you mean?"

"Let's just say that if it wasn't for you, the rest of these jackrabbits would still be living very boring lives."

"I made them Kindle?" Melanie looked shocked—almost like someone had slapped her.

"What's your gift, Stephens?"

"Augmenting—oh my gosh!" Melanie's face lit up.

"You mean I got my powers genetically from my Aunt Nicole. And when I Kindled I basically Augmented Conner and Lexa somehow and made them Kindle too?"

"Yup. Of course, they had to have Light inside of them—had to be good wood for your spark to start a fire. But you started it. Think about three matches lying together. If you light one, and the other two are close enough, what's going to happen?"

"They'll light on fire too." Melanie started to cry and laugh at the same time.

Are you okay? Conner asked.

Yes! Sobs and giggles interrupted her thoughts for a minute. *I'm not just the secretary!*

What?

Nothing. It just means a lot to me.

"So is this why Madi is showing signs of Kindling?" Lexa asked.

"Uh-huh," Lee said. "It's a little early for sure, and that's why people have been surprised. But no one's surprised that she's demonstrating Magi powers—only that they're coming out at such a young age. It's probably tied to Melanie. Stephens, you're such a strong Augmentor, you've basically lit the neighborhood on fire."

The crashing of the orb called everyone back to attention, and Dr. Seo walked to the witness box.

"What did you find, Doctor?" Madame Cumberland asked.

"The Light Timothy produced is a positive match to the previously unidentified Light signature from Dauphin Island."

"Dr. Seo, can you please make it very clear what this means?" Madame Cumberland asked.

"Well, it means that Timothy can use Light. And it means that he did perform Lightcraft at Dauphin Island," Dr. Seo said.

"Does this evidence support Timothy's assertion that he was trying to leave Umbra?"

Dr. Seo frowned. "I don't think it proves anything, but yes, I would say this evidence supports Timothy's story because Darkhands can't use the Light."

Lexa cheered.

Conner wondered a little about her excitement. He still wasn't convinced that Timothy should be freed. He'd had a sad life for sure. But Conner didn't trust Timothy. He'd done too much, been too bad for too long. Even if he truly wanted to change, Conner didn't know if he could.

CHAPTER 29

RENUNCIATION AND INVESTITURE

LEXA STRUGGLED TO CONTAIN HER EXCITE-ment as they followed Madame Cumberland down to Timothy's cell. Now the tribunal would end and everyone would get back to finding Dr. Timberi. Her theelings told her two things: Timothy would be released and he had an important part to play in the quest to save his father.

She'd tried head-talking with Conner, but he seemed grumpy, and Pilaf wouldn't talk about anything except the fact that Melanie had made them all Kindle. Melanie had been preoccupied since the whole surprise about her being Dr. Timberi's niece. Lexa didn't understand why that seemed to upset Melanie much. To her, it seemed really cool. In fact, she might be more than a little jealous. But she forced herself not to think about that.

When they arrived in Timothy's cell, a spark of hope gleamed in his midnight eyes.

Madame Cumberland started to cry. "Oh, Timothy,

I'm so sorry for all you suffered." She tried to hug him, but the bubble around him crackled and she let go. "When Morgan first found out you were actually alive, he was beside himself with joy—and then nearly went mad with grief at the thought of what you'd suffered." Her words faded into tears.

Timothy remained stiff and rigid. It reminded Lexa of the way Dr. Timberi reacted to hugs.

"I think we can persuade them to let you go free," Madame Cumberland said. "Oh, Timothy, there is so much ahead of you! So many wonderful, wonderful things."

The sharp sound of the guard's staff hitting the door outside interrupted them. The door creaked open, and Notzange walked up the steps.

"Hello, everyone." She smiled. "I apologize for disturbing you. I would like to speak with Timothy if I may."

"We'll just wait outside," Conner said.

"No," Timothy said. "You might as well stay. You're the closest thing I've got to friends." He looked at Melanie. "Or family."

Notzange nodded. "I shall be direct. Timothy, before today, nearly everyone thought you should be executed. A few who were extremely charitable advocated imprisonment. After your testimony today, opinion has softened.

"However, there is a great concern among some of the Council. A large contingent fears this is all part of an elaborate plot. And given Lady Nightwing's history of elaborate plots, I cannot condemn this line of thinking."

Lexa noticed that Madame Cumberland stopped smiling and grew stiff as Notzange continued.

"All of this causes great confusion about what to do. None of our options seem to be good ones. You are an admitted Darkhand with a record of great evil. How can we simply free you? On the other hand, after all you have suffered, execution seems cruel, and imprisonment only a little less so." She paused. "You know about Renunciation?"

The corners of Timothy's eyes grew tense and the lines heavy. "Yes. It would mean giving up my powers forever. I couldn't use Light or Darkness."

"But even that raises objections."

"And they are?" Madame Cumberland's voice had grown chilly.

"Investiture."

Madame Cumberland threw up her hands and snorted. "You must be joking!"

Pilaf raised his hand. "Excuse me—"

Madame Cumberland answered his unspoken question. "Investiture is where one Magus gives up his or her powers to another. It is a *theoretical* way around Renunciation. It happened once in all of Sodality history—back in the Victorian era. A dying husband reportedly—reportedly!—gave his powers to his wife. Notzange, this is ridiculous! We don't even know if Investiture is a real thing. No one in living memory has ever done it, and the records might be incorrect."

"There are actually three recorded instances," Notzange said in a calm voice. "And yes, it is largely unknown. But given the number of unusual and almost impossible things Lady Nightwing has done in the past, we cannot dismiss the possibility."

"But surely you don't think—"

Notzange raised a hand. "What I personally think does not matter because I am not free to act for myself. There are grave concerns about the security and safety of the entire Sodality, perhaps the world. I must balance all those concerns." She stepped forward, a few inches away from Timothy. "Look me in the eye."

Timothy looked up as she placed a hand on each side of his head.

"Tell me you have given up on Umbra, renounced being a Darkhand."

Without blinking, Timothy held her gaze. "I swear on my father's life that I have given up Umbra. I have forsaken the Dark and all its works."

Considering how often he tried to kill his father, I'm not sure how much value he puts on his father's life, Conner thought to Lexa.

Notzange continued to stare for several seconds and then nodded.

"There is only one way I can think to conclusively prove your innocence. What do you know of sigils?"

"Not much. I mean, I've seen Magi shoot them in battles."

"A sigil is part of your soul. Literally. The Light gives it form. A sigil can be used in combat, as you have seen. But they can also do other things. A sigil cannot lie. It represents who you are, expressing the truth of your soul. If you organized a sigil and allow the council to inspect it, I believe it would prove your innocence."

"How do I do that?"

Notzange smiled. "Here are three newly trained Adepts." She nodded at the Trio. "They have recently gone through this process themselves. Perhaps they could teach you. Now, I really must leave."

She nodded at Madame Cumberland with a smile. "Mona."

A pang of sadness jabbed Lexa as she witnessed the tension that had grown between the two old friends. The hopeful, inviting smile on Notzange's face stung Lexa. It was an obvious attempt to make peace. Dr. Timberi had given her the same sort of smile right before she told everyone how much she hated him.

Lexa grew even more uncomfortable when Madame Cumberland gave a curt nod but no smile. Lexa felt as if she was watching one of the biggest mistakes of her life on instant replay.

After Notzange left, Timothy looked at the Trio. "Can you teach me to do a sigil like she said?"

"Yes!" Lexa shouted at the same time Melanie said, "We can try," and Conner said, "Probably not."

Madame Cumberland stood up. "I'll leave you all to work. I have some things I need to do." She gave Timothy another smile and then left the room.

Timothy took a deep breath. "Well, this isn't easy. But I'm sorry—for everything. That doesn't do much, but I don't know what else to say."

"It's okay," Melanie said. Her well-bred, Southern-girl politeness came almost as natural to her as crying. Somehow, Lexa had missed that part of growing up in Tennessee.

"We're sorry too," Lexa added, trying to be polite. Conner glared at Lexa and Melanie. *It's okay? We're sorry? For what? We didn't do anything to him!*

I was just trying to be polite, Lexa said. People say a lot of polite things they don't mean. Everyone knows that. Sheesh, Con.

"You don't have anything to apologize for," Timothy said. "But thanks anyway." He leaned forward, grabbing Lexa with the intensity in his eyes. "Get me out of here," he whispered with fire in his voice.

"Excuse me?" Lexa said. She hadn't expected that.

"Get me out. Help me escape. Now. Before they kill me or make me Renounce."

"Would that be such a bad thing?" Conner said. "Renouncing, I mean."

Lexa glared at him. *Conner, that's terrible! I'd rather die than lose my powers!*

Conner glared back. *Then don't try to kill people and no one will take them away.*

Timothy interrupted Conner's glare. "How can I defend myself from Umbra when they come after me? And you know they will. Can I really count on the Magisterium to protect me for the rest of my life? And can I count on them to find my dad? How can I rescue my father if I Renounce? Because we all know they won't. But I can save him—I'm the only one who can."

The thrill of watching her theelings coming together made Lexa tingle all over. "Do you have a plan? Do you know where he is?" She struggled to contain her exuberance.

Timothy dropped his voice even lower. "Maybe," he said. "But I can't tell you anything unless I know for sure you won't tell anyone. I need to know you aren't spies for the Magisterium. For all I know, the reason the Supreme

Magistrate told you to help me with my sigil was to have you spy on me."

"That's not true!" Conner said, stepping toward Timothy. "We're not spies for anyone."

"Prove it," Timothy said, stepping toward Conner. "Teach me this sigil thing. If you help me with that, then I'll trust you."

"You prove it," Conner said, stepping toward Timothy. They glared at each other, just an inch or two apart. The bubble around Timothy crackled and Conner stepped back. "Prove you've really changed."

"How? I'm going to try to learn to do sigils."

"Give us some information. Like, what's the stuff Darkhands shoot—how is it different than regular shadows?" Conner asked.

Timothy looked a little surprised. "It's shadows mixed with hate or fear or anger. Hate's the strongest. It usually comes out as black fire."

That's what dragged you under the water at Dauphin Island! Melanie said. *The natural shadows in the water mixed with your fear when you thought you felt something. Without you realizing it, you created a monster that attacked you.*

Conner nodded as understanding clicked in his brain. That made sense. It all made sense. Especially the pillowcase and the hornets. Shadows were the pillowcase, the vehicle. Hate was the wasps, the engine that propelled it all. That explained the struggling, mixed-up feeling he got when he reached out to the Darkness.

His gut said Timothy had told the truth on this one. That reduced Conner's distrust by a few degrees—enough that he agreed to join the effort to teach Timothy how to do a sigil.

They spent a few hours teaching Timothy and practicing. He managed to shoot some Light but never managed to create a sigil.

When the guards came to tell them they needed to leave for the night, Lexa looked at Timothy. "We'll be back tomorrow," she said with a wink.

THE ADUMBRATORS OFFICE

MELANIE DIDN'T SAY ANYTHING AS ONE OF the guards led them on the long walk from Timothy's cell to their rooms. As they walked, Lexa went on and on, head-talking about how she just knew they'd all be working together to free Dr. Timberi. She made it sound like it would all be over by suppertime.

Lexa was convinced that her theelings were coming true, but Melanie wondered. Did Timothy really have a plan? Or had Lexa's outburst in the tribunal given him the idea of manipulating her into helping him escape? He seemed shrewd enough to do that, and Lexa was definitely desperate enough to take risky steps.

Melanie didn't know what to think about helping Timothy. To be honest, she didn't know if she trusted him. She didn't think so.

But her dad had told her to help Timothy if she could—something she now understood. His only sister's only child. A nephew he thought had died.

And, as she thought about it, Timothy probably did know things that could help them find Dr. Timberi.

"Evening, y'all." Lee emerged from a side hall and grinned at them. He saluted the guards. "I'll escort them the rest of the way. Dismissed." The guards saluted and walked away. Lee lowered his voice. "Stephens, how'd you like to take a trip to the Adumbrators office and get that info you wanted?"

"They said we could come?"

Lee grinned even wider. "Not exactly. But you heard the Supreme Magistrate today. She told Hortense to cooperate. That's good enough for me. We gotta strike while the iron's hot. Let's go have a look-see."

"What will Hortense say?"

"Hortense won't be there this late. The whole idea is to let you peek into the networked horloges and find out what you need without her causing a fuss. If anyone says anything, we'll just work it out later."

Lee led them to the main entry hall of the château and then up to a thick wooden door, guarded by the gray-cloaked guards with the silver staffs.

"The Supreme Magistrate ordered these four to the Adumbrator office," Lee said. The guards nodded, scanned them with the staffs, and then let them through the door into a circular tower at the bottom of a long spiral staircase. They followed Lee up the stairs to another heavy door set in a wall of thick stone. The shape of an eye had been carved into the rock above the door with rays of light around it like straight eyelashes. An ancient-looking inscription said, "Et vigilantia lumina." Melanie looked at Conner, who said, "Vigilance and light."

"Nice job, Dell," Lee said. "How'd you know that?"

"My Latin teacher is super hard core and makes us memorize lots of vocabulary. He always said we'd thank him one day."

Lee opened the door. "Hurry on up," he said. "We don't usually let junior Adepts poke around top-secret intelligence-gathering operations. And, remember, I didn't exactly get permission to do this."

As they walked into the office, Melanie struggled to know where to focus her eyes. Along the stone walls, hundreds of horloges made of thousands of hoops spun inside nooks and niches that had been carved into the rock. With every hoop spinning in a different pattern, trailing and flashing Light, the horloges created a visual spectacle of color and movement unlike anything Melanie had ever seen.

Looking away to avoid sensory overload, Melanie noticed rows of desks occupying the middle of the room—desks with computers and other twenty-first century equipment.

A massive plasma screen mounted to the wall near the door seemed to be a digital version of the universal view from the horloge, showing the constantly shifting total levels of Light and Darkness.

Below that display, rows of numbers and graphs also fluctuated, as if they were monitoring the condition of a patient in a hospital.

A door opened, and everyone jumped as Hortense stepped out of an inner office. "May I help you, Colonel?"

"Well," Lee drawled, "today in the tribunal, the Supreme Magistrate said—"

"Morgan is dead," Hortense said. Her voice sounded firm but contained more compassion than Melanie would have expected. "I'm sorry. I know it is difficult to accept. But we have verified that account."

"You've seen the body?" Lexa asked.

"Excuse me?"

"Did you personally see his body?"

"How about DNA?" Melanie jumped in. Arguing with authority figures made her feel downright evil. But she pushed that aside. "Or dental records?"

"He's not dead," Lexa said. "But I almost think you want him to be since you won't do anything to help him."

Hortense glared at her. "Morgan's arrogance seems to have rubbed off on his students. How dare you come in here and imply that I have not done my job?"

Melanie bit back a sharp retort. Her mom always said you caught more flies with honey than vinegar. "Madame Benet, I just want to look in an horloge that will show me—"

"No. That is quite impossible. One does not simply peer into top-secret devices on whim."

"But you can stand here and watch me. I just need a few minutes." Melanie's pulse surged as she pushed her normal caution and deference aside. "If he's really dead, then it can't hurt. And if he is still alive, it could help. What do you have to lose?"

"That is quite enough," Hortense said. "You will leave at once or I will call security. You have no authority here, Colonel."

"Excuse me, Madam Director." A deep, rich voice

floated through the room. Melanie turned her head as Notzange walked in.

"Your Eminence." Hortense's eyes narrowed and she gave a curt nod. "What may I do for you?"

"I came to ask a question, but I seem to have interrupted something."

"They were just leaving," Hortense said, glaring at each of the children—and then Lee.

"Really? I did not hear you answer their questions," Notzange said in a soft voice. "Please do not let me interrupt you. I can wait."

Hortense's face burned the same fuchsia color as her robes, and for a moment Melanie thought she might hit someone, even with Notzange watching.

"No," she said. "We do not have DNA or dental records. We have not recovered a body. But we have a credible account by a witness. A double agent, one of our people who has infiltrated the enemy and works for Umbra. Giving more details would compromise this person and put them in great danger."

"And they saw, with their own eyes, Morgan's body?" Notzange asked.

"I have never had reason to doubt this person," Hortense said, fire blazing in her eyes.

"Yes, I am sure of that," Notzange said. "And yet, if they did not see it personally, it seems that the account could be a rumor. Or perhaps deliberate misinformation. Of course, I am not a trained Adumbrator, so perhaps I am missing something. But I should think you would want to follow any possible leads. I am told that Lexa continues to have a mental connection with Morgan."

Notzange smiled. "It's all very confusing. I rather suspect that it will come up in the tribunal tomorrow."

"Of course." Hortense nearly spit the words out.

"Thank you, Madame Director." She turned to leave.

"You said you had a question for me, Your Eminence?" Hortense said.

Notzange smiled. "Did I? I do not recall. Good night, everyone."

After she left, Hortense's eyes narrowed into slivers as she glared at Lee. "It is almost as if someone sent for her."

Lee shook his head. "Boy, ain't that a funny coincidence. You know, Hortense, some people would feel obligated to follow the Supreme Magistrate's orders. But not you. You just keep charging ahead in your own path, no matter what anyone says."

"Enough!" Hortense snapped. "Leave!"

"I always respected you, Hortense," Lexa said.

"Excuse me?" Hortense glared at Lexa.

"That was Dr. Timberi's sigil," Lexa said. "Sometimes his words jump out of my mouth. Dr. Timberi really respected you. I know you had your issues, and I know he could be difficult, but he respected you a lot." She put a hand on Hortense's tight, tanned arm.

The anger on Hortense's face wilted.

"He's alive, Madame Benet," Lexa said. "I can feel him, and I'm not lying. Please believe me. You examined my memories once—a few months ago when I had visions of Notzange being kidnapped. Can you do that again? Just look into my mind and check on Dr. Timberi's sigil."

Hortense nodded, put her hands on Lexa's head, and closed her eyes. As the Light connected them, Hortense's face softened. "It appears he might still be alive," she said.

"Might be?" Lee asked.

"He's alive!" The sharp edge in Hortense's voice could have sliced a hair in half. "Our source was wrong." Hortense frowned for a few seconds, and Melanie sensed a fierce internal struggle. "Melanie, what is it you want to know?"

Melanie explained her theory. "I need to be able to see places where Darkness has stopped in a dramatic way recently." She prepared to argue with Hortense, go get Notzange, and do whatever it took to get Dr. Timberi back.

Don't argue with her, Lexa said. *I have a theeling—she won't back down. I understand her a whole lot better now. She's not bad. But she needs to feel respected.*

"Please?" Melanie added. "I would be so grateful if you'd allow me to do this." Melanie didn't care for the way humility tasted in her mouth.

However, Hortense surprised her by nodding. "I owe you an apology, Melanie." It looked like she had to chew on razors to make the words come out. "I truly believed Morgan was dead. I felt that keeping false hope alive was cruel. And I truly worried about betraying our person who infiltrated Umbra." She paused. "But I was wrong." She pulled herself to her full height and sent sigil after sigil into the air. Within seconds, comets began shooting into the room, filling the office with Magi. Hortense looked at her staff and said, "New information has been established that Morgan Timberi is alive. Finding him is now the highest priority of this office. To work! I want access to the data from the horloge network on the monitor."

As the office crackled with energy, Hortense pointed to the plasma screen. "This monitor connects to a supercomputer that records and analyzes data from horloges all over the world—including some we have in satellites. The information you want should be easy to get, Melanie." Looking over her shoulder, she said, "Display the general global view."

"Yes, Madam Director," someone replied, and the abstract blobs of Light and Dark on the screen formed themselves into a map of the world.

"Superimpose the locations with the most consistent Dark activity during the past three months," Hortense said.

Red dots appeared on the map, labelled with the names of the location: Mexico City; Halifax; Belem; Pittsburgh; Dusseldorf; Lisbon; Guatemala City; St. George, Utah; and the Aleutian Islands.

"Now, show us the consistent locations of Dark activity today."

The stars marking the Aleutian Islands, Pittsburgh, and St. George, Utah, vanished.

"St. George, Utah, was where we knocked out that listening post," Lee said. "That's why Darkness disappeared there."

"That leaves Pittsburgh and the Aleutian Islands."

Lee nodded. "Now we're getting somewhere."

"He's in a place called the Abyss," Melanie said, "so it's probably not Pittsburgh."

Hortense nodded. "Zoom in on the islands." The map zoomed in on them. Hortense pointed to a dark area in the water near the islands. "There is an ocean trench there—the Aleutian trench."

"Perfect hideout," Lee said. "I'm guessing those islands are pretty scarcely populated. Okay, I'm going to send some folks to Pittsburgh and poke around just in case. But I'm taking the Phalanx to the Aleutians, and I'm going to request some serious assets to back us up. Hortense, can you give me the exact coordinates?"

She nodded and someone tapped a few more keys. The coordinates popped up on the screen. Lee nodded. "Okay. Got 'em." He looked at Hortense. "Thank you."

She smiled. "You are welcome." Then she looked at Melanie and Lexa. "Thank you. Thank all of you. You saved me from making a terrible mistake. I would not have been able to live with myself."

"Now listen," Lee said when they stepped out of the Adumbrators office. "Can y'all find your way back? I'm heading over to the Phalanx barracks to get things going." He looked at Conner. "Dell, you up for another fight?"

"Wait!" Lexa said. "What about us? That's not fair."

Lee shook his head. "Lexa, honey, I'm sorry. But this place is gonna be guarded by the best of the best. Your brother has a special skill we can use. He might save people's lives, so it justifies putting him in serious danger. No way can I justify taking the rest of you."

Lexa opened her mouth, and Melanie sensed the argument forming like a storm about to burst. But then Lexa shut her mouth. A few seconds later, she said, "Okay. I see your point."

Melanie smiled. Lexa had worked so hard to keep her promise. She'd been fighting every tendency that made her a drama queen sometimes.

Lee smiled and tapped her forehead with a finger. "Good girl. I know it's tough. I promise we'll keep you posted, and you can come over as just soon as we get the place secured. Promise."

"Come on, Dell—Conner, not Lexa." Lee jumped into a flip, turning into a comet before he finished.

"Awesome!" Conner shouted. He jumped into a flip too—and fell on the ground. "Okay, not quite ready for that." He got up and ran a few steps, disappearing in a red comet.

"Good job," Melanie said to Lexa, patting her back. "I know it was hard not to argue."

"Oh, that?" Lexa waved her hand. "I just didn't want to get them suspicious or waste time arguing. There's no way I'm missing out on helping to rescue Dr. Timberi. We're going to go see Timothy," Lexa said. "I want to hear what his plan is."

"What?"

As Melanie stared at Lexa, Pilaf's eyes blinked like strobe lights. "Lexa!" he said. "You can't do that!"

Shhh! Lexa hissed. *Oh yes, I can. We can. Lee's right about the Magisterium. It might not be bad, but it's too slow. And I don't trust them to do the right thing. I don't trust them to make the right decision about Timothy, and I don't trust them to find Dr. Timberi.*

"But you can't help a prisoner escape!" Pilaf said. He turned and looked at Melanie. "Right, Melanie?"

Melanie paused. A fundamental part of her recoiled

at the thought of doing something so radical. Illegal, in fact.

But Timothy was her cousin. Her blood.

She thought of her amazing Aunt Nicole. Would she just stand around hoping the Magisterium managed to free Dr. Timberi? For that matter, if Melanie had been languishing in some Darkhand prison, would Uncle Morgan wait for anyone else to—she couldn't even finish that thought. It was too ridiculous.

Her dad had told her to help Timothy.

She grabbed Pilaf's arm. "Come on, Pilaf. We can't wait anymore." She sprinted down the steps toward the dungeon, dragging Pilaf behind her.

CHAPTER 31

CONNER'S TRIP

FILLED WITH FURY AND A SENSE OF HELP-lessness, Conner pounded a hole in the rock wall of the château.

How could they leave him out?

Lexa? Melanie? Where are you guys?

Conner? Melanie's voice came into his mind. *Why aren't you with the Phalanx? Aren't they gone yet?*

They're not taking me after all.

What? Lexa joined in now. *Why not?*

The head military guy—Lee's boss—ordered him to leave me. Too dangerous. Lee tried to argue, but without telling him about what I can do with Darkness, he couldn't persuade him. With growing frustration, Conner punched another hole in the rock wall.

Ouch. He shook his knuckles. Just because you could punch a hole in rock didn't mean it was a good idea.

I'm back in my room. Where are you?

The pause that came made him suspicious.

225

We went on a walk, Lexa said at the same exact time Melanie said, *We're going to see Timothy.*

Seriously, what's going on? The fact that Lexa just withheld details worried him.

We went on a walk to go see Timothy, Lexa said. *We're going to help him with sigils.*

This late at night? What are you up to, Lexa? The sparks of Conner's suspicion flared to large flames. *Oh my gosh, tell me you're not going to talk about helping him escape.*

Silence.

Lexa! You have got to be kidding. That's crazy! Melanie, you have to stop her. I'll be right there.

Conner, I actually agree with Lexa on this one. Melanie's thoughts sounded different. Much stronger and more decisive than usual.

Conner nearly choked. Hortense must have used some secret brain-scrambling weapon on them. They'd lost their minds! Gone completely crazy in the few minutes he'd been away. Help Timothy escape? The man who had tried to kill them—and Dr. Timberi—time after time?

Here I come, he said. *Don't do anything!*

Hoping he wouldn't get in too much trouble, Conner streamed into a red comet, blasting at top speed toward the dungeons.

Conner only collided with one person—an elderly cleaning lady who smacked him several times with a wet mop, even after he apologized. After that he ran instead, leaving a trail of cold, dirty water behind him. The lost time frustrated him, but he didn't want to risk crashing into a guard or someone who could cause real problems. He pushed himself to run faster. Their rooms and the dungeons were on opposite ends of the castle, so he had a long way to go, and he was terrified Lexa would do something stupid before he got there.

But she couldn't, right? Surely the Magisterium guarded Timothy better than that. No way a couple of thirteen-year-old Magi-in-training could break him out. What could Lexa and Melanie do? Melanie had intelligence and Augmentation. Lexa's abilities as a Seer didn't exactly lend themselves to neutralizing a—

Pilaf. Pilaf could neutralize Light . . . Pilaf, who adored Lexa.

Conner ran faster now, fighting the sinking feeling inside of him.

Even if they got Timothy out of that protective bubble somehow, they couldn't leave the castle. Not like—

Lexa had Translocated Blinson. But that was impossible. But she'd done it. But only because he and Melanie had helped, right?

Lexa! Melanie! he called out. No answer.

Pilaf! If you can hear me, don't help them! Don't let them do anything!

He sped up even faster.

And what about Timothy? What were his plans? Darkhands could do sigil traps. Conner had seen them. If your sigil got inside of one, the trap forcibly reunited your body and sigil, bringing you together as if you were attached to a rubber band that had been stretched out. A sigil trap could transport your body anywhere in seconds.

What else could they do? Conner realized he knew very little about Darkhands. What other powers did they have that Conner didn't know about?

As sinking fear turned to panic, Conner found himself streaming down the hall. He muttered an apology in advance to any other cleaning ladies. But he couldn't mess around anymore.

DECISIONS

LEXA HAD WORRIED THAT THE GUARDS
might stop them, but no one said anything. Having
the Supreme Magistrate on your side opened a lot of doors.
Including the door of Timothy's cell. They opened it, and
Lexa bounded up the stairs.

"Timothy!" she said. "Timothy, wake up!"

He sat up, blinking his eyes and squinting. "What's
wrong? What time is it?"

"Timothy, I need to know your plan," Lexa said.
"What's your plan if we can get you out of here?"

He looked at her with a piercing stare she had experienced many times from Dr. Timberi.

"What's going on?"

"They found the Abyss," Lexa said. "The Twilight Phalanx is headed there now. But I want to be part of it. You
said you had a plan. I want to know what it is."

Timothy's gaze grew more intense. "The Phalanx will
never get in," he said. "Never."

"How do you know?" Lexa asked.

"The entrances to Umbra's bases are impossible to find. Impossible."

"They got to the place in the desert where you were keeping Notzange," Lexa said.

Timothy smiled. "Yes, but only because you got there through a sigil connection, and they tracked you."

"Wait!" Melanie said. "We got there because Lexa's sigil went into a sigil trap. That pulled her body through time and space to reunite with her sigil, right?"

"Yes," Timothy said.

"Why don't we do that?" Melanie's voice shook with excitement. "You can make a sigil trap here. Lexa can extract Uncle Morgan's sigil into the trap. That will bring his body here. Easy! We can save him. If you do that, I'm sure they'll let you go."

Lexa nearly jumped out of her body. "Yes! Yes, that's it! Oh my gosh, Mel, you are brilliant! Why didn't anyone already think of that?"

"Because only Darkhands do sigil traps," Pilaf said. "I learned that while I was studying for my test. Magi don't know how."

"That's right," Timothy said. "Of course, I can't actually do it because of this." He gestured to the bubble of Light around him. "Not to mention any use of Darkness would probably get me instant execution."

"If we get Dr. Timberi back, it won't matter," Lexa said. "They couldn't execute you for helping to save him. Pilaf, make the bubble go away."

Pilaf frowned. "Conner told me not to help you do anything until he got here."

"Pilaf, please!" Lexa grabbed him by both hands. "You have to!"

He shook his head and pulled his hands away. "I think we'd better wait for Conner. Why is this is so urgent anyway? Why not let the Phalanx find him? Or at least wait and see what they find?"

"Pilaf, I have to!" Lexa said. "I swore the Magi's Oath that I would find him. Please, Pilaf. I have to do this. It's my fault he's gone."

"No," Timothy said. "It's mine. Pilaf, please. The Phalanx will never get inside that base, I guarantee that. There will be all kinds of booby traps. At best, they won't find anything. Most likely they'll be slaughtered. But if you can deactivate this bubble somehow, I think I can—"

"No!" Pilaf said, folding his scrawny arms across his chest. "Not until Conner gets here."

Lexa screamed and fell to the floor as pain tore through her, removing her ability to stand or move or even breathe. The pain seemed to loosen her spirit from her body, prying them apart in a real and literal way.

Her vision merged with Dr. Timberi's, and once more she fought the dizziness that came from a shared consciousness.

"Oh dear," Lady Nightwing wheezed. "I turned it up too high. How clumsy of me. Another blast like that would kill you, Morgan. And what would be the fun in that?"

A warm tear dropped onto his cheek, forming a stark contrast to the fires of pain still smoldering throughout his body.

Nothing. He. Would. Say. Nothing.

"Do you know what this machine does, Morgan?" Even scarred and injured, Lady Nightwing's malicious energy gleamed through her eyes. "It's truly amazing. You know how the Shadowbox works, correct? It causes great spiritual suffering. And you know that a refraction collar causes great physical pain. Some people think that emotional suffering is worse than physical pain. But I decided that was a false choice. Why settle for just one?

"This invention allows you to feel it all! It generates mental images that cause you emotional and psychic pain. These electrodes then send signals to this box, which translates emotional distress into an equal amount of physical pain for your nerves! They amplify each other—synergy, if you will!" She patted a black box with copper-colored wires running from it. "So much neater and efficient than the old ways."

Lexa struggled to keep her thoughts together. The waves of pain blurred every line between body and spirit, tearing through her consciousness. Not only physical pain. Not only horror and emotional suffering. Massive waves of both. Great, burning wildfires that roared everywhere, in and out—Dr. Timberi passed out, and the connection ended.

As Lexa came back to herself, she struggled past the dizziness she felt. She looked around the room. Conner had joined them, a pained expression on his face as he stared at her.

"Guys," she said. "We have to do something. Now! I'm serious. It's really bad. He won't last much longer."

Lexa staggered and almost fell as the connection jumped back open, forcing and clawing its way into her mind. She managed to stand only because Melanie and Conner caught her.

The blackness faded, and Lady Nightwing's voice came back. "Now, Morgan, you get so sleepy all the time! I didn't want the fun to end so soon." She pulled a syringe away from him, and Dr. Timberi's pulse pounded, running at a speed far beyond normal as the chemicals took effect. "This will keep you awake and conscious for a nice long time! I'll give that a few seconds to work, and then we'll start again with my new toy!"

Lexa, is that you? he whispered.

Yes, I'm here!

Don't stay. Please. Too awful for you. Won't last long now.

She could feel him struggling to pull his thoughts together and focus. The pain—and the effects of the drugs—smashed through his attempts at coherent thought like twin wrecking balls.

He managed to say, *Love you all.* Then he closed the connection.

Lexa looked at Melanie and Conner, who still held her, cables of Light linking their heads together.

"Did you guys see any of that?" she asked.

Melanie and Conner nodded.

Conner looked at Timothy. "Can you get him out of there with a sigil trap?"

Timothy nodded. "I think. I can't promise. I don't know what kind of security Lady Nightwing might have around him. But I don't think she would expect us to try that, so it might work."

Conner looked at Pilaf. "Can you neutralize the bubble around Timothy?"

SIGIL TRAPS

"WAIT," MELANIE SAID. "WE NEED TO BE super careful. That sigil is our only link to Dr. Timberi. If we lose it, we have nothing."

"When I did the sigil trace to find Notzange, everyone linked their sigils to mine," Lexa said. "Couldn't we do that? Connect our sigils to his? Then we wouldn't lose track of it."

Melanie nodded. "That's a good idea."

"How do I extract it?" Lexa said.

"You just tell it to go out," Pilaf said. "A sigil can't stay in your soul without permission. It's against the Light." He smiled. "I read that when I was studying for my test."

"As soon as it's out, everyone link to it fast," Melanie said.

"How long will it take to do a sigil trap?"

Timothy shrugged. "A minute. Maybe more. They're complex."

"What if there's some kind of sensor attached to the

bubble?" Conner asked. "Will alarms go off if Pilaf makes it go away?"

"We have to take that risk," Lexa said. "Seriously, we can't waste any more time. Just get the trap made and I'll send out his sigil. But I don't want to do it until the trap is done. You guys get ready to link your sigils to Dr. Timberi's."

Melanie held her breath as Pilaf walked up to Timothy. He reached out and grabbed the shield as if he was pulling a sheet off a bed. The Light vanished.

Timothy's hands flew in front of him, weaving and twisting. A tiny spark of Darkness flew from his fingers, then faded away.

"What's wrong?" Lexa yelled.

"I can't connect to the Darkness!" Panic echoed through Timothy's voice.

Outside, piercing alarms shattered the silence, followed by shouts and pounding footsteps.

"Hurry!" Lexa yelled.

"I can't do it!" Timothy flicked his hands over and over, but nothing came. "The Light's too strong in here."

The door started to open, but Conner streamed over, slamming it shut.

"Hurry!" he groaned. "I can't hold this forever."

The shouts and pounding outside grew louder.

Conner groaned as the door shook with something like a battering ram. "They'll blast through this in a second," he yelled, "and they're not going to be happy with us."

Amid all the panic and noise, the symbols on Melanie's whiteboard clicked into place. "We need to Translocate him like we did when you sent Blinson to the dumpster," she yelled. "He can't use Darkness in here." Melanie pushed Timothy down to the door.

"Where to?" Lexa asked.

"Outside the gate, hurry!" Melanie said.

"I need you and Conner."

Conner groaned something that sounded like, "Hurry!" He yanked his hand away as an ax came through the door, and then pushed back against a different part of the door.

Lexa closed her eyes, facing Timothy. Yellow sparks crackled in the air around her. Melanie grabbed her hand, and pink sparks joined the yellow.

"Now, Conner!" Lexa yelled.

Conner grabbed Melanie's other hand. As soon as he did that, a flash of Light tore through the room. Red, pink, and yellow, it looked like a sunset had exploded. Timothy vanished.

Get out of here! Conner shouted. *I've got Pilaf!*

As the door flew open, the guards shot hot blasts of Light into the room. Melanie ran, turning into a comet, then shot up through the ceiling. Up into the assembly room, then outside the thick walls. She passed through the shield that surrounded the château with a whistling shriek.

Lexa landed at the same time as Melanie, with Conner's red comet a second behind. As Conner faded back to his human form, he shook Pilaf off—Pilaf, who with his rubber gloves, was strangling Conner.

Timothy's hands had already started weaving. Darkness swirled and spun in front of him, sparkling like black glitter in whirlwind. It spun into the shape of an hourglass, which stretched out, growing taller and taller.

"Done!" Timothy yelled.

"Now!" Lexa closed her eyes and flicked her hand out. A pale, ragged swan made out of golden Light shot out of her chest.

"Hurry and connect to it!" Melanie linked her unicorn sigil to the swan with a thin cord of pink Light. Lexa's yellow dolphin and Conner's red German shepherd followed right behind.

Shouts filled the grounds of the château, punctuated by whistling shrieks as dozens of comets streamed out of the shield.

The swan floated into the column of shimmering blackness, followed by the unicorn, dolphin, and dog.

Dr. Timberi did not appear—and Melanie knew something was wrong.

The Darkness shook and trembled, and Melanie's soul seemed caught in a tug of war. She'd felt that before. The first time they'd encountered Timothy, he'd put them under some kind of compulsive spell. As the tug grew stronger, Melanie could no longer think or talk.

A whirlpool of Darkness opened inside of the sigil trap. It grew bigger, exerting an irresistible pull.

He tricked us! Conner yelled. *Let go! It's a trap—*

The warning came too late.

Melanie's body snapped into her sigil, following it into total darkness.

REUNITED

DARKNESS SURROUNDED LEXA, PRESSING down on her chest until she couldn't breathe. It rushed in through her mouth and nose, clogging her lungs and throat. From there it forced itself into her mind and heart, filling her soul with a terrible and growing fear she could not understand or explain.

Strange and terrible noises filled the Darkness like nightmares on a microphone: gurgling, growling shrieks, distorted laughter, and screams.

Darkness flashed, with each flash somehow darker than the surrounding Darkness in the same way the cherubim seemed brighter than lightning.

Did the cherubim have counterparts, creatures made of Darkness who had their own realm?

Terrible wails sent waves of despair roiling through and around her.

One of her last thoughts was that Timothy had tricked them. Or had Lady Nightwing put some special shields around Dr. Timberi? With mounting depression, Lexa realized she knew almost nothing about what the Darkhands could do.

And then it ended.

Lexa's feet landed on something hard. Her vision cleared, and some of the Darkness left. It still filled the air all around, but she no longer felt it inside of her.

Through the haze, she saw a man stretched out on a metal table, covered by a web of wires. A woman in black turned around with a surprised look on her scarred, shrunken face. After a second or two of shock, she laughed. "Did you really just walk into another trap? Haven't we done this once before? You didn't think you could just pull him out with a sigil, did you? I wondered if anyone would be stupid enough to try that." She laughed a wheezing, rattling laugh.

Lexa raised her hands to shoot, but no Light came out. She couldn't connect to her gateway, so instead, she jumped, tackling Lady Nightwing and knocking her down to the floor with a satisfying thunk. Balling her hands into fists, Lexa pounded Lady Nightwing, fuelled by the pent-up anger and frustration of the last long weeks.

She became aware of Melanie doing the same thing, then Lexa's hand hit the metal floor as Lady Nightwing began to fade into smoke.

"No, you don't!" Pilaf yelled, accompanied by the snap of rubber as he tore his dish-washing gloves off. He jumped through the air and grabbed a fistful of smoke, neutralizing it so it faded back into the surprised face of Lady Nightwing.

Lady Nightwing shrieked and thrashed, but Pilaf

clung to her left foot like a koala bear grasping a branch in a hurricane. With Pilaf neutralizing her powers, Lexa and Melanie continued to pummel her.

"I've got him!" Conner yelled, and Lexa looked over her shoulder to see Dr. Timberi slumped against Conner's back, almost like he was getting a piggyback ride.

As much as I like the idea of you two pounding Lady Nightwing into pulp, I think we need to get Dr. Timberi out of here, Conner said. *Any ideas?*

I've still got his key to the Otherwhere, Melanie said.

Can you open a portal? Conner said.

Melanie stopped hitting Lady Nightwing long enough to pull a chain from around her neck with an old-fashioned key dangling down. *Hold her tight, you guys,* she said. *Don't let her get away.*

Melanie thrust the key into the air in front of her—and nothing happened. She tried it again.

Lady Nightwing laughed. "You can't open a portal to the Otherwhere here. Was that really your plan?" She pulled her right foot back and smashed it into Pilaf's face.

The blow knocked him backward and he let go of her. Lady Nightwing faded into smoke and spun out of the room in a cyclone. As she disappeared, Melanie thought she saw a second cyclone—vanishing just seconds after hers.

When Lexa ran over to Conner and Dr. Timberi, her throat swelled with so much emotion she thought she might choke. Dr. Timberi was barely alive. Had they come too late?

"Are you okay?" Melanie asked, grabbing his pale hand.

Dr. Timberi's mouth fluttered into a weak, tattered smile. "Yes. Now." His voice had grown hoarse and ragged.

Conner, Melanie said. *Is that collar still on him?*

I tore it off already, Conner said.

How about the ticks?

Barbecued. Conner nodded at several charred spots on the floor. *But it took almost all my strength just to zap those tiny bugs.*

We need to get some Light into him right away, Melanie said. *I'll try to Augment him, but I need your help. I can hardly open my gateway.*

Melanie took Conner's hand, then grabbed Lexa's.

Lexa closed her eyes and sent as much Light as she could into Melanie. She sensed Conner doing the same. It took far more effort than normal. Instead of a raging river, Lexa felt like she squeezed out a few drops.

She opened her eyes and saw that Conner's face looked like it did when he wrestled. Melanie looked like she might pop something.

Are you guys having a hard time? Lexa grunted.

Yeah, I can barely do anything, Conner grunted in return.

A small cloud of soft pink, yellow, and red Light flowed out of Melanie's hands into Dr. Timberi.

It shouldn't be this hard, Conner said. *I thought we were supposed to be super powerful together.*

I think we are, Melanie replied. *I don't think anyone else could have used the Light at all.*

Dr. Timberi opened his eyes and smiled a weak but genuine smile. "Thank you, Melanie," he said in a voice more like his old self. "How did you do that? It's impossible to use the Light down here. Well beyond the strength of any Magus." His voice sounded soft and faint, like someone had turned a recording down low.

"We have a lot to tell you," Melanie said.

"I will be interested to—" Dr. Timberi seemed to notice that he was draped over Conner's shoulders. "Awkwaaard," he said, pulling himself onto his own feet.

"Are you okay?" Conner asked as Dr. Timberi staggered, then toppled over.

Lexa went to stabilize him, but Melanie got there first.

"I will be fine," Dr. Timberi replied. "But perhaps I could lean on your arm. That infusion of Light helped. But I am embarrassingly weak."

"I'll help—" Lexa stepped forward, but Melanie got there first again, stepping between Lexa and Dr. Timberi.

Melanie wrapped her arm around Dr. Timberi's waist and then put his arm around her shoulder. "Lean on me, Uncle Morgan."

Dr. Timberi beamed at Melanie. "You found out!"

Melanie nodded. "It all came out at Timothy's tribunal."

Dr. Timberi's pale, worn face lit up. "Then you got him away safely? Have they sentenced him yet?"

Melanie sent out tiny cables of Light with a private message for Conner and Lexa.

Should we tell him?

Tell him that the son he gave his life to rescue just betrayed him again? Conner said. *No way. If we get out of here, there will be time.*

Lexa said nothing. She didn't trust herself to speak at that moment. The feelings she struggled with needed a thick wall of silence.

Melanie looked back at Dr. Timberi. "Madame Cumberland's working on that. Right now we need to get out of here."

"How did you get in?" he asked.

"We used your Last Sigil to do a trace," Melanie said. "We attached our sigils to your swan and then—" She stopped and looked at Pilaf. "Wait a minute, how did you get here, Pilaf?"

Pilaf giggled and waved his gloves in the air. "When that dark vortex appeared, I figured something bad had happened. I didn't want to abandon you, so I slipped my gloves on and grabbed hold of Conner. I'm getting really fast with the gloves."

Dr. Timberi looked at Pilaf. "Gloves?"

"The rubber insulates my power so I don't neutralize Light. Or Dark."

Looking at Pilaf, Lexa noticed gooey blood all over his face. "Oh, Pilaf," she said. "Your nose! I think it's broken." Crooked and swollen, it now matched his enormous glasses—which also looked broken. He shrugged. "Yeah, she kicked pretty hard. It was worth it, though, to watch you two hit her." He giggled again.

"You two did what?" Dr. Timberi asked.

Once more Lexa opened her mouth. But Melanie spoke before her. "Lexa and I pounded Lady Nightwing like bread dough." At that point, Lexa realized that Melanie wasn't being rude. It was a two-person conversation. Dr. Timberi was talking to Melanie, not to the group.

Dr. Timberi smiled. "I wish I had been more conscious. The drugs she gave me to keep me awake left me groggy and unable to focus."

"We really need to get out of here," Melanie said. "Conner, can you break down the door?"

Conner took a few steps back and ran, throwing

himself against the door, which smashed open after just a few tries. Apparently his strength wasn't diminished by the Darkness. Maybe because it was inside of him, like music that had already been downloaded, instead of a song on the radio that could be interrupted. Hopefully their other gifts were intact as well: Lexa's theelings and Melanie's ability to Augment. Those could be important.

Conner walked through the door, followed by Melanie and her Uncle Morgan.

"I am glad you found out, Melanie," Dr. Timberi said. "It has been difficult to not say anything. You are so very like Nicole."

Lexa struggled to keep her boiling feelings contained inside the wall of silence. This had not gone according to plan. She would rescue Dr. Timberi, who would thank her for her heroic efforts. She would apologize, and he would cry and tell her he owed his life to her and say that he would be eternally grateful—

Stop it. Lexa tugged on her ponytail. *Stop it!* She realized with terrible embarrassment that she had written a little drama and cast herself as the star. It had all been about her. Her chance at redemption. Her chance to be the hero. Her chance to be Dr. Timberi's favorite again.

Ashamed of herself, she tried to push those thoughts away. But they didn't leave. Every time Lexa heard the words "Uncle Morgan," she felt like another level of a wall had been built. A wall that kept her outside. Again.

I can't hear you! Lexa shouted at her thoughts. *I'm not listening!* She pasted a smile on her face, telling herself how wonderful it was that Dr. Timberi had found his niece.

If she couldn't stop thinking unpleasant thoughts, she would choose not to act on them.

Conner helped Melanie and Dr. Timberi through the broken door, then Pilaf. Then he looked at Lexa. "You okay, Lex?" he asked.

"Yeah, fine," she said with a bright smile. "Just thinking. How are we going to get out of here?

"I don't know," he said. "But if I ever find Timothy, I'm going to make what you guys did to Lady Nightwing look like a day at the spa."

Dr. Timberi's cell led into a large circular room made entirely of black metal panels between black metal beams. Lexa figured it had to be at least half a football field in diameter. A single, small door across from them looked like the only exit.

I don't like this, Lexa, Conner said. *There's so much Darkness. I've never felt it this strong except when*—"Run!" Conner yelled as terror and panic sprinted across his face. "Get out of here!"

All around them, the metal wall panels slid down, revealing windows.

Conner threw his hands over his ears.

"NO!" he shouted as the walls slid away. Outside the thick, clear walls, dark water surrounded them, filled with shadows squirming like maggots on dead meat.

"It's a Shadowbox!" Conner yelled, pushing everyone forward to the door. "We walked into a giant Shadowbox!"

THE SHADOWBOX

COLD, PARALYZING FEAR GRABBED CONNER. He'd been through this before. And it had nearly driven him insane. He couldn't stand it again. Either his soul would become twisted and evil, or his mind would snap and break forever. This time, the cherubim couldn't give him extra protection. He would end up crazy or really become a Darkhand, doomed to hurt and destroy.

Images of what he'd done before burst into his mind, images of Melanie sobbing in a heap on the floor. The things he'd said to her slithered back into his mind. The ugly, destructive words he'd used to shred her emotions into torn and bleeding—

Conner. Conner, come join us! Free the shadows in your heart.

As the shadows called him, a terrible, sweet poison coursed through his spirit, coaxing him, luring him. He wanted to do this. Wanted to—

NO! he yelled. *No! No!*

But the shadows grew stronger. They pulled at him, taunting him, reminding him, and showing him new, even worse visions.

And then they stopped.

"Conner, are you okay?"

Conner looked up into a face with a swollen crooked nose and two blinking eyes.

"Pilaf?"

"Sorry, it took me a minute to get to you. My glasses fell off and I can't see."

A bright red rash sprung up across Pilaf's face. Conner realized what had happened. Pilaf was neutralizing the Darkness, stopping the Shadowbox.

"Pilaf, you can't—"

Pilaf grinned. "Yeah, right. Like you wouldn't do the same thing. I need you to help me find the others. I can't see very well." Melanie screamed, followed by Lexa sobbing.

"But, Pilaf, you can't absorb all that Darkness—

"Conner!" Real anger flared in Pilaf's voice. "Which one of my friends should I leave down there to suffer? If you could carry everyone out of here but it would make you sick, would you even hesitate? Stop wasting time. We'd better start with Dr. Timberi. He's the weakest."

Conner shut his mouth. He'd just been schooled by Pilaf. "You're right. Dr. Timberi's right here."

Keeping hold of Pilaf's right hand, Conner pulled Dr. Timberi up and placed Dr. Timberi's right hand in Pilaf's left. Dr. Timberi sighed. "Oh, thank you, Conner. Thank you, Pilaf. I don't think I could have held on to sanity much longer." He shivered and wiped some sweat off his face with his free hand. Conner wanted to ask what he'd seen but stopped. The Shadowbox made you see yourself doing the worst things you could imagine, so it was very personal.

They found Lexa next, and Conner helped her up and put her hand on Pilaf's left arm. Lexa sniffed and rubbed tears out of her eyes. "That was awful!" she said, still crying.

"It's all right, Lexa," Dr. Timberi said in a soft voice. "It's over now. It won't hurt you anymore." He started singing the lullaby Lexa had recently sung to him.

Conner picked Melanie up. She didn't make any noise, but her whole body trembled, and her skin had grown so pale it almost glowed in the dark. When Conner attached her to Pilaf's right arm, she hugged them. "Thank you," she said in a small voice. "I'm so sorry."

"For what?" Conner asked.

"That you went through that. For more than a minute or two. How awful." She held on to Pilaf with tight fingers, but she also gripped Conner—something he didn't mind at all.

They tried to move in the direction Pilaf thought he remembered seeing the door. But the room had no light, so he couldn't be sure. They had to shuffle at a slow crawl because if anyone let go of Pilaf, the agony of the Shadowbox returned with a vengeance.

The crawl slowed as Pilaf hunched over, growing sicker and weaker with every step.

With Pilaf hunched over, it grew harder to keep connected to him. Someone seemed to let go of him every few steps, falling to the ground, and shrieking until contact with Pilaf had been reestablished.

After Dr. Timberi had stumbled and let go for the third time, Pilaf said in a shaky, queasy voice, "Conner, tear my shirt off."

"What?"

"You need more surface area of skin," Pilaf said between gasps. "And I want to keep my pants. My shirt's the only option."

Careful to keep one hand on Pilaf's skin at all times, Conner tore Pilaf's shirt off, freeing up more skin for people to touch.

Then Pilaf stumbled and fell. For a terrible, panic-filled moment, the shadows filled Conner. He heard everyone else scream as well. It stopped when Pilaf reached up and re-touched his hand. Conner grabbed Melanie and reattached her. Pilaf found Lexa's hand, and she got Dr. Timberi.

Pilaf vomited, his pale, bony shoulders heaving and shaking. Conner started to cry as he watched this tiny, blinking kid making himself deathly ill to stop everyone else's suffering.

"I'm sorry. I can't walk anymore," Pilaf whispered. Conner scooped him up, cradling him like a baby.

"Take my shoes off," Pilaf gasped. "And my socks."

Melanie and Lexa did as he asked. Pilaf put an arm around Conner's neck and gave the other one to Dr. Timberi. Lexa and Melanie each grabbed a foot.

"Pilaf," Melanie said, "can you control how much Darkness you filter from each of us?"

"Maybe," he whispered. "Why?"

"What if you just reduced the Darkness instead of eliminating it? Make it so we have some bad stuff, but that it doesn't overwhelm us? If you neutralize less Darkness, maybe you won't be as sick."

"I'll try," Pilaf whispered.

Shadows slid back into Conner's mind, but this time, they didn't overpower him. They just scared him.

The room changed from the Shadowbox room to a circus where clowns with sharp-toothed smiles flew at him with sharp power tools.

He screamed as a clown with a chain saw came right next to him. But nothing happened.

The clown came again and again. But nothing happened. The other clowns did the same. But still, nothing happened.

Conner realized he had gone into a terrible nightmare but nothing worse. Unpleasant. Upsetting. But not like the Shadowbox. The shadows could scare him but not hurt him. They couldn't get inside of him. It was the difference between dog-paddling in a hurricane and being in a boat.

CHAPTER 36

BACK TO SCHOOL

"WAIT!" MELANIE YELLED. "EVERYONE stop." She took a deep breath, trying to clear her mind and ignore the slimy things with hundreds of bacteria-rich legs crawling all over her. "Okay, I think I figured something out. We're all seeing different things. Our own nightmares, right? Pilaf's dampening the Shadowbox so it's only scary, but it's still unique to each of us. If we're going to get out of here, we need to get on the same page and have the same nightmare."

"How do we do that?" Lexa asked.

"Well, I have an idea," Melanie said. "Two, actually. First of all, everyone needs to connect their thoughts to each other." She paused as thin strands of colored Light shot through the Darkness. "I'm connecting to Pilaf," Conner said.

Okay, Melanie said, *can everyone hear me?*

Everyone answered that they could.

Here's the next part. I hope this works.

Lexa screamed as a zombie clown with an ice pick ran at her. *Conner! I don't like your nightmares,* she said.

Melanie took another deep breath, trying to stop her thoughts from scattering. *Everyone think of the most miserable day you had in middle school. Exaggerate it and make it worse than it really was.*

Melanie remembered her first day in middle school and the anxiety she felt as she went to a new building, leaving behind the safety and comfort of Mrs. Beuter's fifth grade homeroom. Now she'd have multiple teachers. What if they were mean? What if she got bad grades? What if people made fun of her?

She focused on her fear of the big kids. What would those giant eighth grade boys do to little sixth graders? And what about the older girls? She'd heard they could be really mean on Facebook . . .

The swamp in her nightmares vanished, replaced by the main entry hall of the middle school at Marion Academy. The halls were dark, lit only by spooky red light glowing from the exit signs.

There's the front desk where Mrs. Lehman sits! Lexa yelled.

A little flutter of hope jumped in Melanie's chest. The middle school—even in creepy light—felt like home. But the second that feeling came, the school faded, replaced by twisted swamp trees hiding creepy, germ-ridden reptiles—

Melanie refocused on her bad school memories, and the middle school came back into view.

Keep focused on your bad memories, she said. *Don't let anything happy come into your mind or you'll lose it. We have to trick the Shadowbox by making it think we fear the middle school.*

Melanie walked up to the front desk in the lobby. *Okay, let's make sure we're seeing the same things.* She held up a pad of paper. *What do you see in my hand?*

Mrs. Lehman's demerit pad! Lexa shouted.

That's what I see too, Conner added.

Me three, Pilaf said in a soft, weak voice. But he didn't sound as weak, Melanie thought. Or maybe she just hoped.

Don't get excited! Melanie said. *Stay focused on bad stuff. Remember the Shadowbox reflects our fears.*

I am so terrified of a warm beach and Mexican food, Conner muttered.

Now what? Lexa asked. *How do we get out of the Shadowbox room?*

Melanie paused to think, willing her whiteboard to life. *We saw the exit to the Shadowbox, so we know it's somewhere. I'll bet it's incorporated into our nightmare. I think we should start by finding all the exits in the building,* Melanie added. *One of the exits in our bad dreams has to be the real exit. Right?*

But there are like four or five different exits in the middle school, Lexa said.

Right. We have to try them all.

A terrible noise interrupted them as zombie clowns with hedge trimmers rode toward them on giant centipedes.

Just hold still! Melanie shouted—mostly to herself. *They can't hurt us.*

She gritted her teeth as the terrifying stampede rushed up . . . and then vanished.

Let's start with the front doors, Lexa said. *They're closest.*

Huddling together, they turned around and walked across the lobby to the front doors. Conner pushed them open—and they stepped into Mrs. Grant's English classroom.

Endless sentences appeared on the board, waiting to be diagrammed while nightmare-Mrs. Grant cackled something about Conner never playing sports again. Then she grinned at them with pointed teeth and turned into a monster.

Staying connected to Pilaf, they shuffled out of Mrs. Grant's room and went down the stairs, heading for the nearest exit. Walking down stairs while keeping four people connected to Pilaf required them to move at a very slow pace. Halfway down, Pilaf shouted, "Close your eyes! Right now!"

Melanie clamped her eyes shut. Conner laughed.

"Conner!" Pilaf yelled. "I told you to close your eyes."

"Sorry," Conner said. "I tripped."

A few seconds later, Pilaf said, "Okay, you can open them."

Melanie looked at Conner with an unspoken question. He whispered in her ear, "Pilaf dreamed he came to school in his underwear."

Melanie shuddered. She hated that dream. And to have it in front of everyone—she tried to change her thoughts before the Shadowbox picked up on it and made that happen.

There's the exit! Conner pointed to an emergency exit that led to the parking lot.

They ran through the doors—and found themselves inside the theater.

Melanie recognized a nightmare version of the battle when they'd fought Lady Nightwing, the night Dr. Timberi gave himself up to save Timothy. In the nightmare, Lady Nightwing stood there, holding a knife at Timothy's throat, laughing.

The nightmare version of Dr. Timberi shrugged. "Why should I care?" He walked offstage, leaving Timothy in Lady Nightwing's clutches.

Melanie looked up at the real Dr. Timberi, who cringed and closed his eyes. As he groaned, Melanie said, *Hurry, we need to get out of here!*

They stumbled through the theater exits—which led into the cafeteria, where another dream-version of Dr. Timberi stood, frozen as Timothy sent all the knives from the kitchen hurtling toward dream versions of Melanie and Lexa.

It was exactly what had happened last April.

Just as he had in real life, Timothy threw shadow knives at nightmare-Dr. Timberi's back.

Except, this time, dream-Dr. Timberi shielded himself, leaving Melanie and Lexa unprotected with kitchen cutlery rushing at them.

"No!" real Uncle Morgan shouted. "NO!"

CHAPTER 37

LEXA'S NIGHTMARE

IT HIT LEXA WITH FLASH-FLOOD FORCE THAT Dr. Timberi's nightmares involved letting people down. In his worst dreams, he put himself before others.

She admired that. So different from her nightmares, which no one had seen yet because no one could.

Lexa's deepest fears didn't involve reptiles or zombies. What terrified her was nothingness. Not mattering. Being invisible. Left out. Alone.

No one saw her nightmares because in her most terrifying dreams Lexa didn't exist, and no one cared or even noticed. Everyone she loved most went on with happy lives, without her. Being nothing and not mattering terrified Lexa far more than anything she could think of.

They tried exit after exit. Each time they ended up somewhere else in the school, with no apparent logic or pattern.

Nightmares kept attacking them. When mean girls posted terribly embarrassing pictures of Melanie on every social media platform possible, Lexa screamed, "Conner! Behind you!"

Conner jerked his head over his shoulder. "What is it?" he said

"It's gone now," Lexa replied. "Just a monster."

"Oh, okay," he said and then checked on Pilaf, who looked worse and worse.

"Conner didn't see," Lexa whispered. Melanie squeezed Lexa's arm. "Thank you," she whispered back.

They turned a corner, maybe twenty yards from the last exit, the only set of doors they had not yet tried.

"Come on, guys, this has to be it!" Lexa tried to imitate a cheerleader. "We can make it!"

With escape in sight, they shuffled forward, and Lexa hoped they weren't too late. Pilaf's spells of unconsciousness lasted much longer. Dr. Timberi moved like a crippled old man, shaking and moaning, and his color had grown worse.

Almost there! Lexa said. *Once we're out of the Shadow-box, it will be better. The Twilight Phalanx is here somewhere. We'll just send them a sigil and—*

With a triumphant flourish, Lexa pushed the bar on the door.

Nothing happened. She struggled again, then looked down and saw chains appear, wrapping around the handles, cinching the doors together.

Let me try, Conner said. He kicked one of the doors, and the chains jerked tight. He kicked again, and Lexa thought the door handles might have bent a little.

Another kick. The handles bent a little more.

Melanie, do you have any Light left? Conner asked. *If you can Augment me even just a bit—*

A pale, pathetic cloud of pink floated out of Melanie's chest and into Conner.

He kicked again. The handles bent more noticeably.

One more kick, and this time, with a screeching shriek, the handles tore away, allowing the doors to swing open.

They limped through the door—and found themselves in the gym. They were still trapped.

A smog of despair filled the air as hope evaporated. No one said anything. They collapsed on the wrestling mats, too exhausted to talk or cry. A tiny moan parted Pilaf's lips. Then he went still.

The Trio sent Light into him, but it dribbled out of them in such tiny little flecks that it seemed like treating cancer with ibuprofen.

How long had they been playing Lady Nightwing's sick cat-and-mouse game? Did they even know that there was a way out?

The image of quicksand flashed in Lexa's head. The more you thrashed and flailed, the tighter you got sucked in. Was this place like quicksand for the brain? Would it become more tangled the more they thought about it? Maybe Melanie's calculations hadn't worked because the Shadowbox wasn't linear or logical.

What kind of prison could be more effective than a prison of the mind? If you didn't know what reality was, you could never escape.

Lady Nightwing had created the ultimate prison for Magi.

For Magi.

A theeling sprouted in Lexa's heart and mind—a flicker of knowledge that burst from a spark into a blazing, blinding light. Lady Nightwing had created an unbreakable prison for Magi. But only Magi.

A regular person wouldn't be trapped. A regular person would escape like a tiny fish swimming through a net made for a shark.

Another theeling came now, one that made Lexa cringe and shrink.

She couldn't bear it, couldn't go along with it.

"Dr. Timberi's almost gone!" Conner yelled. "Can you Augment him or something?"

Melanie touched Dr. Timberi and then shook her head, crying in frustration. "I don't have any more. It's all gone."

As his hand fell away from Pilaf, Dr. Timberi writhed on the ground, screaming as the Shadowbox overcame him.

They stumbled around, trying to reconnect him with Pilaf, and Lexa remembered Dr. Timberi's nightmares: being selfish and not protecting those who needed him.

She looked at Pilaf, who was no longer breathing, his skin whiter than her mother's wedding china.

Lexa realized she didn't have any choice. And she knew exactly what to say. The words appeared in her mind. Raising her arm to the square and struggling to squeeze each word out, she said, "I, Alexandra Louise Dell, hereby Renounce my powers as a Magi—I mean Magus. I bind myself to this course with all the power of the Light within me."

"Lexa, no!" Melanie and Conner yelled together. Dr. Timberi parted his lips and whispered something.

Lexa doubled over as something rushed out of her—physically, mentally, spiritually, and emotionally. She couldn't breathe, and her whole being screamed as part of her soul was sliced away. The loss of whatever had rushed out left her smaller, diminished, and weak.

Warm arms encircled her.

"Lexa, are you okay?" Melanie asked.

Lexa tried to stand, but her knees grew weak and wobbly, and she fell.

"Lex?" Conner put his arm around her and pulled her back up.

Lexa fought through a growing forest of emptiness and despair. She had work to do. Blinking, she looked around at the newly revealed location.

The nightmare Marion Academy had vanished, replaced by a large, round chamber made of metal beams framing enormous windows that looked out into the black water. Cobwebs of copper wires dangled from the beams all around the room.

There was nothing else.

Lexa walked over to the door. "What am I standing by?" she asked.

"The basketball hoop," Conner said at the same time Melanie said, "The bleachers."

"It was all a trick," Lexa said. She walked back to them and helped Melanie pull Dr. Timberi to his feet. "Follow me."

She led them to the door, which opened after Conner pounded it several times. They walked through the doorway and into a long hallway, where every metal surface had been painted silver.

"What do you see?" Lexa asked.

"We're at the end of a long silver hallway," Melanie said.

Lexa nodded, afraid to allow shattered hopes to torment her again. "What are the walls made out of?"

"Huge glass windows," Melanie said.

"With big metal beams in between them," Conner said.

"And outside is dark water that looks very deep and probably very cold," Melanie said.

"I think we're out of the Shadowbox," Lexa said. "We made it."

Out of habit, Lexa raised her arm and tried to send a sigil. Nothing came. Except searing sadness.

Oh yeah. She didn't have powers anymore.

Lexa had become nothing.

"Can one of you send a sigil?" Lexa asked. "If we can let Lee know we're here, maybe we can go home."

Melanie raised her hand and sent a pink unicorn through the glass walls. But it dissolved when it hit the water.

"It is very difficult for Light to stay together this far underwater," Dr. Timberi wheezed. He looked a little better now that they had left the Shadowbox. But not much. "It's one of the reasons they choose this location."

"Wait!" Lexa said. "I saw Melanie's sigil! Does that mean my powers are coming back?"

"I'm sorry, Lexa," Dr. Timberi said in a soft voice. "Renunciation is final. Your powers can't come back. I'm so sorry." He put an unsteady hand on her shoulder. "But you have grown accustomed to seeing the Light. Your eyes are awakened to it, and I don't imagine that will change."

"At least there's a little light out here," Melanie said, pointing to the florescent lights above. She closed her eyes and sent pale clouds of pink light into both Dr. Timberi and Pilaf.

Pilaf didn't open his eyes, but his breathing seemed to

become more regular. Dr. Timberi sighed and didn't look as likely to die in the next few minutes. "Thank you, Melanie," he said. "But please be careful—after that ordeal, you can't have much Light to give. Don't wear yourself out."

They walked forward, surrounded on both sides by the endless, dark underbelly of the ocean. It made Lexa feel heavy and closed in.

Progress was slow because every few yards they had to step through thick steel frames—big rectangles of steel with an opening in the center like what she'd see on a submarine in the movies. The openings were each about a foot off the ground, difficult for the weakened Dr. Timberi and for Conner, who carried Pilaf.

At the end of the silver hallway, they climbed through one more doorway and found themselves at the intersection of two passageways. The silver hallway continued straight ahead of them. Another hallway, this one painted red, ran to their right and left.

Melanie looked down the red hallway. "The passageway on each side of us is a giant circle," she said. "Right, Lexa?" Lexa nodded. The red hallway on their right and left circled away, forming a huge glass ring around a massive pillar of rock that disappeared in the black water above and the blacker water below. The silver hallway in front of them led straight into the rock about fifty yards ahead of them. Additional rings connected to passageways above and below them, all growing out of the massive rock formation. All the tubes and tunnels reminded Melanie of a giant hamster habitat.

"This structure is made of acrylic and steel. They have special cells and Shadowbox suites projecting out into the ocean," Dr. Timberi said. "Each tube has its own color to make navigating easier because there are no other land-marks out here. That's what we just left. Lady Nightwing gave me a tour before she locked me up. She wanted me to see her triumph. That cliff is an underwater mountain housing Umbra's base of operations. The whole structure is designed to enhance Darkness by providing maximum exposure to the darkness of the ocean. I do not know every-thing they are doing, but Lady Nightwing is conducting all kinds of research here. None of it, of course, is good."

"How do we get out?" Conner asked.

"The only way out is straight ahead, through the moun-tain, and up to the surface," Dr. Timberi said. "Which means we had better hurry before someone notices we are not where they want us."

They walked forward, stepping through another of the double metal frames. Lexa noticed big, red buttons behind glass on both sides with "EMERGENCY" painted above them in red letters.

"What are these?" she asked.

"This far underwater, the pressure outside is immense," Dr. Timberi said. "The tiniest leak could cause the whole structure to implode. Each of these frames has a heavy door above it. In case of a breach, doors will drop down and seal off any leaking sections. A complicated series of pumps then work to equalize pressure and prevent a leak in one area from destroying the rest of the structure. She was quite proud of this system, bragging incessantly about every detail—watch out!"

The smell of sulfur and smoke filled the corridor. Lexa looked up and saw a burning ball of blackness rushing down the silver hall at them.

THE BLACK SWAN

CONNER THREW HIMSELF ON THE GROUND, shielding Pilaf with his body. He worried that even a little Darkness might be enough to finish Pilaf.

Another blast followed the first one, filling the air with sparkling, sizzling Darkness.

As the fire sped toward Pilaf, Conner reached out with his mind. Shadows mixed with anger, one cold, the other hot. He felt the seam, the place where they met, and imagined a knife slicing them apart. A small gap in the fire appeared, and he imagined a meat cleaver hacking away at the connections.

As he felt the seam weaken, he called to the shadows. *Come here!* he commanded.

With a rushing sound, the shadows separated from the fire. They whooshed toward Conner, leaving black sparks that hung in the air before fading and falling to the ground as ash.

He directed the shadows to a nearby corner, a place

where shadows pooled. They twisted into a long, snake-like vine, slithering into the shadows below.

More blasts of fire and Darkness came, but Conner sliced through them without any trouble. That was all he had to do—remove the shadows, and the Darkness faded.

"Conner!" Lexa yelled and pointed. A large group of guards emerged from the black rock at the center of the structure and ran down the silver hallway in front of them.

"Those emergency doors!" Melanie yelled. "Trap them!"

Conner reached out. Shadows flickered everywhere, filling the ocean. Now that he could tell the difference between Darkness and darkness, the darkness didn't scare him. And the ocean happened to be full of darkness.

Calling on the shadows, Conner imagined a giant fist pounding through the windows several yards in front of the guards running down the passageway. The shadows obeyed, forming a giant fist that crashed into the acrylic. The windows cracked, and jets of water sprayed into the passageway. The guards retreated as alarms sounded and a massive metal door slammed down in one of the frames, blocking the hallway ahead of them. Within seconds that silver passageway had been sealed off.

A smoky cyclone appeared in the red hallway to their left, fading into Lady Nightwing. She pulled her hands back, crackling with Dark energy. Thrusting her arms forward, she spit twin streams of black fire at Dr. Timberi.

Conner reached out in his mind, connecting to the fire, which seemed especially strong and toxic.

It took more effort than he'd anticipated. Lady Nightwing's flames burned with a furious hate, resisting his efforts to connect. By the time he found the seam in the fire and pulled the shadows away from her violent hate, the tips of the first flames hit Dr. Timberi, who collapsed with a groan.

"Uncle Morgan!" Melanie ran over to him.

The fire vanished as the shadows flew to Conner's hand, and hot sparks fell to the metal grate below.

Lady Nightwing stepped back, her face betraying shock. "That's impossible."

"Nah," Conner said. "It's actually a little gift you gave me. A souvenir of my time in the Shadowbox." Anger raged inside of him. Because of this woman, Lexa had no powers. Conner had almost gone crazy. Dr. Timberi had been tortured. Pilaf was almost dead—

He hurled a blast of red Light at Lady Nightwing. She dodged Conner's Light, so it hit a window behind her. However, as she ducked, a bolt of pale green fire hit her shoulder. Conner couldn't tell if the fire was Darkness someone had illuminated or Light that had been darkened.

Lady Nightwing screamed and hit the floor.

Following the trajectory of the Light backward, Conner saw Timothy Timberi appear in the red passageway to their right, fading out of his cyclone and lowering his hands.

"You're finished, Emily," he said. "The Phalanx is fighting their way down here now." He flashed a grim smile. "Someone let them in, I guess. The whole Magisterium will be here soon."

"Traitor!" Lady Nightwing hissed. "You'll never get out of here." She jumped to her feet and shoved her palms forward. Thick Darkness billowed out from each hand, rushing toward Timothy.

He scowled, and more pale, green fire exploded out of his hands, pounding into the oncoming Darkness with a shrieking crash.

With the sound of metal tearing into metal, Timothy's fire pushed against the Darkness, shoving it back toward Lady Nightwing. But then her Darkness churned and boiled, pushing back against the green flames.

The Darkness shoved the green fire back an inch, then two, three, and four. Both Lady Nightwing and Timothy shook and trembled, clear signs of strain on both their faces.

We need to move Pilaf and Dr. Timberi, Conner said. *I'm afraid they might get hit in the crossfire.* He carried Pilaf, and Melanie and Lexa helped Dr. Timberi away from the intersection, a few steps backward into the silver hallway.

Back in the red hallway, Lady Nightwing's Darkness gained a few more inches, and Timothy dropped to the ground. Without his fire to block it, Lady Nightwing's Darkness rushed past where he had been standing. The sudden lack of resistance surprised Lady Nightwing, and she fell forward, stumbling.

A sharp cracking noise split the air. Behind Lady Nightwing, a small fracture appeared in the acrylic where Conner's Light had hit the window earlier.

Water sprayed through, and in just seconds, the tiny crack burst into a huge gash.

Lady Nightwing screamed and lunged forward as a heavy metal door dropped down in the doorframe behind her, sealing off the red passageway to their left. She managed to get through just in time. Another second and she would have been trapped in the flooding section.

Now she stood a few yards away, and Timothy laughed.

"Do you find death by drowning amusing?" Lady Nightwing snapped.

"Not exactly," Timothy said. They glared at each other like two cowboys in a movie getting ready to shoot. "But I just I realized that I'm not afraid of dying anymore. And I think you are. That's what's funny." Timothy vanished in a strange blur—a combination of the shimmer that came from a phasing Magus and the smoky cyclone of a Darkhand. Lady Nightwing took a few steps forward, hands poised to shoot as soon she found him.

He reappeared, just behind her, arms extended. A stream of the green Light burst out of his hands, hitting her in the back.

She fell down, motionless and still. After a few seconds, he lowered his hands. "Ironically, you taught me that move, Emily." He ran past her, into the silver hallway where Melanie worked to revive Dr. Timberi. "Dad? Dad! Can you help him?" he asked her, obvious anxiety in his voice. "I'm sorry about leaving earlier. I wanted to let the Phalanx in before anyone figured out what was going on. I thought that was the best chance of getting you out of here."

Dr. Timberi's eyes flickered open. Unfocused at first, his eyeballs darted around. And then they saw.

"Timothy! Timothy!" Grabbing Melanie and Conner, Dr. Timberi pulled himself to a sitting position. Timothy took his hands, helping him to stand, and Dr. Timberi threw his arms around his son.

Neither Timothy nor Dr. Timberi spoke. They just held each other.

Focusing on the reunion, Conner didn't notice Lady Nightwing until she had pushed herself up on her knees and sent two knives flying through the air toward Dr. Timberi's unprotected back.

Conner screamed and shot at the knives, but his efforts came too late. So did Melanie's.

Timothy's face registered the threat, and without breaking the hug, Timothy whirled around, switching places with Dr. Timberi as the knives arrived.

Timothy gasped, went rigid, and then fell the ground.

"No!" Dr. Timberi's yell echoed through the ring, and Conner thought it might tear the whole structure apart.

Dr. Timberi jabbed his hands forward, sending pale gold Light out of his hands. Lady Nightwing twirled, disappearing into a cyclone and missing the Light.

But Conner had anticipated her movement, and he yanked the shadows away from her.

Lady Nightwing crashed into the floor, and both Melanie and Dr. Timberi sent blasts of Light at her. Stunned, she didn't respond, and their combined Light pummeled her in the chest.

Lady Nightwing's body flew backward, her face frozen in a malicious sneer.

As she fell, a burst of black fire belched out of her fingers, but her aim was off. Conner could tell that it wouldn't hit anyone, so he didn't worry about it. Nor did he worry when she sent one last blast into the only open hallway—the red passageway to their right.

She hit the ground at the same time as her last burst of black fire hit an acrylic window.

And then Conner realized she hadn't been trying to hit anyone.

She had aimed for a window to their right.

Everyone retreated back toward the Shadowbox as water rushed in through the crack and one of the steel doors slid down in the red passageway, blocking them from the water.

The emergency doors protected them, but now the hallways in front and on either side of them were flooded and sealed off, leaving them trapped at the bottom of the Aleutian trench.

"Timothy," Dr. Timberi moaned, sinking down to cradle his son in his arms. "Timothy!"

A noise Conner had never heard burst out of Dr. Timberi's mouth: a haunted wail, a sharp lament. A bitter song of unbearable pain.

Timothy's eyes opened. He smiled a peaceful smile and then struggled to raise his hand. Something blurred around his fingers but faded away.

Timothy's smile faded, and he wiggled his fingers again. This time he managed to summon up a few sparks of the strange Light he shot. He looked frantic as he jerked his arm around.

"Mel," Lexa said, "I think he's trying to do a sigil. Can you Augment him?"

As Melanie reached down and touched her cousin, pale pink Light glowed around Timothy.

He smiled and stretched his hand out again. This time something shot forward, flying through the air.

A black swan—made of dark Light. Not Darkness—but Light that happened to be dark.

Timothy had organized his sigil.

ᴛʜᴇ Bʀɪᴅɢᴇ

As Melanie fought tears, Timothy's sigil hovered in the air. Exactly like Uncle Morgan's, only black instead of gold.

The sigil spoke. "I love you, Dad."

Uncle Morgan's lips quivered. "Oh, Timothy. Why did you do that?"

"Because it needed to be done. And you already gave your life for me once. It was my turn."

The sigil begin to fade.

"Forgive me, Timothy," Uncle Morgan said.

"For what?"

"I should have protected you. I should have been there and never let them take you. I should have saved you."

"You did, Dad. You brought me back from the Darkness."

The black swan faded even more, but Timothy's voice continued. "I know I'm free of the Dark because I'm not afraid to die. I hear singing and I see Light. Me and mom will be waiting for you." The sigil looked at each of the Trio, focusing especially on Melanie. "Take care of him."

The black swan faded like smoke in a breeze.

Uncle Morgan's face crumpled, and he pulled Timothy closer, rocking back and forth as his shoulders heaved. As he held Timothy, Melanie knelt down behind Uncle Morgan and hugged him.

After what seemed like a very long time, Uncle Morgan let Timothy down, laying him on the floor with the gentlest touch Melanie had ever seen. He straightened and smoothed Timothy's hair, then kissed Timothy's forehead. "Good night, sweet prince," he whispered. "And flights of angels sing thee to thy rest."

After several silent moments, he stood, straightening himself slowly. Lexa threw herself into a hug, followed by Melanie and Conner.

"Thank you," Uncle Morgan said. "Thank you all." After a minute or two, he stepped away. "We really must find a way out of here. I don't know how long our oxygen will last—and I'm not entirely sure about the structural integrity of this portion of the ring since there have been so many breaches."

"I guess you can't just open a portal into the Otherwhere?" Conner asked.

"No, I'm afraid not. The Darkhands surround their lairs with demons and Darkness—just as we surround our sanctuaries with cherubim and Light. It would be impossible for a human to pierce."

A screeching, scraping sound pulled everyone's attention away, and Melanie screamed as the flooded red section to their left crumpled, imploding under the relentless pressure of the ocean. She looked at the flooded hallways in front of them and on their right. How long until their section crumpled too?

"The good news," Uncle Morgan said, "is that the Darkhands will never get at us that way."

It wasn't all that funny, but it felt good to shake off the nightmares and the terrible things that had happened. So everyone laughed: loud, long, and perhaps a little hysterically.

After the laughter ended, it got quiet as the gravity of their situation began to sink in.

Conner stared out the massive windows. It looked like he was concentrating.

"What are you thinking?" she asked.

"There are shadows everywhere down here," he said. "I have to be able to use them, right? There must be something I can do. But what?"

Melanie looked out into the darkness of the ocean. A light glowed as a bioluminescent fish swam by the window. The fish's light was small, but it broke up the complete darkness, illuminating one of the darkest places in the world.

Luminescence.

Melanie's whiteboard started to hum. She remembered the cherub's words: *Sometimes you must be the bridge that brings the light into the darkness. Sometimes you must be the light that glows in the darkness.*

"Conner," she asked, "when the Lucents came and healed you a few months ago, what images did they show you?"

"Light and dark. And doorways and bridges."

Melanie froze as symbols danced on the whiteboard, pirouetting, spinning. She remembered the day Conner had been pulled underwater, far enough that he almost drowned. She remembered the night Conner had become magnetized to both Light and Dark, had a clear mental image of him floating in the air, half covered in Darkness, half in Light. A bridge.

"Conner, what if we were wrong this whole time?"

"What?"

"We assumed that being a gateway between Light and Dark meant you could control both. We thought your greatest power was to control shadows and use Darkness when it was light around."

"Yeah."

"What if it's different?" She paused, trying to translate into words the ideas crackling in her brain. "What if your real power isn't using Light when it's dark? What if being a bridge means you can reach out and bring the Light into the Darkness—like a bioluminescent fish?"

Conner nodded. "Okay, so, if you're right, what does that mean in practical terms?"

"How did you get away when you were drowning in the Gulf of Mexico?"

The flooded section to their right creaked and groaned, and their little passageway swayed and shook.

"The Lucents came."

Again the cherub's words came to her mind:

Because it is very difficult for us to move in your world. Lucents move there more freely than cherubim, but even they cannot simply appear anywhere. They need Light as a foundation before they can come. Your sigil gave them something to which they could connect, an anchor for them in a hostile world.

"But the cherub told me that Lucents can't just appear anywhere. Something has to open the Shroud for them. And they need something to anchor themselves to. Even if it's small, they need a foothold. What did you do before they came?"

"Nothing. I was drowning." Conner stopped. "That's not true. I sent a sigil, but it faded away. I didn't think it actually did anything."

"Your sigil may have been what allowed the Lucents to come," Melanie said.

"But you already sent a sigil and nothing happened," he said. "Light can't stay together in the water. It's too dark."

"But you have special powers I don't. The cherubim chose you to go into the Shadowbox. The Lucents have saved you twice. You're a bridge between Light and Dark. Try it."

Conner looked out of the windows.

He closed his eyes and stretched his hand out.

Nothing happened.

"I'm not strong enough," he said. "Not on my own."

He grabbed Melanie's hand, and she poured all the remaining strength she had into Conner, trying to help him do whatever he needed to do.

"Lexa, we have the body and the brain," Conner said. "We need the spirt as well." Melanie looked over her shoulder in surprise. She'd sort of forgotten about Lexa, who had faded into a shadowy corner.

"I don't have my powers any more," Lexa said in a quiet voice.

Conner held out his other hand. "You still have a spirit, and you still can sing, Lexa. You don't need to be a Magi for that."

Magus, Melanie thought.

Whatever, Conner replied as Lexa took his hand. "Sing the lullaby, Lexa."

Lexa opened her mouth and sang, soft and rich. "You came from a land where all is light, to a world half-day and a world half-night "

Conner closed his eyes again, appearing to focus on the black depths ahead of him as Lexa continued to sing.

"To guard you by day, you have my love, and to guard you by night, your friends up above."

Conner began to glow, pale at first, then brighter and brighter. Soon he blazed with red Light edged with pink. Melanie even thought she saw a little yellow.

A large, red German shepherd appeared, bounding out of Conner's heart and charging into the depths outside. The sigil began to fade, and everyone concentrated harder. It flashed and then vanished, dissolving in the heavy darkness.

The water returned to blackness. Uninterrupted by even a bioluminescent fish. Darkness everywhere.

Everyone collapsed, overwhelmed by the effort combined with the powerful depression now pushing down on all of them.

Melanie had been so sure. How could she have—

Melanie blinked and then rubbed her eyes. In the dark distance of the ocean, a tiny Light appeared. Another bioluminescent fish?

Another spark appeared. And another. And another, glowing like Christmas lights floating in the water. More and more of the Lights appeared, coming nearer and nearer.

"Lucents!" Melanie yelled. "Conner, you did it!"

"We did it," Conner said in soft, awe-filled voice.

The lights continued toward them, multiplying almost exponentially, interrupting the darkness all around.

While floating nearer, the Lucents gathered together, swirling until they created a cyclone of Light.

The cyclone tilted down, creating a spinning horizontal tunnel with a fiery opening that stretched toward them until it filled the hallway.

Conner hefted Pilaf into his arms and stepped inside while Melanie and Lexa helped Uncle Morgan into the flaming portal.

Inside the tunnel, music entered into Melanie's mind and heart, making her want to laugh and cry at the same time. The exquisite melody blended with harmonies so complex and deep she thought it must be math turned into music. Warmth surrounded her, filling her with a peace deeper than the water from which they'd just escaped.

Bright, blazing lights flew past her now, and she recognized cherubim.

One of them paused.

Thank you, Melanie, she said. *Thank you for saving my family. I am proud of you.* Recognition exploded through Melanie. She knew that voice. It was the cherub that had visited her earlier.

An image appeared in her mind: long red hair and dark brown eyes that glowed with light and life and love.

Aunt Nicole?

Take care of him, please. The pathway he walks will not be easy. I must go now. Time is limited.

The cherub flew away from Melanie, hovering around Uncle Morgan, whose head jerked up. Shock burst across his face, followed by disbelief, and then bright, beaming joy. A second light joined the first, and together, they stayed near an increasingly joyful Uncle Morgan until the tunnel began to fade.

CHAPTER 40

THE MENORAH

As September plodded into October, Lexa accepted that no miracle would restore her powers. As the last clinging leaves dropped from the trees, her last secret hopes also fell.

When Halloween blurred into Thanksgiving, Lexa gave sincere thanks that Pilaf had recovered and that Umbra had been destroyed in the battle at the Abyss. She also said a special prayer of gratitude for the considerate kindness that Conner and Melanie showed her.

Just after Thanksgiving, a tribunal established Timothy's innocence. Based on documents taken from the Abyss, it became clear that Timothy had left Umbra. In light of that, the Magisterium ruled that Timothy truly believed he could rescue his father and had been surprised at the trap.

Lee testified that Timothy had let the Phalanx into the Abyss. The entrance was impossible to find, and the Phalanx very nearly died in a trap. Timothy chose to let them in, believing that would be the best way to help his father. He didn't know about the Shadowbox and had assumed that Dr. Timberi and the Four Musketeers would be safe until he returned with the Phalanx. His plan had not worked in the way he'd intended, but his actions enabled the Magisterium to crush Umbra, which had built a fortress with no escape routes, trapping themselves with their own arrogance.

Timothy was awarded a posthumous medal and became a hero in the Magi world.

Still, Lexa felt bleak and barren like the empty, skeletal trees all around. Both her powers and Dr. Timberi were still gone. One was gone forever, while the other clung to life with uncertainty.

After their escape, Dr. Timberi had collapsed. The trauma of what he had endured in the Abyss, topped with the loss of Timothy, had left him near death. For weeks, it looked like he would follow Nicole and Timothy, and everyone prepared for that possibility. Then, with excruciating slowness, he turned a corner. He regained consciousness but required a lengthy stay in a special Magi hospital as his mind, spirit, and body began to heal.

School had just dismissed for Christmas when Lexa's mom walked up the stairs and opened her door.

"Madame Cumberland just called." Her mom smiled. "He's home, Lexa!"

Lexa insisted on going to see him, and her mom drove her over. When they arrived at his townhouse, Melanie's mom answered Lexa's knock on the front door. It took Lexa a few seconds to figure out why.

Oh yeah. Mrs. Stephens was Dr. Timberi's sister-in-law.

"Hello, Lexa!" Mrs. Stephens hugged her long and tight. People had been doing that since they'd heard what Lexa had done. "Morgan is resting, but he'll want to see you."

She led Lexa into Dr. Timberi's living room, where he slept in a large armchair next to an enormous Christmas tree dripping with lights and ornaments. A large menorah sat next to an intricate Nativity on a table near him. Every other surface of the room had been covered with some kind of Christmas decoration, and a stereo filled the air with the rich, nostalgic sounds of a choir singing "White Christmas."

Lexa's eyes moved to the bookshelf that held a family portrait of the Timberis: a young, handsome Dr. Timberi, a gorgeous Nicole, and a chubby Timothy, all smiling and full of life and joy.

The smiling faces in the picture slashed through Lexa's heart. The difference between the lives the Timberis had hoped for and the reality they encountered seemed cruel beyond words. Just when things were getting good for them, a bitter twist of fate had ended it all.

And while Lexa didn't consider her loss to be anywhere near Dr. Timberi's, it still hurt, and, like his, it seemed so unfair. She, Conner, and Melanie had learned they had powers of unusual strength with the promise of an incredible future—and then it had ended.

Just like Dr. Timberi's family. It was just getting good, and then—

"Lexa!"

She looked at Dr. Timberi in time to see a warm, surprised smile spread across his face. The genuine affection in his voice soothed some of the scars in Lexa's heart.

He held out his hands to her, and she grabbed them. "Oh, Lexa! Thank you. Thank you for saving me—for saving us all. You amazing, wonderful, courageous girl!"

Lexa tried to say something but realized that she'd cry. So instead of saying anything, she hugged him instead.

He didn't get tense. Instead he patted her head with fingers that no longer felt awkward.

When she trusted herself to speak, she looked up at him. "How are you?"

He smiled. "Thank you for asking. Physically, I'm nearly recovered. Just tired, but that will pass."

"How about emotionally?" Lexa asked.

"That recovery may take a little longer." He swallowed, blinking several times and looking away. "Now, Lexa, the real question is how are you doing?"

"I'm fine," she lied, hiding behind a forced, bright smile.

"Lexa." He chuckled. "Surely you don't think a fake smile will fool me. Tell me, really, how are you?"

Lexa's chin quivered as the tears welled up inside her again. Her words ran out, mishmashed together.

"It hurts. It really hurts. More than anything ever has." She quickly added, "Don't get me wrong, I'm glad I did it. But it's really hard to not have powers anymore. Conner and Melanie will get to be Magi, but I won't and I think I was the one who was most excited anyway . . ."

Sobs won a temporary victory, and her words melted into one big glob of tears. Dr. Timberi patted her hand but didn't say anything.

He reached below his paisley blanket and pulled a handkerchief from his bathrobe pocket, which he used to wipe her tears. "I cannot imagine how you feel. But thank you. Thank you. None of us would have survived without your sacrifice. You and Timothy both gave everything you had, and I wish I could give you more than my thanks."

Lexa nodded. She knew that she had done the right thing, but her heart hadn't quite caught up yet.

"The worst thing is that I feel guilty," Lexa said. "Like I've ruined the Light's plans."

"What do you mean?"

"Ever since we Kindled, you've said that the three of us would do something really great and important. We just found out we're incredibly powerful all together. Who knows what the Trio could have done? Now we'll never know."

"Lexa . . ." His gentle voice cut through her tears. "You saved my life. And brought my son back to me. To me, that was great and important. Perhaps that was the plan all along."

Lexa paused to think. She'd never considered that possibility. "You mean the universe would go to all the trouble to arrange everything that's happened just to help two people?"

He smiled. "I can't pretend to know. But, yes, I believe that. I believe it very much." Dr. Timberi held up his hands and the menorah flashed gold, then floated over to his outstretched fingers.

"A dear friend gave this to me many years ago. Her name was Miriam Kushner. She was the daughter of a rabbi and one of the best Magi I ever knew. Miriam and I worked in the Adumbrators office and had many discussions. She was devoted to her faith, as I was to mine." Dr.

Timberi pointed at the Nativity set. "But we were both interested in religion, and we discussed our beliefs often. I attended Shabbat dinners at her family's home, and she spent many Sunday dinners with us. " Dr. Timberi used a corner of his blanket to polish part of the menorah.

"When Nicole died and Timothy was taken, I experienced a bleakness that I cannot describe. Remember, I thought Timothy was dead. I didn't find out he had lived for many years. The deep tragedy of my loss plunged my world into constant night. I walked in an unyielding darkness of mind and soul that nothing could relieve or even soothe. I began to surrender to despair.

"Miriam took me to see her father and asked him to tell me the story of Hanukkah. He told me about brave people risking everything to fight for faith and freedom and winning against impossible odds. The story was inspiring, and, of course, it ends with a miracle. A supply of oil that should have lasted only one day burned for eight, giving light that should not have been possible: a miraculous light shining defiantly in dark times. That is why Hanukkah is sometimes known as the Festival of Lights.

"At the end of his story, Miriam's father clasped my hands and said, 'Morgan, light will always come. Even in great darkness, light will always come. And sometimes, we even get miracles.'

"I pointed out that no miracle could bring my family back to me. He shook his finger and said, 'And your story is already finished and written that you know the ending so soon? Watch for the light, Morgan. Watch for the light, and hope for miracles.'"

Dr. Timberi paused and looked at the menorah.

"Do miracles still happen?" Lexa asked. "I mean, it seems like the really big ones all happened so long ago." And, while she didn't want to say it, no miracle had ever reunited Dr. Timberi's family.

Dr. Timberi nodded. "Perhaps that's because they believed in miracles a long time ago. Could it be that miracles follow belief as opposed to the other way around?"

He paused. "Today I see that Rabbi Kushner was right in every way. The miracles were not obvious. Nicole did not come back to life, and I wasn't ever able to raise Timothy. But today I feel connected to my family in a way I could not have anticipated. I miss them keenly, but they are real and present, and I feel certain I shall be with them again beyond this life. Even my loss, bitter though it was, ended up as miracle because it triggered the series of events that ultimately brought down Umbra.

"I realize that experiencing Nicole's love was a sort of miracle, as was the fact that our love brought a life into this world. It was a miracle that Timothy came back to me, healed and free from the Darkness.

"Another miracle occurred when you, Conner, Melanie, and Pilaf walked into my life. Your Kindling ended up rekindling love and light in my heart as I came to love the four of you like my own children. Certainly that is a miracle."

Dr. Timberi smiled and polished another spot on the menorah. "I've always remembered what Miriam's father told me. When I doubted, when I faced dark times, I looked at the menorah and tried to believe his words. Sometimes trying or hoping was all I could do. I wanted to believe, and hoped I someday could. Eventually, I believed I could believe. And now, time has proven him right. Miracles do happen, Lexa. And they illuminate darkness, even when it is the darkness in our own hearts."

Dr. Timberi ran his finger along the top of the empty menorah. As his fingers brushed each candlestick, a tiny gold flame appeared, dancing in the air over each branch. When the entire menorah glowed, he smiled and said, "I learned from Miriam's family that the lighting of the Hanukkah candles is sometimes known as kindling. For the Magi, that is an interesting coincidence, is it not?"

Dr. Timberi looked in Lexa's eyes with a piercing, searching look. Keeping his eyes fixed on her's, he pressed the menorah into her hands. "Watch for light, Lexa. Watch for light, and hope for miracles."

And then, with a little smile, he closed his eyes. His head rolled forward on his chest, and soon, his shoulders rose and fell in a steady, regular rhythm.

Lexa straightened his blanket and then, in a soft voice, she sang,

"So sleep, sleep, till the Darkness ends,
Guarded by your angel friends,
So sleep, sleep, till the Darkness ends,
Guarded by your angel friends."

MELANIE'S PLAN

ON CHRISTMAS MORNING, MELANIE SAT UP in bed, trying to keep from shouting. The symbols on the whiteboard had been buzzing and humming when she'd gone to sleep, and now, as she woke up, they clicked into place—and she just knew.

Conner! Conner! she called out. *Conner!*

What? His thoughts came several seconds later—thick and groggy.

I figured it out!

Figured what out?

I know how to fix Lexa's powers.

Are you serious?

Yes!

Okay. So what do we do?

Well, it's a little complicated. I need you to get Lexa to the choir room.

Why the choir room?

Because Uncle Morgan's still recovering and school's out,

so no one will disturb us there. I'm pretty sure that no adult would approve of what we're going to do, so keep it quiet.

Okay, this is starting to sound interesting, Conner said.

He listened while Melanie explained the rest of the plan.

What do you think? she asked.

Brilliant. Or crazy. It will either work or blow up the universe.

She waited for him to laugh and say, "Just kidding." But he didn't.

When everyone arrived at Dr. Timberi's classroom that afternoon, Lexa looked around, narrowing her eyes. "Okay, this doesn't look like a surprise party for Dr. Timberi. What's going on?"

"Sorry, Lex," Conner said. "I said that to get you here."

"The truth is even better!" Melanie smiled and grabbed Lexa's hand, struggling to contain her rising excitement. This would be the most amazing thing ever. "You and Conner originally Kindled because I Augmented you, right? I basically made you Kindle. So if that worked once, why not again?" She paused and let it sink in. "But this time, Conner's going to help me, so it will be even stronger. Think of this as sort of like jumping a car. Lexa, your battery is dead. We're going to recharge it."

Lexa nodded. "That makes sense. Do you think it will work?"

"Positive," Melanie said, "Lexa, you need to concentrate on Kindling again. Think of Kindling and try to open your gateway. Conner, get as charged up with Light as you can."

"What do I do?" Pilaf asked. "Just cheer?"

"That's a really important job, Pilaf," Conner said.

"Okay, Lexa, hold your hands out in front of you," Melanie said, closing her eyes and extending her hands as well. She concentrated on the image she'd planned, sending strands of pink Light out of each finger, connecting with Lexa's. Additional threads ran out of her forehead, attaching to corresponding places on Lexa's head.

"Okay, Conner," Melanie said. He pushed on the accelerator, so to speak, and his Light poured into her, warm and strong, like him. Melanie Augmented and magnified his Light, enhancing it and adding her own before sending their combined Light into the cables that linked her to Lexa.

"Can you feel the Light, Lexa?" she asked.

"No—not yet," Lexa replied.

"Okay—a little more, Conner." He sent more, and Melanie focused harder on sparking something inside Lexa.

"Still nothing," Lexa said.

More Light flowed from Conner, and Melanie turned up the wattage, Augmenting even harder.

"How about now, Lex?" Conner asked.

Lexa shook her head. "I'm sorry. I don't feel anything."

"Turn it up all the way, Conner," Melanie said. "Everything you have." He did the equivalent of flooring the gas pedal, and energy flooded into Melanie. She, in turn, funneled every ounce of energy and power she could through the cables towards Lexa.

"Um, Melanie." Pilaf's voice got her attention. "Should that be happening?"

Melanie opened her eyes. Pink sparks crackled all over Lexa, and the Light cables connecting them had swollen and bulged. Clearly the Light rushing into them was not going anywhere.

"Conner," Melanie said, "Maybe we should—"

An explosion cut her off, interrupting her words with alternating blasts of pink and red Light like a fight between fireworks. Everyone threw themselves to the ground as Light exploded through the room, blowing up chairs and pictures and anything at all.

As the explosions stopped, a gold comet shot into the room, fading into Uncle Morgan in pajamas and a smoking jacket. "What ARE you doing?" he roared.

A few stray sparks crackled in the air as Melanie looked up at him. She wrinkled her nose as a combination of shame, confusion, and frustration all tackled her tongue. She couldn't talk—and Conner, Lexa, and Pilaf all stared at her.

"Will someone please tell me what is going on here?" Uncle Morgan asked, whipping out his famous stare.

Melanie gulped and stood up. She'd never felt so foolish—or frustrated. Her mental whiteboard had never let her down before! She hated being wrong.

When she managed to speak, the words came out in a tiny voice. "We were trying to re-Kindle Lexa."

"What?" Uncle Morgan bellowed. "You could have killed her! And blown up the school, yourselves, and perhaps this part of the city!" He gulped down a large lungful of air and held it for several seconds before letting it out in a long, slow stream. "Forgive me for yelling. But what you did was incredibly dangerous."

"I thought since I made her Kindle in the first place—and if Conner added his Light, since they're twins . . ." Melanie's words tripped out as muddled as her thoughts.

Uncle Morgan took another calming breath, bringing his voice back to normal levels. "Melanie, that is one of the most brilliant ideas I have ever heard. But there is a minor flaw."

Melanie's heart leapt inside of her, jumping like an antelope. "I knew it was a good idea! What did I miss?"

Uncle Morgan smiled, sad but warm. "The fact that Renunciation cannot be undone. It is impossible. Otherwise, it would not be such a heavy penalty." He put his hand on her shoulder. "Do not feel too badly. Making mistakes is part of being human, and you must learn to accept that. Humility, my dear Melanie, is more important than perfection, and of the two virtues, it is the only one to which any of us may reasonably aspire."

He was right. As always. She nodded and managed a smile. "You're right," she said. "Sorry, Lexa."

"It's okay." Lexa looked away and didn't turn back again.

Uncle Morgan looked around the room. "As I recall, my classroom was blown apart in the first big battle after you had Kindled—back at the beginning of this adventure." His voice sounded wistful. Was he was thinking of Timothy? "Very fitting," he whispered.

What did he mean by that?

"Please, dear ones, promise me you will not try to re-Kindle anyone's powers. Once Renounced, they cannot come back. The only way around it is Investiture—which involves the cherubim in a complicated process that has only been done three times in recorded history. Now, possums, please help me clean up this mess." He started singing "Sunrise, Sunset," and then pulled out his conductor's baton. He pointed it at a broken chair, which jumped up and put itself back together. Melanie and Conner joined in, using the Light to repair broken objects all around the room.

CHAPTER 42.

GIFT OF THE MAGI

As everyone else used Lightcraft, Lexa pretended to smile. *It's okay,* she repeated to herself. *You can still have a good life. You can still be happy. You did what had to be done.*

Dr. Timberi waved his baton, mending broken glass and picture frames and a hundred other things, sending gold flashes of Light everywhere.

The flashes kept coming near her, which seemed strange since all the broken objects nearby had been fixed. Puzzled, Lexa looked around, realizing that gold Light swirled around her feet in gentle coils. The Light lifted her up, encircling her, spinning faster and faster. What was going on?

As she opened her mouth to ask what was happening, complicated, amazing harmonies filled the air, sung by voices so rich and beautiful that her brain couldn't begin to grasp all of the beauty.

Dots of colored Lights appeared, one here, one there.

Ten, dozens, hundreds, and thousands of colored Lights hovered around her, spinning in time with Dr. Timberi's gold column of Light.

Lucents! What were they doing?

Happiness, peace, and deep love washed over Lexa, followed by images: a grandfather telling a story to a young child; a father rocking a new baby; a doctor bandaging a knee. More and more, faster and faster—images that showed men in the act of nurturing and loving children.

More lights appeared. Brilliant and blazing white lights filled the air between her and the Lucents. A tiny gap in the layers of light from the Lucents and cherubim revealed that Dr. Timberi had lowered his arm, although gold Light still cocooned her.

Wrapped in three layers of spinning Light, Lexa felt a little like a neon corn dog.

Greetings, Lexa Dell. One of the cherubim spoke in her mind, a strong and powerful feminine presence. Something about her seemed familiar to Lexa.

"Hello," Lexa said. She couldn't head-talk anymore. Hopefully regular speech would work just as well.

Another cherub spoke, a male this time, and he sounded younger than the first. *You are sad, Lexa Dell.* He also seemed familiar.

"Yeah," Lexa said. "I'm not mad or bitter or anything. But I'm still sad."

Lexa Dell, the male voice said, *if we allowed you to turn back the clock and to choose once more, would you make the same choice?*

"Can you do that? Go back in time?"

You did not answer our question, Lexa Dell, the female said.

Lexa paused. Would she give up her powers again? Would she accept the isolation, the loneliness, the feeling of being less of who she was? Would she choose to live the rest of her life watching Conner and Melanie and even Pilaf do cool things with the Sodality? Would she make the same choice?

Lexa remembered the joy of streaming, the excitement of theelings and visions, the adrenaline that came from kicking Darkhand butts in battle. And then she remembered Dr. Timberi, ragged and nearly dead in the Abyss. She thought of Pilaf's skinny, unconscious body, sick and not breathing.

Would she make the same choice?

"In a second," she said. "I'd do it again in a heartbeat."

Well chosen, Lexa Dell, said both voices.

"So was that like a quiz or something?" Lexa asked. "I mean—"

Her nervous system hummed like busy telephone wires as energy crackled through her. Up and down, inside and out. The Lucents seemed to open a little window into her soul and Lexa squealed—a gateway! They had opened her gateway again, and Light poured into her spirit like water running out of a dam.

She shivered, and her spirit got goose bumps. It felt better than a hot shower after being in the cold. Better than a hot meal after being hungry. Better than a million other things.

The cherubim vanished, and the Lucents reversed their spiral formation, fading away as Lexa floated down to the ground. Life and energy galloped through her, in greater strength than she'd ever felt before Renouncing.

As the power surged inside of her, she couldn't resist raising her arm. It floated up nearly on its own, a channel for the Light surging inside.

Lexa's sigil exploded out of her arm, a dolphin, leaping and diving through the air, alive and free and—gold.

Not yellow. Gold.

She looked at Dr. Timberi as understanding dawned.

"Did you—" She couldn't speak the thought that now filled her mind.

"Yes, I did." His smile said far more than any words could have.

Lexa ran to him so fast that she thought her tears probably flew behind in horizontal ribbons. Throwing her arms around him, she tried to pour out the gratitude she couldn't express in the energy of her embrace.

He hugged her back. No awkward arms, no stiff fingertips—a real, honest hug, and she thought she felt a few warm drops fall on her hair.

After a minute or two, Lexa looked up into his eyes, laughing and weeping at the same time.

A few months without the Light had nearly killed Lexa. And she'd only been doing Magi stuff since last April. Dr. Timberi had been a Magus for thirty or forty years. How must he feel?

"But—why?"

"Because I owed you a debt, Lexa. The night Lady Nightwing threw me in the Shadowbox, you stayed up all night singing and kept the Darkness at bay. Without your song, I would have gone mad or worse. You brought light in my darkest hours and hope when I despaired. You sang about being guarded by angels, and that's what you were to me. You risked your life and gave your powers up to save me. How could I do anything different? I'm only sorry that I was not strong enough until now." He blinked several times, then smiled. "It's not as if I'm dying. I will still teach, and I can even work for the Sodality as a researcher or historian or something."

Lexa managed to stop crying, but a deep, aching sadness throbbed inside. Dr. Timberi without his powers seemed like a bird that could no longer fly or a horse that couldn't run.

"I'm not exactly a bird that cannot fly or a horse that cannot run," he continued.

Lexa stared up at him. "Wait," she said. "Why did you say that—about the horse and the bird?"

He wrinkled his forehead. "I don't know exactly—the image just came into my mind. Why?"

"Just curious," Lexa said as a theeling began to grow.

"At any rate," he continued, "It's not a tragedy. Life often presents us with—"

Pink and purple polka dots, Lexa thought.

"—with pink and purple polka dots," Dr. Timberi said, then stopped. He shook his head and blinked.

"What did you just say?" Melanie asked.

"I'm not entirely sure. Fatigue, I guess," he replied, still looking a bit surprised.

But, in a flash of insight, Lexa understood. She had carried his sigil inside her, and now he'd Invested her with his powers. There must be a link between them. He apparently heard her thoughts, but since he wasn't a Magus anymore, he didn't realize it. It must be more like a strong subliminal message.

Lexa paused for a few more seconds, thinking through an idea. This would require some care. She might only have one chance to do this, and it had to last the rest of his life. It would have been better if she could have rehearsed it, but she didn't know how long the link would last. It might fade the longer he went without being a Magi.

Hoping he would receive the message in his unconscious mind, she said, *Dr. Timberi, you are the awesomest teacher who has ever lived. You gave up everything for me and I will never forget it. As long as I live, you'll be my hero, and when I'm a mom, I'll tell my kids about you. And my grandkids.*

Even without Magi powers, you are a hundred times cooler than anyone else. I love you, Dr. Timberi! All of us do. Me, Conner, Melanie, Pilaf—we love, love, love you and we'll always be there for you. Whatever you need, for the rest of your life we're here for you. Think of us as your kids.

Dr. Timberi looked startled—then his chin started to quiver and his lips trembled. He looked away, but for a few minutes, his shoulders shook, accompanied by a gasping noise.

Lexa, did you just plant that message in his mind? Conner asked.

Yeah, she said.

He gave her a fist bump. *Nice job, sis. I'm proud of you. Seriously.*

Melanie beamed at her too. *That was incredible, Lexa.*

Can you help me do one more thing? Lexa asked.

What? Conner said.

Lexa organized her sigil—a gold dolphin. *I want a sigil to take that message inside him. I want it to stay there for the rest of his life, so it will need lots of energy.*

Conner pointed his hand at the sigil, and red Light glowed around the gold, followed by Melanie's pink.

Lexa gave the sigil instructions: *Go inside of him and stay there. Whenever he's sad, remind him of what I just said. Make him feel it. Make him* know *it. Forever.*

The glowing dolphin sailed into Dr. Timberi, shining with red, pink, and gold Light.

When Dr. Timberi turned around, his eyes still glistened, but his face gleamed with the biggest smile Lexa had ever seen there. He stood in front of a window, and Lexa realized with a chill that it was the same spot he'd stood right before their first battle with the Stalker, right after they had Kindled. Golden afternoon light poured in, painting Dr. Timberi with a soft glow. Outside the window, feathery snowflakes floated down as if they'd fallen from angel wings.

"Uncle Morgan, are you okay?" Melanie asked, taking his right hand as Lexa took his left.

"Yes, thank you," he said. "More than okay. In fact, I don't think I've ever been happier."

Lexa knew exactly what he meant.

Appendix

FROM THE FILES OF THE MAGISTERIUM

Virtus et Lumen

MAGI SERVICES:
OFFICE OF ASSESSMENT AND EVALUATION

MEMORANDUM
To: Supreme Magistrate
Office of the Supreme Magistrate

Your Eminence:

I am happy to inform you that I have finally completed the project you suggested three years ago. Written in three volumes, my report on the unique triple Kindling of Melanie Stephens and Conner and Lexa Dell is now complete. The report begins with the earliest manifestation of Conner's powers in the gymnasium at Marion Academy and concludes with the Investiture of Lexa Dell.

Since you were closely involved in the events, I wanted you to be the first to receive a copy of this, the final volume.

Compiling these histories has led me to think it would also be valuable to detail the unique events that led you to your position today.

Respectfully,

Pilaf

Olaf Larson, MD, PhD
Director, Office of Assessment and Evaluation

Virtus et Lumen

OFFICE OF THE SUPREME MAGISTRATE

My Dear Pilaf,

Thank you very much for your note. And thank you even more for your prodigious efforts in compiling this multi-volume record. As I perused them, I relived many happy memories and a few tender ones as well.

It so happens that I was back in Nashville this weekend, and everyone sends their love. Lexa invited me to watch her students perform *The Sound of Music*. She is a brilliant director and truly gifted teacher, and I enjoyed spending time with her and her husband. The baby will be here any day.

Conner and Melanie certainly have their hands full. Imagine a house full of children who inherited both Melanie's brainpower and Conner's mischievous nature, coupled with his speed. It is a potent combination, indeed: master criminals who can run very fast. I am joking, of course. They are wonderful children, but, indeed, a handful.

I also thank you for your interest in my own story. And you are correct: becoming the first Supreme Magistrate without current Magi powers is certainly unique, but I think there is enough about me already contained in the three admirable volumes you have written. We will let that suffice for now. Besides, who really wants to hear the bureaucratic exploits and misadventures of a large middle-aged man? Another time, perhaps.

Again, thank you for your excellent work. My love to Madi and the children.

Fondly,

Morgan

Morgan Timberi
Supreme Magistrate

$\int$CK$\int$OWLEDGME$\int$TS

I AM SO DEEPLY INDEBTED TO SO MANY PEOPLE that I struggle to know where to begin. First, I am grateful to Deseret Book for graciously allowing me to use the lovely lyrics for "Angel Lullaby." I am also grateful for my mother, who sang it to me as a child.

Writing this trilogy required some research in areas where I have no expertise. I am grateful to the following for their professional expertise: Professors Michelle Wooten, Scott Bergeson, J. Ward Moody, and Todd Richards all answered important questions. Gary J. Smith, M.D., Lisa Morgan, M.D., Aaron Norton, and Ken Folger also provided important technical information and were very patient with my repeated inquiries and "what if" questions.

This book benefitted from the candid critiques of my students and former students: Leah, Denee, Annie, and Meg. This author benefitted from their sweet sincerity and genuine responses.

Finally, my family has been endlessly helpful. My parents and grandparents have provided significant support. My daughter allowed me to talk through the plot as we drove to and from school, and then she read and commented on early drafts. My sons patiently allowed me to work, and my wife supported me in every possible way with tremendous grace and generosity.

Discussion Questions

1. The word *luminescence* is defined as "the emission of light by a substance not resulting from heat." Why do you think this was chosen as the title of this book?

2. When the author was writing this book, he mentally used the title *The Redemption of Lexa Dell*. In what ways does Lexa redeem herself?

3. In this book, Lexa struggles with guilt. She blames herself for what happened to Dr. Timberi. Those around her try to tell her she is not to blame. What do you think?

4. During the book, it becomes obvious that Dr. Timberi has many friends who risk their lives for him and who would do anything to save him. What qualities does he have that leads to this kind of loyalty? What qualities do you think are important in a friend?

5. Does Timothy redeem himself in the end? Dr. Timberi thinks so. What do you think?

6. Lady Nightwing tries to inflict both physical and mental or emotional pain. Which do you think is the worst?

7. Lexa makes a very difficult decision toward the end of the book. She doesn't regret the decision—but it doesn't stop being hard for her. Have you ever made a decision you felt was right but still struggled to make?

8. What do you think of Dr. Timberi's decision at the end of the book? Did it surprise you? Did he do the right thing? What are the consequences likely to be?

9. Many of the characters in this book make sacrifices for others or do things that are difficult but need to be done. Who do you think is the greatest hero in this book? Why?

ABOUT THE AUTHOR

DURING HIS MIDDLE SCHOOL YEARS, Braden Bell was the least-stable, lowest-achieving student in the history of the world. He shocked every former teacher by graduating from high school and college and then going on to earn both a master's degree as well as a PhD. A teacher by day and a parent by night, he is around teenagers 24/7. He teaches music and directs plays at a private school, much like Marion Academy in the Middle School Magic series. Whether he fights evil after hours is something he cannot disclose. You can contact him at www.bradenbell.com.